PRAISE FOR *OLEANDER CITY*

"With austere prose, compelling characters, and a gripping true story, *Oleander City* bears down on its characters like a category five storm, forcing three lost souls to discover who they truly are. More timely than one would think, this tale of natural catastrophe, racial injustice, and lawlessness ultimately illuminates the humanity that motivates and unites us all. A certifiable page-turner, *Oleander City* pulls at you with the dark undertow of an America that isn't quite bygone."

—ADAM JOHNSON,
Pulitzer Prize–winning, *New York Times* bestselling author of *The Orphan Master's Son*

"Set against the sweeping backdrop of dramatic action . . . this book will keep you reading into the night."

—Chris Offutt, author of *Shifty's Boys*

"In *Oleander City*, Matt Bondurant takes the carbon of history and, with the pressure and heat of beautifully crafted prose, sensitively drawn characters, and a gut-wrenching, heart-wrenching narrative, creates a brilliant diamond of a novel. Bondurant hurls readers through the Galveston hurricane of 1900, past figures as legendary as Jack Johnson and Clara Barton, into collision with the Ku Klux Klan, and straight toward the dark, murky truth of the American Dream. *Oleander City*, like all diamonds, is a gift to last forever."

—SNOWDEN WRIGHT,
author of *Play Pretty Blues* and *American Pop*

"From the catastrophic chaos and horror of the worst natural disaster in US history, Matt Bondurant extracts three very human stories of individuals who found themselves caught up in the aftermath of unimaginable tragedy. His portraits of these three disparate souls dramatize the valuable poignancy of tenderness cast against the necessary toughness of dedication, the sweetness of dreams, and the unwavering commitment to purpose, to life. This novel surprises with its perceptiveness and astonishes with its poignant illustration of the deeper and more sustaining values of beauty and truth and love."

–CLAY REYNOLDS,
author of *The Vigil, Franklin's Crossing*, and *The Tentmaker*

"*Oleander City* is a surreal blend of the real and the imagined, where broken lives traverse the ravaged landscapes of hurt and loss. Matt Bondurant depicts characters who carry the great weight of tragedy, and he reminds us that where there is heavy burden, there is also the strength to bear it."

–MICHAEL FARRIS SMITH,
author of *Nick* and *The Fighter*

"Bondurant weaves together fascinating backstories with vivid descriptions of the storm and its aftermath, showing that it takes many types of courage to fight for what is right."

—*BOOKLIST*

OLEANDER CITY

BOOKS BY MATT BONDURANT

Oleander City
The Night Swimmer
The Wettest County in the World
The Third Translation

OLEANDER CITY

A Novel Based on a True Story

Matt Bondurant

BLACK STONE
PUBLISHING

Printed in the United States of America

First edition: 2022
ISBN 979-8-200-83116-6
Fiction / Historical / General

Version #1

CIP data for this book is available
from the Library of Congress

Blackstone Publishing
31 Mistletoe Rd.
Ashland, OR 97520

www.BlackstonePublishing.com

For Ford, Emmy & Griff

PART 1

The churches, the great business houses, the elegant residences of the cultured and opulent, the modest little homes of the laborers of a city of nearly forty thousand people; the center of foreign shipping and railroad traffic lay in splinters and debris piled twenty feet above the surface, and the crushed bodies, dead and dying, of nearly ten thousand of its citizens lay under them.
–Report of Red Cross Relief, Galveston,
Texas (1900–1901), written by Clara Barton and various members of the Galveston Red Cross relief team.

That peculiar smell of burning flesh, so sickening at first, became horribly familiar within the next two months, when we lived in it and breathed it and drank it, day after day.
–Fannie B. Ward,
American Red Cross

We kept running into so many dead bodies that I had to go forward with a pike and shove the dead out of the way. There was never such a sight. Men, women, children, babies, all floating along with the tide. Hundreds of bodies going bump-bump, hitting the boat. I was sort of in a daze picking them out of the way.
–Phillip Gordie Tipp,
Galveston, Texas

HESTER

SEPTEMBER 8, 1900

GALVESTON, TEXAS

The Sisters of the Incarnate Word decided to tie the girls together with a length of clothesline.

When they filed into the kitchen for tea that afternoon the sky outside the rattling windows was churning with lashing rain. The girls huddled together at the long tables with their bread and butter, watching sinuous columns of red ants winding up the plaster walls. Then the front door came off the hinges and brown water gushed in over the threshold and swirled around their ankles so the sisters moved everyone to the second floor. They tied the girls together in long lines with one of the sisters on each end so that no one would be swept away. There were ninety-three girls at the St. Mary's Orphan Asylum, and nearly as many young boys in the boys' wing next door.

Sister Henrietta stood in the stairwell watching the murky flood that roiled through the bottom floor. She looked back over her shoulder at the lines of children linked together by the white cord.

Girls! Listen to me now. Remember your faith!

Sister Lucy struggled to loop the cord around Hester, the last child in line—a tiny girl with a sullen face and flaxen hair.

Hester! Please hold still!

Hester ducked, again slipping her head out from under the loop of rope, and Sister Lucy said a word under her breath that Hester had never heard before. Sister Lucy had her other arm clamped around Little Cora, the three-year-old that Hester shared a bed with. All afternoon, the sisters led the girls in hymns to keep them calm, and when Sister Margaret started another chorus of their favorite, "Queen of the Waves," Little Cora's small tremulous voice joined the others:

"Queen of the Waves, look forth across the ocean,
From north to south, from east to stormy west . . ."

The building groaned in the shrieking wind and Hester looked into Little Cora's dark eyes then twisted free from Sister Lucy's grasp. The next moment the floor shuddered as the foundations shifted, beams snapping with the sound of cannon fire, and the girls and the sisters were thrown to the floor. Hester got to her hands and knees as a fishing trawler passed close by the window, spinning down the street like some kind of impossible monstrous toy, the bow smashing through the second-story windows of the mercantile exchange across the way.

Pray with me, girls! Sister Henrietta screamed. Pray for absolution!

The lines of girls collapsed into each other while the sisters tried to gather around them in a protective ring. The building lurched again, the floor tilting, and it seemed to Hester the orphanage was bobbing like a cake of soap in the bathtub. The walls bowed and flexed, plaster cracking with the strain, and then the windows exploded inward in a heavy gush of glass and water and all went dark. Hester crawled against the steep incline of the floor, jamming her fingernails in the cracks between floorboards, moving toward a gray patch of light above her. Stretching out a hand, she caught the doorframe to Sister Henrietta's study, pulling herself up as a desk, chairs, and books tumbled past. She kept climbing up toward the window on the side of the house. We are sideways, she thought. The orphanage is rolling over!

My girls! Sister Henrietta screamed in the darkness below. If this is our end let us meet our Lord in glory!

There was a terrible roaring sound and the building shuddered as half of it was torn away in the flood. Hester pulled herself up through the window and onto the side of the house. Clouds laced with flashing webs of lightning roiled just above her head and the cold rain made her gasp for air. The orphanage was on the far western side of the city, just a block from the beach, and looking east Hester saw the city of Galveston swaying and twisting as the ocean coursed through it, ripping buildings off foundations, tearing them apart. She watched houses, apartments, shops, schools, and churches disintegrate in the flood; boats, wagons, sheds, barrels, light poles, and entire trees flowing in a mad tumult down the street. Where the boys' wing of the orphanage once stood was now a swirling maelstrom of shattered material. A woman stretched flat on her back on a delivery wagon came spinning past, her mouth open in a soundless scream. A section of roof rushed by with a half dozen people clinging to the exposed rafters. Clouds of splintered wood fired through the air at incredible velocities and Hester curled up, covering her head with her arms.

Moments later, the remaining structure of the orphanage fell apart and Hester rode a slab of clapboard siding into the rushing water. Powerful currents and battering underwater wreckage tore at her body and shredded her clothes but Hester clung to the boards until they surged back to the surface. She was vibrating from the shock and cold and all she could think was that this was surely the end of all things. She adjusted her grip on the boards, her hands and fingers numb and stiffened into claws. It must be over soon. Please, God, let this be the end. But she did not let go; the roar of wind and water filled her ears as her eyes closed and she drifted into darkness.

Hester was jarred awake when her raft of boards collided with a vast logjam of drowning longhorn cattle—hundreds of them in a mad panic, their curved horns clacking against each other as they arched their necks, bellowing in anguish. Amid the cows she saw a man with a small boy on his shoulders, trying to push a woman into the limbs of a pecan tree. As soon as she found a hold he let her go, and at that moment the logjam of cattle broke loose and they were carried away from the tree. When Hester's raft of boards bumped along nearby, the man dragged himself and the boy onto it. They had been badly slashed by cattle horns and the man's face was covered with blood. The boy called out for his mother, now a distant silhouette waving from the branches of the tree until she disappeared in a rush of white water. They were sucked along with the mass of dying cattle into a vicious rapid that funneled them through the mangled wharfs along the bay, several times pulling them fully under as if some petulant watery hand had plucked at the raft from below. Hester clung to the boards, pressing her forehead to the planks as the cold rain rattled down. Why won't this end? she thought. How long can it go on?

They were pushed into calmer water and the man flopped on his back, coughing and retching. The little boy was gone. The man sat up and looked around, spotting Hester on the other end of the boards. He wiped the blood out of his eyes and stared at her for a moment without comprehension. She was used to a baffled expression when people really looked at her for the first time. Hester was six years old but looked years younger, her growth stunted from malnutrition as an infant. When she arrived at the orphanage they thought she was a newborn, until she took a bottle and bit down on the nipple with a complete set of teeth.

Then suddenly the sky was lightening, the winds stalling out and she could hear the crunching, rending sounds of the city being ground apart. Above their heads, the stars emerged so quickly that Hester wasn't sure if it was real. Around the edge of this quiet circle in the sky, like a lens into some other world, the storm still raged. The man turned his back to her and they sat silently for a few moments. Hester opened her mouth to say something but the words caught in her throat. She swallowed and tried again, but before she could make a sound, the man slipped off the boards and disappeared under the dark water.

***

In the morning, Hester found herself on the sandy banks of Offatts Bayou, a couple of miles west of the city. The bayou was clogged with splintered wood pilings, smashed boats, and other debris. She was naked and covered in insect bites, scrapes, and lacerations from exposed nails, angry red furrows in her puckered skin that did not bleed but itched terribly. Her lips were swollen and blistered and the skin on her hands and feet was gray and spongy. The landscape to the east toward the city was a rolling tableau of destruction, water-molded formations of wreckage and muck, so many buildings wiped away that the bell tower of St. Patrick's Church a couple of miles away stood alone like a broken finger. Thin trails of smoke crept skyward, bleeding into low dark clouds.

Hester began to encounter bodies immediately. Mute forms with awestruck expressions, twisted into horrible shapes amid the wreckage. She walked through a grove of pale elm trees with a dozen bodies dangling from the branches. Clouds of mosquitoes tormented as she slogged through brackish water and black mud. It was as if she had passed over into the sinister hellscapes that the sisters spoke of in their sermons. It occurred to her then that she must have died sometime during the night.

On her way back to the city, she found a dress half buried in the muck. Hester knelt and smoothed the fabric until she could see the color: robin's-egg blue. A little doll was tied to the waist with a cord. The doll was made of feed sacking dyed a dark brown and stuffed with small seashells. Its eyes reminded her of Little Cora. She rinsed the dress in a puddle and shrugged it on, her body shaking with cold. It was too large and gathered about her ankles and wrists, but it was warm. Hester inspected the doll, fingering the small seashells inside until she stepped on something soft. Lifting her bare foot she saw the curled fingers and white palm of a small hand half buried in the mud. She backed away and ran through the flattened clumps of grasses.

Later Hester crouched at the edge of the bayou, the water still flowing seaward. She put her face between her knees and rocked, hugging the doll to her neck, moaning and shuddering with cold.

The first day and night she saw mostly children, flitting about the piles of wreckage, moving over the debris like the shadows of spiders, the pale orb of a face in the empty eye socket of a window. Hester did not acknowledge the children, looking away as soon as she saw them, and when anyone tried to approach she ran and hid. She was sure they were all dead, just as she was, all of them somehow trapped in this world where they didn't belong.

A few hours later, men began to emerge. Wandering like sleepwalkers, they started dragging bodies out of the wreckage and piling them in the street. A shirtless man in a straw hat carried a jug of whiskey, and each time a man brought a body he gave them a slug then took one for himself. They piled boards on top of the bodies and poured kerosene over everything and lit it on fire. Hester squatted behind a rain barrel and watched the yellow blaze climb and roar as some of the men wept and others lay down in the mud and went to sleep.

Hester focused on moving, staying out of the light, like a crab scuttling from hole to hole, exploring the rubble of buildings, looking for a place to hide. If they found her the men might pile her body with the others to be burned. In the remains of a house she picked through the wreckage of the kitchen while being watched by an enormous old hound dog with reddish-brown fur and a dark muzzle. The nuns never allowed dogs near the orphanage and told the girls terrible stories of vicious packs that roamed the city, hunting unwary children. But this dog just seemed tired, and he licked his crusted jowls with a gray tongue and gazed at her with melancholy eyes. Hester had a can of green peas in her pocket—the only food she had been able to find. She found a sharp-edged brick and chipped away at the lid until liquid began to seep out and the dog brought his massive head low and sniffed, smelling the peas and salt. Hester poured some of the peas through the jagged opening onto her palm, and the dog slurped them from her hand, and she poured out more until the can was empty. His tongue felt warm and soft, and he licked the liquid between her fingers and up her wrist then sat on his gaunt haunches, watching as Hester searched the rubble of the kitchen for food. Everything was gone or ruined. In a drift of wet sand in the pantry she found a book with an embossed leather cover, the pages thickened and warped, covered with blurred abstract shapes of watery ink. She took it with her when she left and the dog followed.

Hester decided this was a spiritual test, the kind the sisters spoke of, and she must do something to make things right again. Perhaps I can make it go back, she thought. Maybe the whole world will go back to what it was before. She remembered the words of the sisters: *What doth the Lord require of thee, but to do justly, to love mercy, and to walk humbly with thy God.*

On the second day, Hester found a narrow spot in the rubble of the Lucas Terrace apartment building on Seventeenth and Market, overlooking the beach. The stench of bodies was overwhelming in the city, but the offshore breeze by the beach kept the mosquitoes and biting flies at bay and sometimes made it possible to close her eyes and sleep without the searing reek of death flaring in her brain. Hester also figured that if the sisters were right and Jesus was coming, then he would surely walk across the waters of the Gulf bearing a basket of bread and clean water. He would take her by the hand and lead her back to the orphanage where Sister Lucy would be making redfish soup in the kitchen. The other girls would bathe her and comb her hair and take her to her bed where she would snuggle with Little Cora. She would wait by the water and keep watch.

Hester stuffed her shelter with dry pieces of carpet, curtains, and clothes that she found, creating a sort of burrow to crawl into with a board to pull over the opening. She lay in her little cocoon and in the gray light filtering through the wreckage turned the pages of the book, imagining the words that might once have been there. The dog lay just outside, looking at her with his doleful eyes until she made room and he came in gladly, circling then wedging himself against her and snoring within seconds. He was warm and smelled like sand and grass and other scents she could barely remember. She closed her eyes and chanted the rosary with her fingers inside the doll, rubbing the small shells between her fingertips.

As it grew dark the second day, the sunset was luridly colored, purples and reds spreading obscenely over the horizon. The occasional sound of gunshots rolled over the city. The beach was usually two hundred feet of clean sand to the waterline. Now the water was high and thick with bobbing debris and bodies, extending east and west beyond the visible distance. She didn't understand where all the bodies had come from. She didn't know there were so many people in all the world! The storm must have passed over all of Texas and now the whole world was ruined. Anyone she ever knew—the Sisters of the Incarnate Word, the boys in the wing next-door, Little Cora, her real parents, the new family she might have had—they were all out there, lost forever, rolling like restless sleepers in the dark water.

JOE

Leon and his Magnificent Trained Donkey were almost finished, and that meant it was time for someone to get hurt. The rain hammered on the tin roof of the converted tobacco warehouse so powerfully scented with cured leaf that everybody in the building had a throbbing headache. It was raining when they arrived in Victoria that morning, and a couple inches of standing water ebbed backstage where Joe lay sprawled on rolls of sodden carpet, shirtless and wearing black tights with a gold sash. His hands were packed in six-ounce boxing gloves and his eyes were shut. He was breathing in long, slow draws. Lying on his chest was a folded telegram. Onstage, Leon's donkey brayed a series of sounds uncomfortably close to human speech, and the audience roared with laughter. Patterson, Joe's longtime sparring partner, was sleeping on a table in his wool bathrobe, head resting on his gloves. The beer kegs were mercifully empty, poured into the bellies of a hundred Texas cotton farmers at five cents a glass.

The crowd roared again and Salazar started honking on his trombone while Leon and the donkey were making their exit, the animal doing a heavy-hoofed version of "The Cuban Drag" down the aisle. McCarthy started warming up the crowd and Joe had about five minutes before he went on so he read the cable again. The telegram was from Jack Curley, a fight promoter and manager that Joe had worked with over the years.

```
Lansky says they got big fresh negro name Jack
Johnson down in Galveston bragging too much
want to shut him up $1500 plus expenses knock
him out early if you want
```

Is there a man, McCarthy shouted from the stage, in the noble hamlet of Victoria, Texas, who has the *grit* to take the challenge? I say, is there a man among ye?

McCarthy hoisted the waist of his pants and prowled the ring, the megaphone held to the side of his mouth without the cigar, the oil in his hair draining in streaks of gray down the back of his neck. The crowd laughing nervously, men pointing and shoving each other.

Any man that lasts just three rounds with Chrysanthemum Joe, the California Terror—that brave man will be awarded the grand sum of five hundred dollars! Three rounds!

Lying backstage, Joe put his arm over his face to block out the gaslight that flickered on the wall. Maybe tonight, he thought, no one would volunteer. Patterson would do his exercise club routine; the twins would sing their song while Phil the monkey rode his bicycle; then they would shut down Chrysanthemum Joe's Scientific Boxing Revue and go back to the hotel and to bed.

Joe composed his reply to Curley in his mind:

```
Offer is appreciated but must decline no longer
in game officially a civilian yours Joe
```

Must I appeal to the *womenfolk* present? McCarthy bellowed. Perhaps *they* would have the starch to take on the man who fought James Jeffries to a draw. The man who beat Joe Walcott, the man who's been in the ring with every great heavyweight fighter alive! This is your chance at history, Victoria, Texas!

Patterson moaned in his sleep. A stray dog wandered through the cramped backstage area, stepping delicately through the water. Joe's hotel room had a comfortable upholstered armchair and a two-week-old copy of the *San Francisco Call* on his nightstand, folded to the theater reviews. A hot bath in the copper tub in the basement. An unfinished letter to his wife, Louise. Maybe this would be the night no one volunteered. Joe sent a quick prayer to the Hebrew god he did not believe in.

Chrysanthemum Joe. A head of lustrous golden hair that he kept swept back over his high forehead, running down to a curl at his collar. Faint pads of scar tissue orbiting his eyes, nose flattened and slightly askew, a notch in his lower lip where his cornermen cut away a hunk of flesh during the famous "Battle of the Barge" with Gentleman Jim Corbett. He was the son of Polish Jews who settled in California—his father, Isador, a Yale graduate, newspaper editor, and poet who spoke nine languages and ran an antiquarian bookstore on Gary Street in

San Francisco. Joe's mother, an Englishwoman of genteel birth, taught Joe to play Mozart on the waterlogged upright piano under the stairs. As a boy Joe served coffee and rolls to Bret Harte and Samuel Clemens in the parlor where Isador convened a literary salon. In the evenings, Isador paced the floor reading aloud in a theatrical manner from Balzac, Emerson, and Frederick Douglass, his heavy tread on the floorboards keeping time as he declaimed passages from *Incidents in the Life of a Slave Girl* while Joe and his brothers cowered on the rug, steadying the wobbly oil lamps with their white hands.

Isador Choynski died from mouth and throat cancer, croaking out his final hours in a ward in San Francisco General while Joe battled Kid McCoy for twenty rounds. McCoy was a known flimflam artist, who laced his gloves with itching powders and faked injuries. Joe's corner second was drunk that night and McCoy's people managed to switch out Joe's water, and after round eight Joe drank six ounces dosed with chloral hydrate. The last twelve rounds felt like fighting underwater. It was a brutal, bloody affair that left both men covered in gore. Joe broke McCoy's nose and three ribs, putting him on the floor sixteen times. The referee and the timekeeper were known anti-Semites, and McCoy benefited from some long counts and early bells, but Kid McCoy and his famous "corkscrew punch" battled back late, in the process giving rise to the expression "the real McCoy." Joe lost the decision and arrived late for his father's funeral, his noble face battered so badly that his mother didn't recognize him.

Chrysanthemum Joe.

The crowd roared, and Joe opened his eyes. He flexed his hands, stood up, and shook out his shoulders. He jogged in place, sending ripples of water across the backstage area, under the table where Patterson snoozed and the stool where Salazar sat staring dreamily at the ground, a towel around his neck and his golden trombone cradled in his lap. The backstage door stood open and the rain beat lashing patterns in the black mud. Phil the monkey in his cage covered with a feed sack, rattling the door mechanism with his little hairy fingers. Somewhere in the back, Leon was singing to his mule while feeding her ground oats and brown sugar.

> *Hello, my baby, hello, my darling, hello, my*
> *goodtime girl.*

Finally! McCarthy screamed from the stage. There is an ounce of manhood left in Texas, ladies and gentlemen! Let's welcome our challenger!

It was easy to understand why they sent for him. A popular veteran at the end of his career, Joe was a gatekeeper for young comers and projects that needed a true test. He was also one of the only top-level fighters who would cross the color line. But it was the *principle* of Curley's proposal that bothered him. *Shut him up.* The feverish, yellow-eyed, nut-cracking rabble, fortified with whiskey and a watertight certainty of the innate superiority of the white race. *Kill that got-damn Negro!* Joe had been in such fights before, and it never worked out the way they thought. When the man was bloodied and put down the crowd uttered something like a collective sigh, and it seemed as if everyone just wanted to lie down and close their eyes. It reminded Joe of the moments after he had lain with a woman. He'd given that up, too.

Joe jogged out onto the stage and vaulted into the make-shift ring. The crowd surrounded him on three sides, rows of faces stretching off into the dark recesses of the warehouse—mostly cotton farmers getting cranked off the cheap beer, but also wives sitting with their purses in their laps and barefoot children wandering the aisles. The women in the audience gazed at Joe with naked interest. He was a rare creature, a lumines-cent pearl in a sea of gray oyster flesh, his body like some kind of ancient form that visionary Greeks worked in marble with an iron spike and a wooden mallet. Just under six feet tall and 175 pounds—one of the smallest heavyweight boxers in the game. But his chest was broad and his torso segmented like the thorax of a beetle. You couldn't pinch a finger of fat anywhere on the man. Then the glossy mass of his blond hair, the jut of his chin, the sleepy, heavy-lidded mountain-blue eyes. The enig-matic half smile.

McCarthy was in the corner lacing up the challenger, a massive fellow in canvas pants and hobnail boots. Joe figured this fellow outweighed him by at least sixty pounds. He could tell by the hump of muscle around his neck that the man was a dockworker, likely a loader or cotton-squeezer—those tireless hulks who jammed cotton bales into the deep holds of blue-water ships. He grinned at Joe, his eyes watery-pink, a glass of beer in one gloved fist.

Ladies and gentlemen, McCarthy bellowed, please welcome to the ring Augustus, ready to defend the honor of Victoria! It's real simple, folks. Ol' Gus here just has to survive three rounds!

McCarthy pulled a paper out of his jacket pocket and flapped it in the dockworker's grinning face before walking around the ring, displaying it to the crowd.

I have here a bank order for five hundred actual American dollars, paid in full by the Bank of Victoria. Just three rounds! C'mon, let's hear it for him, folks!

Salazar started kneading Joe's shoulders, murmuring Spanish in his ear. Joe bounced on his toes and fired off a couple jabs. The six-ounce exhibition gloves felt like pillows on his fists. The dockworker waved to his pals in the crowd, then upended the beer into his gaping mouth and tossed the empty glass into the audience. It shattered somewhere in the dark and there was a high-pitched scream and a chorus of shouts and curses and Salazar hit the bell. Joe found himself walking forward with his hands up and a kind of simmering quiet taking over his thinking, focusing on the emotion of the moment. That was the fuel he had to burn, and the emotion that Joe felt was rage. Rage against the heavy yoke of unalterable fate that conspired to set him in this place, to do this terrible thing.

Augustus came rushing out, swinging heavy and wide. Joe sidestepped and tapped him behind the ear as he passed, and Augustus went into the ropes, getting tangled up and nearly bringing the ring down. A good laugh from the crowd, and Joe bobbed in the center of the ring, his hands far apart, eyes half closed. The first round passed this way—Joe slipping the dockworker's awkward throws, slapping him across the cheeks or tapping his kidneys. The nature of exhibitions was to draw the thing out; give the lunker some fair shots, let his friends and family see him in action against a real boxer. Joe always found this difficult to tolerate. It was like doing something halfway, making it impossible to find the sweet rhythm of the fistic arts. He had to resist the swelling urge to let his hands go. He had to choke it off at the root.

Do not look at his face. Watch the gloves and feet.

In the second round, Joe could feel the restless nature of the crowd, who were already tiring of this dancing display. They wanted someone to *hit* somebody. Augustus panting and red-faced, the good-natured smile replaced by a scowl of frustration, and Joe knew that the man was determined to hit him at least once. So after a minute he squared up, his hands held wide, and invited the man in. Augustus obliged with a sweeping haymaker and Joe bobbed slightly, the glove passing through his tousled hair, then Joe smacked him with a hard straight right, snapping his head back. Augustus put his hands to his face as a delicate fan of blood sprayed from his nose. Joe stepped to the side and rotating from the hips dug into the kidney, following with a tight hook to the side of the head that sent the dockworker sprawling to the floor.

The crowd whistled and howled and Augustus got to his feet, still holding his nose, helped by McCarthy, who was yelping into the megaphone something about will and courage but Joe heard only the throb of blood in his temples, the stentorian exhalations of his lungs. The world became centered on the present, everything else falling away. McCarthy wiped Gus's face with a towel and the dockworker came forward again, and this time Joe stood in front of him, picking off his punches with his gloves. When the big man paused, bewildered, Joe faked a straight left then hooked the floating rib, his fist sinking deep in the dockworker's ample flesh. Augustus went down and rolled over, gasping for air. More than a minute left, but Salazar hit the bell and McCarthy helped the man crawl to his corner.

One more round, folks! Can Augustus make it? Let's hear it for him, folks! One more round!

The crowd roared, and Salazar scampered about with a push broom as chicken bones and beer glasses began to rain down in the ring. Augustus sat on an overturned bucket, his back heaving, blood draining from his face and forming a puddle around his feet. Everyone in the place was out of their seat, hollering with distorted mouths and wide eyes in a wave of bloodlust and horror. The man's nose was broken and the rib shot would make it hard to breathe for a month. His buddies outside the ring urged him on, slapping his arms and back, pantomiming unorthodox punches and ridiculous feints. Just behind this group of men, a plain stone-faced woman in a calico dress and bonnet held the hand of a small girl whose mouth was crusted with blue cane sugar. The woman was staring at Joe with a look that inspired some deep thinking. It seemed her eyes were a question, locked onto him as she wrestled with some essential principle played out on this poorly lit stage perched on the edge of her world.

> *The fire-eyed maid of smoky war.*
> *All hot and bleeding will we offer them.*

Joe looked at Salazar, who nodded and hit the bell, and Augustus rolled to his feet and shuffled forward, blinking like a mad toad, his nose and the middle of his face one swollen, blood-smeared mass. Many boxers in this situation would allow the duffer to get one—some kind of glancing blow at least—and professionals had plenty of ways to make a punch look heavy and true. Half the game was illusion, principles of misdirection. But there was five hundred on the line and Joe was not this kind of man. He was irritated with the whole ordeal, the farcical nature of it, and Joe's passion to hurt the man passed beyond rage and circled back around to something almost like devotion. So Joe stood in front of the big man with his hands down and let him swing, rotating from the hips and using small motions of his neck and shoulders to slip a dozen shots as the dockworker pawed at him, exhausted and desperate, eyes bulging, spraying blood across Joe's chest with each gasping exhalation.

Then there was the moment, a brief interlude between lunging punches, when everything slowed down and Joe made the mistake of looking at Augustus's face just when the man seemed to gaze at Joe with a kind of innocence, his expression open like a child. He was reduced to a craven, lurching system of blood vessels and nerves, but to Joe, for just the briefest moment, a flash in the lights, the man was achingly beautiful.

Joe tapped him on the forehead with a left and when Augustus ducked Joe twisted and driving from the knees and snarling through gritted teeth he unloaded an uppercut, catching him bang on the chin. Augustus immediately stiffened, hands dropping, head rolling back, falling as if he thought the ground was going to catch him, his calves, buttocks, shoulders, and head all hitting the floor at the same time. A froth of bloody bubbles at his lips, arms floating up stiff in the dead man's clutch, like he was reaching for something from beyond the grave.

The crowd went completely silent. Joe looked at the woman with the little blue-lipped girl, who was still staring at him, unmoving.

Yes, he said with his eyes. You see the true nature of things.

People in the audience began to scream, someone shouting *he killed the man!* and then more yelling *dear God he's dead get somebody he killed him!* People began to run up the aisles, knocking over chairs, climbing over each other to get to the exits. McCarthy yelling over the din, his blood-spattered shirt torn down the front to his navel.

Folks! Listen to me! He's gonna be just fine!

Salazar vaulted into the ring and dumped a bucket of rainwater on the unconscious man, who spasmed once, craning his neck, looking around with rolling eyes. Joe dancing on his toes in the corner, still throwing combinations, his heavy eyes half shut, exhaling through his nose.

Look! McCarthy shouted. He just took a little nap! See? Now, come on back and sit down, folks! We'll have him up and about in a minute.

The crowd began to come back, murmuring down the aisles, sheepishly returning to their seats, half of them a distraught mess, unsure of the strange, barbarous magic they had just witnessed. Joe jogging in place and repeating the combination: straight left hand, dip the shoulder and quarter turn, twisting up and in with the right. They looked at him slack-jawed, blinking. He did the combination again, slower this time. Then he did it again. The crowd staring at him, silent. A little boy ran up the aisle waving a white handkerchief, peanut shells crunching under his feet, his face streaked with tears.

***

Later that night Joe had his newspaper and a cup of ginger tea sitting on a little table next to the copper tub in the basement of the hotel. Salazar tossed a handful of sea salt, lemon peel, and bitterroot into the steaming tub then went upstairs to bed. It was near midnight, the only sounds the reluctant settling of the old hotel and the occasional clink and gush of a water closet. The basement was cold, damp, and dimly lit, with steel water tanks on one side and the hotel's enormous electrical transformer occupying half the room. Joe half dozed, submerged up to his nose, his breath rippling the calm surface of the steaming bath, keeping a cracked eye on the transformer vent. Every ten minutes, the coil would start cycling, grinding to life and spitting out a wad of blue sparks that occasionally landed in the tub.

When the door opened Joe figured it was Salazar returning or maybe Patterson. Instead a man he had never seen before walked to the foot of the tub. He was barely five feet tall and shaped like some peculiar kind of water bird. A snugly tailored black suit, stringy mustache, a bow tie so heavily starched it was a bladed weapon. He bowed at the waist, revealing beneath his thinning hair a jagged white scar that ran across the crown of his pate.

I am sorry to intrude upon you like this, he said in a posh English accent, clasping his hands together in a solemn gesture. But the man upstairs said nothing about a bath. I am Rabbi Henry Cohen, and it is an honor to meet the greatest Jewish boxer in America. I'm here because a telegram was delivered to you today. I represent the Central Relief Committee of Galveston, and I would like to urge you to reconsider the proposition from Mr. Curley.

I haven't responded yet, Joe said.

I told him you would refuse the offer. But I am here to change your mind.

Joe picked up his washrag and began to excavate the crannies of his ear. Better to finish washing before the water got cold.

I'm also here, Cohen said, as the senior rabbi of the Temple

B'nai Israel, representing our congregation and the Jewish people of Galveston. Would you like a cigarette?

I don't smoke.

Cohen struck a match on the bottom of his shoe.

You'll have to forgive me, Mr. Choynski. It's been a difficult couple of days. Couple of months, actually.

Is it as bad as they say?

Cohen blew smoke at the ceiling and picked a fleck of tobacco off his lip.

It is beyond what you have heard, I'm afraid. But we will rebuild.

Joe depended on his ability to analyze the presence and bearing of a man and to determine a kind of threat value that was not limited to their physical dexterity or strength. He concluded that Cohen was a small man who projected a surprising degree of presence.

Be a pal, Joe said, and hand me my robe, will ya?

Cohen picked up the heavy cotton robe from the back of a chair. Joe rose dripping from the tub, stretching out his arms over his head, the full length of his alabaster nakedness steaming. Cohen handed him the robe, then politely turned his face to the wall.

Have you ever fought a Negro in Texas, Mr. Choynski?

Sure.

The opponent in question, Cohen said, is one Mr. Jack Johnson, a Galveston native and worthy opponent. Won his last four contests quite handily. Single-handedly saved a number of people in the aftermath of the storm. He's a local hero. He should rate quite a crowd.

Apparently not everyone likes him, Joe said.

Do you have children, Mr. Choynski?

I do not.

But you are married?

Yes.

Is your wife here with you in Victoria?

San Francisco. She is ill.

I'm sorry to hear that. Do you know who Clara Barton is?

Of course.

The direct beneficiaries of this fight, Cohen said, will be the storm orphans of Galveston, as we call them. Clara Barton and the American Red Cross organization have set up a facility dedicated to caring for the children orphaned by the storm. We feel that your reputation and Jack Johnson's local support will generate much-needed funds.

Cohen spoke in a quick deadpan tone, making it difficult to distinguish satire from sincerity. Joe carefully wrapped his hair in a turban of his own devising. He needed to get upstairs to his room to comb it out.

I'm out of the game, Rabbi, Joe said.

Curley offered you fifteen hundred dollars, correct? What if I say we can double that?

No, thanks.

How about triple that amount? We will house you for three weeks, *and* you will have the opportunity to instruct interested citizens in your scientific boxing methods, at a pay rate of your choosing. I can promise you that the general excitement surrounding the fight will provide several alternative sources of income.

Joe tied his robe. The electric transformer rattled to life, and he took a step back and gestured to Cohen to do the same. The fact was, Joe didn't get good offers anymore. He had already fought everybody, beating most of them, and the ones he hadn't beaten, like Jeffries or Corbett, didn't want to fight him again. He fought Bob Fitzsimmons to a forty-eight-round draw in 1894, the two men furiously bludgeoning each other for more than four hours. Afterward, Fitz refused to be in the same *building* with Joe. "The most devastating puncher I ever faced," Fitzsimmons said. Nobody wanted to get in the ring with Joe anymore, even for an exhibition. He was known as someone who seemed to take every fight personally. Many fighters over the years came into the ring expecting an easy dozen rounds of fancy footwork and pulled punches and suddenly found themselves brutally poleaxed by this oddly articulate blond man with sleepy blue eyes and lightning hands. The two men watched as the transformer gave a convulsive shudder and hawked a gob of sparks that arced across the room and fell into the bathtub with a faint hiss.

I need a comb and a shave, Joe said. Why don't you meet me in the parlor upstairs in about twenty minutes?

Agreed. I was told you are a man of principle.

Did you take in the show tonight?

I did.

Would you say that what I did to that gentleman was the act of a principled man?

I would say that there was an open bargain on the table. There was no attempt to withhold or obfuscate the true nature of the engagement.

And the cheap drink?

That part of the contract he also entered willingly, Cohen said. With gusto.

The humiliation in front of his family? His wife and daughter? Was that the act of a man of principle?

I'm not sure where you are trying to lead me, sir. But the greater part of our lives is determined by such bargains.

No illusions, Joe said. No unearned righteousness. That's all.

***

The next day, Chrysanthemum Joe's Scientific Boxing Revue was packed up and shut down. Joe cashed out Patterson, the twins, and Leon and his donkey. Phil the monkey was shipped back to New Orleans, where he lived a feral existence in the botanical gardens of a wealthy dowager. After wiring money to San Francisco to pay for Louise's care and putting money down on several outstanding notes, he had sixty-three dollars and change left in the money box. Two days later, Joe and Salazar were on the night train to Galveston.

DIANA

Clara Barton and the ladies of the American Red Cross set out on the thirteenth of September, five days after the hurricane, in a private railcar provided by the *New York World*. They would arrive in Houston in three days with medical supplies, the core of their staff, and Liverwright, the *New York World* reporter, and his photographer, who together would document the entire enterprise for the newspaper. Other Red Cross volunteers would meet them in Galveston from points all around the country.

In the railcar were six ladies and one gentleman from the D.C. office, including Diana Longstreet, Clara's personal assistant and director of operations. With assistance from Mr. Lowry, the venerable quartermaster and trusted aide, Diana rigged up curtains to separate the sleeping areas in the car. Mr. Lowry slept in the corner on a straw tick with his greatcoat pulled up to his mustache, while Clara and the other women took the bunks. Liverwright and the photographer sacked out in the aisle. Diana shared a bunk with her younger sister, Cordelia, who was just twenty-four and on her first mission for the Red Cross. Cordelia worked in the volunteer hospital ward in D.C. and had been pestering Diana for years to travel with Clara. Experience had taught Diana that young survivors of a disaster often adopted a feral mode of existence, the shock and horror having disrupted their ability to trust. She figured someone like Cordelia, whose heart was broad and accommodating, could be useful in the orphan assistance effort. Diana knew that her own fondness for children was more like that of her father for his cattle—both were something to be cared for, protected, raised properly. Deep emotional involvement was a weakness that led to poor decisions. Diana was not plagued by this self-knowledge. The *objective awareness of self* was something Clara touted as intrinsic to the development of a mature, modern woman.

The first night on the train, Diana poked her head through the curtain as the two newspapermen lay smoking and chatting in the dark.

We have a long journey ahead of us, gentlemen.

She was in her housecoat, her hair in a single thick braid that reached the center of her back. The glowing red coals of their cigarettes moved in irregular arcs from their mouths to where they rested their hands on their stomachs.

I'm asking you gentlemen to put out the cigarettes and go to sleep. Is this not clear?

Yes, ma'am.

As journalists, you are naturally observant and perceptive people.

That we are, ma'am.

Liverwright whispered something and suppressed a laugh, and the glowing coals moved through the dark again. Diana reached back into her bunk, over the slack form of Cordelia, and grabbed the small water pitcher on the shelf.

Diana, Cordelia murmured from her pile of blankets, what are you doing?

Go back to sleep, Delia.

Diana stepped through the curtain and into the car, walking slowly in the dark until she kicked a bare foot on the floor.

Easy, ma'am, Liverwright said. You'll hurt someone.

Diana leaned over the two men and upended the pitcher of water. They leaped up, sputtering curses.

Miss Barton needs her sleep, gentlemen, Diana said. We all do. Good night.

The ladies of the American Red Cross had only the vaguest sense of what they were heading into. The reports that trickled out of Galveston suggested perhaps several hundred dead—certainly a catastrophe by any measure, but one that the city managers and local institutions could likely handle. When Clara emerged from her office with instructions to mobilize anyone in the D.C. office who could travel, Diana had a feeling that they were embarked on an unnecessary endeavor, needlessly taxing Miss Barton's health. Recently, Clara seemed fatigued in body and spirit, her joints so stiff that she needed assistance in rising from a chair—something that would have seemed unthinkable just a year ago. The week before they left for Texas, Diana found her sitting on the steps of the D.C. office, her eyes closed, resting during the climb to the fourth floor. The woman is eighty years old, Diana reminded herself. Give her the courtesy to age as she must! But Clara could not be stopped once she formulated a plan of action. Diana had seen Clara stride into a phalanx of angry men with rifles and calmly convince them to return home to their families. She worked miracles with rational appeals delivered in a calm, confident manner.

The door that nobody else will go in, Clara was fond of saying, *seems always to swing open for me.*

Diana and all the ladies who worked with her at the Red Cross knew that this was because Clara pushed through that door with her own two hands. As a young teenager growing up in Kentucky, Diana was captivated by Clara's exploits during the catastrophic flood of the Ohio River in 1884, and at age nineteen she moved to Washington, D.C. to join the American Red Cross. In a few years she became Clara's personal assistant, and then at twenty-six the director of operations. She still took care of Clara's day-to-day needs, including waking her in the morning with coffee and giving a final briefing in her bedroom in the evening. For the twelve years she worked for the Red Cross, Diana modeled her professional and personal behavior on Clara. *She is a fully realized, independent person,* she wrote to Cordelia after her first year in Washington. *The model of what a modern woman should be!*

They arrived in Houston on the sixteenth of September. There was still no direct communication from Galveston except the accounts of a few scattered souls who had fled the storm, and their stories were so mixed and strange that nobody knew what to believe. The Red Cross left Houston on a steamer that same night, stopping in Texas City where they were met at the wharf by the Salvation Army who gave them tinned beef, bread, and coffee. They reached Galveston Bay before daylight on the seventeenth. It was so dark and silent that they didn't know they were in the bay until word came down from the captain.

Where is the city? the ladies asked.

The ship's crewmen shrugged and pointed into the darkness. Soon they saw flickering points of light and smelled wood smoke drifting over the water. There was another smell under this, something sweet and cloying, and the ladies held handkerchiefs over their noses and dabbed their watering eyes.

Is the city on fire? they wondered aloud.

A few minutes later, the ferry started nosing its way through a thick floating mat of debris, the hull thudding and bumping as they collided with boards and splintered logs. Diana stood by the rail, trying to descry the outlines of the city. All she could see were fires along the beach and farther inland, but no buildings. Cordelia bent over the rail, peering into the water.

Oh my God!

Cordelia clasped Diana's arm and pointed. Mr. Lowry brought his lantern and hung it over the side, and they could see the white bloated mass that was once a person, facedown and naked, suspended just below the surface of the water. Then another body bumped into the circle of light—a black man, his face twisted in a shocked expression, his eyeballs bulging from their sockets. Cordelia screamed, and Diana grabbed Mr. Lowry's arm to pull back the light.

They went to the bow, where the navigation lights cast a funnel of light on the water. The bay ahead was thick with bodies, the boat pushing through them like a barge through floating lumber. Mr. Lowry was at Diana's elbow, holding a handkerchief over his nose and mouth.

Should we alert Miss Barton?

No, Diana said. Let her sleep.

This was no small crisis, Diana thought. At least a hundred bodies in this section of the bay. The total numbers would surely be well into the thousands. She closed her eyes and swayed with the gentle rolling of the boat, feeling the terrible helplessness of regret. She had brought her sister into this horror.

They disembarked at Galveston into a confusion of darkness, smoke, and wreckage. Spindled mounds of debris loomed in the dark, and men with torches staggered around the docks while shirtless black men pushed wagons full of bodies, followed by more men with rifles. Mr. Lowry helped Clara off the boat while Diana supervised the unloading of their supplies. Liverwright and his photographer stumbled off the boat with their cases and immediately began to inquire about liquor, disappearing into the gloom with a Mexican boy. Despite the activity, it was quiet—just the creak of splintered wood, the groan of settling wreckage, wooden cart wheels crunching over debris. Most of the men moved about listlessly like lost sleepwalkers, and there was a stifling hush about the city, as if no one wanted to raise their voice for fear of waking something.

Clara sat on a stack of crates in her black dress, with a wool coat over her shoulders, reading a stack of telegrams. She hadn't said much, which meant she was shocked by the magnitude of the carnage. When the situation was dire Clara would burrow down into the work, focusing on the logistics, on what mattered now. We are not prepared, Diana thought. This is beyond us.

By the time they finished transporting their supplies to the warehouse designated for their headquarters it was late in the evening and the ladies were torpid and spiritless, wrung out with exhaustion. Clara took a private room on the second floor, and

Diana, Cordelia, and four other ladies shared a large top-floor room. Everyone but Diana immediately slumped into their cots and fell asleep. Cordelia lay on her side, still wearing her coat and boots, gripping her carpetbag with one pale hand. The stone warehouse had survived the storm with minimal damage, but the first floor was swept by the flowing water, leaving the walls and floor coated with a crust of mud. All the windows in the building were blown out by water or wind. Diana carried the rest of their bags to the upstairs room and with Mr. Lowry's assistance she covered the windows with canvas sheets. Their room on the third level was mostly dry but the floor was covered with plaster and bits of broken glass, so Diana swept the floor before wrestling Cordelia out of her coat and boots. Her sister's face was pasty white and her torso was soaked with sweat. The past twenty-four hours had been a terrible shock, and Diana knew that it would only get worse.

Diana knelt on the floor and opened her traveling chest, an ancient, hulking thing of Javanese teak that sailed a half dozen times around Cape Horn with a whaling great-uncle. She had engaged a carpenter in Washington to modify the chest, creating an intricate set of interlocked drawers, boxes with pressure-release lids, sliding cabinets, and file sheaves of sanded pine that expanded outward like a Chinese fan when the latch was released. One-third of the chest held her personal effects, and the rest was correspondence, itemized invoices, organizational protocols, and the detailed records of every humanitarian crisis and relief mission that the Red Cross had taken part in over the past decade. Kneeling on the floor of the darkened room with an oil lamp, she spent a quiet hour arranging her materials before sitting down at the desk by the window to work.

She rolled the window shade up a bit to let in a breath of tepid, odorous breeze. The city was dark, lit only by fires in the streets, and a row of blazing charnel fires on the beach that burned with a bluish tint. The loud crack of burning timbers, the sporadic shouts of men, and underneath it all the constant sound of water trickling, dripping, draining.

Diana opened a bound sheaf of papers containing the manifests for supplies, and the itinerary for the next ten days as laid out by Miss Barton, including tours of the morgues, hospitals, and orphanages on the island. It would all have to be revised to fit the scale of this disaster. There were no orphanages left; they all had been utterly destroyed in the storm. She tried to focus on her work, but the stench of moldering death was like nothing Diana had ever experienced before. Wearing a kerchief and perfume did nothing to stop it. It inhabited her mouth, coating the lining of her cheeks, tongue, and throat as if she were chewing on the rot.

She opened a coin purse and took out a small photograph in a silver oval frame. A thin man with a drooping mustache, his left hand tucked into his waistcoat, his right holding a pocket watch. It was taken six years ago at the sanitarium in Colorado. She carried his letters in a small wooden box, banded together with ribbon, arranged by month. The last month there were only two, both written for him by a nurse.

Diana did a final walk-through of the warehouse, checking the doors and windows before she went to sleep. The Central Relief Committee officials said that gangs of looters were active at night and squads of deputized men patrolled the streets with guns. A contingent of soldiers had arrived from Houston, and more were on the way.

We cannot guarantee your safety, the CRC representatives had told them on the docks.

Clara put her hand on the man's arm.

We are not afraid.

But we are afraid, Diana thought, all of us. Even Clara. Cordelia hadn't spoken a word since encountering the bodies in the harbor. They weren't afraid of looters or anything to do with the living who wandered this broken landscape. They were afraid of the horrors they had yet to discover, the grisly monuments that death had fashioned here.

The front door of the warehouse had been blasted to splinters by the storm but Mr. Lowry nailed together a temporary replacement of water-warped boards, fixed with a rusty padlock. Diana unlocked the door and stepped out onto the front steps. The warehouse stood on the corner of Twenty-Fifth Street and the Strand, and the buildings on the other three corners were shattered hulks of brick and wood barely visible in the inky darkness. The street was two feet of muck, with a few planks laid in antic patterns for walking paths. Smoke drifted slowly down the streets, and she could hear the crackle of distant fires. There was an echoing report, then another—gunshots somewhere in the city.

Something moved in the rubble of the building directly across the street—a shape coalescing in the smoke, a shadow on a shadow. Diana held her breath, holding perfectly still as the small figure came down from the pile of rubble, picking among the bricks until it reached the street. The smoke formed a kind of backlight, and Diana could see the silhouette of a child standing there, looking at her. A little girl in a dress that was too large. Other shadows were sliding behind her in the rubble.

Hello? Diana said.

She stepped into the street.

May I talk to you? What's your name?

The little girl was starting to disappear. Diana blinked hard, her eyes burning and watery in the smoke. Like some kind of vanishing mirage, the girl seemed to be fading back into the darkness. Was she imagining this? Then another shape separated from the gloom and moved toward her. This was not a child, but something lower to the ground. Diana felt a creeping terror rise up her spine. An enormous old hound dog ambled out of the dark and crossed the street to sniff Diana's boots. He turned his head and listened for sounds no human could hear, then loped back into the dark rubble. The little girl was gone.

HESTER

The day the ladies of the Red Cross arrived on the beach, Hester was crouched in her hiding place, watching teams of men pull bodies out of the rolling surf and stack them on the sand. In the first days after the storm they carted the dead from the city to the beach and piled them with the dead already gathered there. A group of black men were marched onto the sand by white men carrying rifles with fixed bayonets, and they spent the whole day loading the bodies on barges. Hester counted seventy-three wagonloads. The barges sailed off over the horizon and returned late the next day, their decks empty. The next morning the bodies began to wash ashore, some with concrete blocks, chains, and sash weights still attached. Many of the bodies had come apart and the shallow surf was a stew of parts sloshing and festering in the harsh September sun. More black men were marshaled at gunpoint to dig a series of large pits stretching down the beach. They piled wood in the pits, stacked the bodies, covered them with more wood, and doused them with fuel oil. As the fires grew more bodies were tossed in. Greasy smoke covered the beach like a creeping fog and the stench grew so strong that men vomited repeatedly. After a few hours most were incapacitated and another crew was brought in. At night, Hester could hear the squeak and scrabble of the masses of rats that crept out of the wreckage and swarmed over the bodies, the delicate smacking of their tiny jaws.

Her thoughts turned to her own hunger. She learned that she could pilfer bread from the relief wagon that parked behind the Methodist Church if she came before daybreak when the driver sat snoring in his overcoat. Hester brought the bread back to her lookout and ate with the intense concentration of a penitent breaking fast, saving a careful portion for her supper. She gave the crusty end bits to the dog then stretched out with the waterlogged book, slowly turning the blurred pages.

At the orphanage the girls were scrubbed and dressed every Christmas Eve and marched to the west side of the city, where the cotton barons and shipping kings lived in grand stone houses with crenellated walls, turrets, and elaborate walled gardens. They would enter one of the residences where the sisters lined them up in a vast gallery filled with huge oil paintings of gilded figures in dreamy sylvan scenes holding scepters and golden spheres in their delicate ivory hands. Then the people who lived there would come down the line and inspect each girl, the matriarch often stroking a cheek before pressing a candy or square of chocolate into their palm. What Hester remembered most were the libraries, the dark oak shelves lining the walls, settees covered with taut red leather, a roaring fire in a fireplace that was taller than the biggest girl at the orphanage. And the endless rows of books—upper balconies lined with even more—some behind glass cabinets, others stacked on carts, heavy tomes left sprawled open on the broad desk that faced the garden doors. The girls were sometimes allowed to silently explore the library for a few minutes while the sisters went behind the closed doors of the parlor to discuss something with the owners, *but do not touch a thing, girls, not a thing!* Left alone the girls spread out and crept along the tall shelves like frightened kittens, silent and wary, letting their fingers hover over the spines, peering closely at the covers. The sisters never said what they discussed with these people, but the girls knew that these were the people who fashioned the world to their liking. The older girls maintained that sometimes one of the girls would be taken into the private conference with the sisters and then never be seen again. They said that these girls were spirited off to some other world, a place filled with warm rooms and unending chocolates and books and families who picnicked on mountaintops and sailed schooners for the coast of Florida. But for as long as Hester could remember, the same number of girls always trooped back toward the beach in the dusk, slumping toward the squared silhouette of the orphanage lit up against the darkening sky, the girls solitary in their thoughts, still savoring the things they had seen.

Last Christmas, Hester found herself alone in a library nook and without thinking, she slipped a book off the shelf and tucked it under her cloak. As they were lined up to leave, the mistress of the house, a grim, skeletal woman with a silver wig and a heavy rope of pearls, came down the row, giving them each a sweet and patting their hair with her clawed hands. Hester stood with her arms clasped in front of her, holding the hefty book against her rib cage, sucking in her stomach, staring vaguely into the middle distance. The mistress of the house paused, dangling the wrapped sweet in front of Hester's impassive face. Hester shook her head, *no*. The old lady's eyes widened, then narrowed, roving down her body, pausing almost imperceptibly at her midsection. Hester's heart seized like a clenched fist, and her vision blurred as she prayed to the god of the sisters. After a moment a thin smile tremored across the mistress's face, and she slowly bent over and whispered, her dry lips brushing Hester's ear.

Only thieves and poets truly exercise free will.

She dropped the sweet into Hester's cloak pocket

But they often die young.

Then the old lady moved off down the line of eager, waiting hands.

At the orphanage, Hester kept the book hidden in an old trumpet case deep in a closet packed with dusty musical instruments. Sometimes after lights-out she and Little Cora would retrieve the book and turn the pages in their bed, looking at the words and engravings in the thin slice of moonlight coming through the window. Neither of them could read, but to the two little girls it seemed as if the story hidden there revealed itself to them all the same. It was always the story of their second life, the new life beyond this one.

The Red Cross ladies came through the piles of rubble onto the beach in two columns, like a formation of soldiers. An austere elderly woman in a dark dress was at the front, stabbing the sand with her cane as she walked, two men hurrying alongside carrying a camera on a tripod. The rest of the ladies wore white dresses with sashes and brimmed hats. Several carried parasols for the sun and held handkerchiefs over their nose and mouth.

Gentleladies, Hester thought. Like a parade of angels.

A tall, slender woman held on to the elderly lady's elbow to steady her as they stepped through the sand. This tall woman was without a hat and had black hair that ran down her back in a thick braid, her forehead flushed pink in the sun. Hester watched the ladies walk onto the beach, the crews of men parting before them, mesmerized by the orderly procession of freshly starched and blindingly white dresses. When the ladies saw the bodies and parts churning in the surf their lines faltered and they huddled together, gaping at the charnel mounds blazing in both directions up and down the beach and at the gangs of men swinging bodies into the flames. When a lady bent over, gasping and retching, the tall hatless woman helped her to her knees and pushed sand over the puddle of vomit with her boot. After the rest of the women staggered off the beach, the tall woman with the braid and the old woman remained, conferring together. Their voices drifted on the wind and between the surf and the snapping fires and the clack and rumble of the horse teams Hester caught a few words. *Committee. Orphans. Diana.*

That was the tall woman's name: *Diana.* Hester rolled it around on her tongue.

Diana called out to a man who was accompanying them, and he ran off and returned with a horse cart. They loaded the old woman into the cart and gave the driver instructions.

Diana. She helps the older gentlelady.

When the horse cart galloped off, Diana turned back to the beach, wiping sweat from her brow with the sleeve of her dress. The sun rose above the sea like a hazy, festering yolk. She turned toward Hester's hiding spot in the ruined building.

They stared at each other for what seemed a long time while

black flakes of ash drifted across the sand at Diana's feet and the men continued to stack bodies like cordwood beside the fires. They were quite far apart but Hester felt that she could see Diana's face clearly—the lines of her eyes, her elegant throat. She looked familiar, like someone she had always known.

Diana gestured to her with one hand, *come to me.*

Hester shook her head, *no.*

When Diana left the beach Hester crept down from her spot and came out in the alley along Thirty-First Street. She followed the ladies as they wound their way northeast to Twenty-Fifth Street and toward the bay, the ladies picking their way through the rubble, holding up their dresses with one hand. After another eight blocks they filed into a three-story stone warehouse with elegant arched windows on the corner of Twenty-Fifth and the Strand. There were women in white dresses everywhere, flowing in and out of the building, carrying boxes and stacks of clothes, food, and bedding. A banner hanging over the door said, American National Red Cross.

A building of women. There was something mesmerizing about these ladies—the white garments, the way they moved with such purpose, their unselfconscious manner. It was like an image of a new, possible world, Hester thought. Maybe it was a future version of the orphanage, as if all the girls had survived the storm, grew up together, and became a family of women.

Hester was crouched in the shadow of a stack of splintered lumber when a few of the Red Cross ladies noticed her. They smiled and held out their hands, beckoning.

Little one, come. Come here.

Hester turned and ran.

JOE

The lights in the dining car were all extinguished except the candle on Joe's table, guttering and swaying as the train heaved across the dark flats of south Texas. The dining car attendants had all gone to sleep and Salazar had slunk off to his bed hours ago. Joe wore a beige linen suit with a silk cravat and matching pocket square, a starched and pressed cotton dress shirt, and cuff links of beaten silver in the shape of an iris. A small glass of plum-colored sherry sat next to a copy of the *San Francisco Call*, turned to the dramatic reviews. The train rattled over a crossing, and the sherry sloshed to the lip of the cut glass, refracting bits of purple candlelight onto the white tablecloth. Joe never drank anything but water, coffee, and milk, but occasionally he liked to order a glass of sherry just to admire the color. Every few minutes he turned the glass to change the pattern of the shards of light that splayed out over the scarred knuckles of his hands.

Just over the rushing and clicking sounds of the train he heard voices, male laughter coming from the next car where a small bar served out steam beer and brandies. Joe pushed the sherry away, gathered his paper, and went down the aisle.

The barman had gone to bed, and two men were leaning on the bar, helping themselves to the brandy which they drank out of water glasses. Oiled hair, wool suits, laughing suntanned faces, decent shoes that needed buffing. Salesmen, Joe figured, working their territory and returning to the company offices with their bags stuffed with receipts. They turned to look at Joe, nodded. Young men in their late twenties, perhaps. Not city men but not yokels, either.

Evening, gentlemen, Joe said. May I join you?

Sure, pal. Whattya having?

Joe walked up between the two men, leaned over the bar, and retrieved a bottle of seltzer and a glass. He could smell the brandy on their breath, the dining car on their clothes. Roast beef and potatoes, then the hint of some perfume. Perhaps a final caress from the wife before departure, Joe thought. But a gentleman should always carry a scent of something more refined than his own salty musk. Joe himself slapped his neck twice a day with a dash of Guerlain's Eau de Cologne Impériale, a perfume first developed for Napoleon III. One man stepped back to give him room at the bar; the other did not. Joe turned to him first.

Joe Choynski, he said.

Ko-in-ski.

The man made eye contact with his friend and smirked. Joe fixed himself a glass of seltzer, added a slice of lemon from a bowl on the bar. He shook out his hair, stretched his neck, and smiled at their reflection in the window. The car shook with the terrible velocity of night travel through an unseen landscape.

Good company is often hard to come by, Joe said, especially in the long, dark stretches of the evening.

The two men looked at each other. One man nodded into his drink and the other murmured something and looked away, fumbling with a book of matches. His forearm brushed against Joe's flank. The other man licked his lips.

Joe raised his glass to the reflection of the three of them, standing there together like old friends.

Gentlemen. To unpathed waters and undreamed shores.

***

The next morning, Joe stripped down in the middle of his room in the Tremont Hotel in Galveston. He stood in a wash basin and scoured himself thoroughly with a brick of tallow soap and a hunk of rough sponge. After rinsing and drying he rubbed his body with a mixture of olive and linseed oils and performed a vigorous half hour of jump rope before scraping the sweat and oil away with a thin strip of sandalwood. On the windowsill sat a tall glass jar of his daily breakfast: a viscous mixture of hand-ground nuts, oils, and spices that Salazar claimed were essential for proper digestion and evacuation. Joe put on his white tights and vest and stood at the window for a few minutes, spooning the nut mixture into his mouth and gazing at the ruined docks and Pelican Island beyond. Joe had come in late and the rail station was only a block from the hotel, so he hadn't seen the full extent of the devastation. Now in the full light of morning the wreckage was astonishing. Two months since the hurricane, and the piers at the port were still smashed to toothpicks, and the rows of massive warehouses on the quay were broken hulks listing badly over the thick soup of flotsam in the bay. Teams of men were picking through the heaps of debris and horse carts snaked down Twenty-Third Street. Most of the lots along Harborside Drive were unidentifiable piles of rubble.

Joe took a sheet of newspaper with him into the water closet and latched the door. He laid the paper on the floor and pulled his tights down around his ankles. He closed his eyes and completed the shameful act in less than a minute. Afterward he balled up the newspaper and tossed it into the smoldering fireplace grate and watched as it flared then settled into ash.

The hotel lobby was mostly full of men in suits having heated discussions over sheets of figures and topographical maps. Joe strode through the lobby to the café, his tights and bare arms drawing curious glances from a table of women in white dresses. While he ordered a coffee at the bar, a tall woman with a dark braid of hair set her teacup in the saucer with a clink and stood up from the table, smoothing the crisp white flanks of her dress. The other ladies in white gathered their bags and followed her out to the lobby. They all wore sashes emblazoned with a red cross.

Joe gulped his cup of black coffee then jogged the twelve blocks south to the beach. It was a cool morning with a brisk wind off the water and low, threatening clouds. The devastation was more complete the closer he got to the ocean, and the last blocks were nearly scraped clean. The few stone and brick buildings still upright, plastered with oceanic mud, stood like lonely sentinels on a wasted plain. The air was rich with the muck of unearthed organic matter from the sea floor and the charred funk of burning trash. Work gangs clearing and sorting wreckage on the sand lined up for a dram of whiskey from a barrel on a wagon, turning to stare at Joe as he jogged past in his clean white vest and tights like some kind of mythic swan taking human form. The ocean was cream-gray, foaming breakers swelling up the beach, where a towering pile of burning debris was stirred with long poles by men stripped to the waist and with rags tied over their nose and mouth. A line of white canvas tents stretched for a mile to the east, the flaps tied back to let in the morning light. Families huddled around smoldering fires in the sand, stirring cook pots and swatting the swarms of black flies. The entire length of the beach was wreathed in drifting banks of smoke.

Joe shucked off his shoes and ran down the beach in a full sprint, arms pumping, knees high. He ran for about a quarter mile then turned and raced back before resting for sixty seconds, hands on his knees, drawing loud, raucous breaths. He repeated this eight times. A group of grubby children gathered in the sand to watch. Joe did a few sets of leaping squat thrusts and the knot of children edged closer. A boy with soot-blackened fingers gnawed at a moldy potato. The others were silent and still as barnacles. After the final set, Joe fired off a dozen one-armed push-ups, grinning at the kids, who stared dumbly back at him. He stood up and took off his vest, mugged a bit, and gave them a flexed bicep. Still nothing. Joe shrugged and walked into the creamy waves.

The bottom was smooth, fine-grained sand—not a single rock or shell—and Joe waded through the chilly surf until he was waist deep. He dived under an oncoming wave, coming up and clearing his nose and smoothing back his hair. The drifting remains of small craft bobbed out beyond the breakers as a dredging vessel chugged east toward the channel, trailing thick gouts of smoke. Small bits of wood and debris clouded the water and stuck to his skin. The horizon was a featureless yellow line.

Joe turned back to the city, the silhouettes of shattered buildings like a maw of broken teeth. The children on the beach were all standing in a line, watching him. A ragged urchin on the end stood apart from the others. She wore a dirty blue dress that was too large for her and clutched a dark-brown doll. She had a wise, knowing look about her and an old lopsided hound dog sat at her feet. Joe waded out of the surf.

What's your dog's name? he said.

The girl took a couple of steps back, clutching the doll to her breast, her face expressionless. Joe stopped and held up his hands.

The girl turned and ran up the beach, the dog loping after her.

***

When Joe got back to the hotel Salazar was standing by the open window in his bedclothes, playing a melancholy tune on his trombone. Sheets of paper covered with musical notations of his own devising littered the floor around his feet. Joe stripped down and lay on his stomach on the floor and Salazar put away his trombone and opened his satchel of oils. Then he slapped and punched at Joe's back before settling into some long strokes from his calves to his neck, pushing hard with his thumbs to dig out the knots. A few minutes later Joe was snoring deeply and Salazar left him there covered with a towel and went to the hotel lobby to get breakfast.

Joe woke precisely forty-five minutes later. He did six sets of push-ups, then dashed cold water from the basin on his face and sat naked with pen and paper in a patch of sunlight from the window.

Dearest Lutie,

The destruction of the city of Galveston cannot be overstated. The smell alone is indescribable. They had to impress gangs of men to handle the dead and they tell me that the fire companies and police refused to touch the Negro bodies because they believe that a Negro body decomposes faster than a white one. The death toll is over five thousand and hundreds more are still missing. There are children everywhere, living on the refuse and sleeping in ruined buildings. A contingent of ladies from the American Red Cross and Clara Barton herself are here to direct the relief effort! My match with Mr. Johnson is designed to bring attention and monetary donations to support their cause, though this is the best offer I've had in some time and so it seems a reasonable way to retire. I will earn at least $4,500 for this fight, plus exhibition fees, so we'll have a nice little purse to celebrate with as well as a bit to put down on our debts. Soon you will regain your strength and we will be hand in hand in the footlights. I believe that people will still pay to see me shuffle around the stage for some years yet and when they see your footwork and hear some of your dynamite warbling "Diamonds and Ropes" will play in New York for a ten-week stand to SRO crowds!

Yours,

Joe

The night Joe Choynski became a professional boxer started with Joe stuffing himself with ice cream at Eddie Graney's sister's wedding reception. It was 1889, and he was twenty-one years old, with the Golden Gate Club Amateur Boxing Champion medal pinned to the lapel of a suit he borrowed from his father. Eddie and the rest of the boys were sending the waiter running back for more beer and bottles of wine, and in the confusion the waiter brought Joe an oloroso sherry in a cut-crystal glass. The sherry was the color of a fresh pomegranate, sparkling with angles of light, and Joe was mesmerized, staring at it as he spooned melting ice cream into his mouth.

Afterward, his crew mustered and set out to the North Beach Athletic Club to see George "the Maine Giant" Bush take on Ed Cuffe in a professional bout. They ran down Russian Hill in a mob, stripping off their ties and chanting popular songs, Joe the only sober man among them. They had just got to their seats when the announcer came into the ring and announced that Cuffe had a poisoned hand and the bout would have to be canceled. The crowd groaned and men began throwing cigar butts and balled newspapers in the ring.

Somebody should volunteer! men shouted. Another man!

Then Joe was springing up, offering to fight Bush. It seemed like the most natural course of action—he was, after all, the reigning amateur champion of San Francisco. Some fighters, like Gentleman Jim Corbett, retained their amateur status because it was seen as the more refined position, the purest form of sportsmanship. Joe was still an amateur mainly because his mother begged him to stay away from "prizefights," where men hammered each other for money in filthy basements under dank public houses. But since he was a young teenager, Joe had been in dozens of finish fights down on the docks when the reward was usually little more than reputation or to settle some minor score. Why shouldn't he get paid? He was in peak condition and hadn't yet met a man who put fear in his bones.

The crowd roared their approval and the announcer beckoned so with Eddie as his corner second Joe stripped to the waist and strapped on two-ounce gloves to take on the professional heavyweight. More than nine hundred people were crammed under the rafters of the gym, the place so dense with cigar and cigarette smoke that Joe couldn't see beyond the first half dozen rows of seats. The air felt like the inside of a sweaty fist.

If he hits me in the breadbasket, Joe said, I'm going to woof up all that ice cream.

Ah, hell, Eddie said. You just work him like you do, Joe.

Joe had barely looked at Bush but now standing in the ring he saw just how enormous the Maine Giant was: six four, 230 pounds, hairy as a badger, with a black handlebar mustache that hung below his jawline. Bush smiled at him, tapping his gloves together, and Joe knew the man considered this a farce. I'm just a skinny little apparition. He thinks he's going to roll right over me. *By heaven, I'll make a ghost of him that lets me!*

The ring announcer introduced him as "Jewish Joe Choynski."

At the bell, Bush came out in a rush and started working overhand rights like a sledgehammer, crashing through Joe's guard. Joe rotated away, but the giant stayed on his port side, hammering him on the temple, shoulder, battering his forearms. After a minute Joe figured the timing and came up with a nice jab to the man's chin but Bush just punched through it and cracked Joe in the face with a right cross, sending him staggering back, blood gushing in a thick rope from his nose. It wasn't the first time Joe had his nose broken, and he shook off the floating black dots in his vision, circling away from Bush, giving himself time to let his legs come back. Joe could hear some in the crowd laughing. *The fancy lad must be stinko! The yellow hair on this yid! Hey, Jew-boy! Look at the little flower!*

Joe came back in a southpaw stance and staying in a low crouch, he laced the giant's ribs and backed him into the ropes. Bush covered up with both hands as Joe worked a quick rhythm of lefts and rights to his generous abdomen. When Joe caught him down the middle with a crunching shot to the solar plexus Bush let out an anguished bark and Joe knew that this was a fight he could win. The bell sounded and Joe went back to his corner. Blood ran down his chest and legs, soaking Isador's pants and filling his dress shoes.

How's the nose? Eddie said.

I got enough red ink for everybody, Joe said.

Bush came out cautious in the second, wary of Joe's speed, and Joe circled and feinted to keep him guessing, working his combinations and slipping punches while Bush lurched around like a winded bear. Joe watched the man's hands and feet, separating them from the boxer so they seemed like appendages of something else. The high, singing feeling was in his veins, and Joe began to swing with malevolent intent. Bush was not a man, not anymore. Just a body, an offering. When Bush stepped to the outside of Joe's lead foot to throw a right hand, Joe slipped to the left and changed the angle, drilling the giant with a couple of hard hooks, and he could feel ribs crack as Bush let out a wincing gasp. Joe stayed patient and toward the end of the round he finally got the opening he wanted. Bush was trapped in the corner with his arms in tight, just peeking over his gloves, and for just a moment his face took on that brief, shining look of innocence and wonder. He was in unexplored territory. Joe let his hands go, battering his guard until he found the giant's whiskers with a vicious straight right and Bush decided that the floor was just the place for him. The referee knelt by Bush's prostrate body, staring up at Joe as if he were some alien form just now appearing.

There was a moment of shock, and then the crowd boomed, rattling the place with cheers, and Joe held out his arms and walked in a slow circle, the shouts and chants coming off the crowd like waves crashing around a point, falling all over him. The smear of dried blood on his face and chest cracked as he smiled, and his heart felt full in a way he had never known before. He was now a professional boxer, 1–0.

Eddie and his pals came over the ropes and they picked him up and paraded him on their shoulders around the ring and then out into the crowd with Eddie holding out a hat. In the end people pitched in seven hundred and sixty dollars to go along with the nine-hundred-dollar winning purse.

Joe came home that evening with the wad of money in a paper bag and his father whooped and hugged him hard with tears in his eyes. When Joe sheepishly handed him his ruined trousers stained with crusted blood, Isador threw open the front door and slung the pants out into the street, bellowing: *Cowards die many times before their deaths; the valiant never taste death but once!*

His mother was so upset she refused to leave her room until morning, when Isador removed the hinges.

The next day, on the front page of the *Public Opinion*, Isador wrote, "We are coming, Father Abraham! The boys of the Jewish persuasion are getting heavy on their muscle!"

DIANA

On their third day in Galveston, Diana and Clara met with the Central Relief Committee to discuss their role in the relief effort. They were brought to the second floor of city hall, with the CRC sitting behind a long table: Albert Lasker, Isaac Kempner, Jens Moller, Dr. George Soper, Edmund Kampf, Floyd Craine, Leo Balestri, Rabbi Henry Cohen, and at the end of the table, the official stenographer, Miss Williams. The men of the CRC were all civic and industrial leaders of the city—an ad hoc group put together to oversee aid and recovery efforts.

We have moved into the warehouse, Clara said. Starting tomorrow we will be available for limited medical treatment, kitchen services, and housing assistance.

Housing assistance?

Floyd Craine's small eyes squinted at the mess of papers spread before him. His face was sunburned and he had a carved ivory pipe clenched in his teeth. He wore a high formal collar that pouched the fat under his chin.

I don't remember seeing that *phrase* in the proposal.

We will try to reunite people with their families, Clara said. If there are no surviving family members, we will accommodate the children as best we can.

Your zeal in providing aid is well known, Craine said. Your work during the War between the States was certainly admirable, considering the, ah, impropriety of it.

We admire your long record of service, Rabbi Cohen said. And we are grateful to have you here.

Cohen was a slight man in a vest and boiled shirt, his fingertips stained with ink. He spoke with an elegant English accent—an Oxford or Cambridge man, Diana assumed.

My cousin's brother-in-law, Cohen said, went to your Office for Missing Soldiers, in Washington. He was looking for his father. It was a great help to him, and I'm glad I have the chance to thank you in person.

Clara nodded. Despite these sentiments Diana was furious. *Impropriety?* Balestri tapped his pencil on a bound stack of papers, which Diana recognized as the Red Cross Charter, written by Clara twenty years ago.

This organization of yours . . . the Red Cross, has come to help feed, clothe, and house the dispossessed?

Yes, Clara said. That is correct.

Balestri flipped a page and moved his finger as he read. Diana shifted in her seat and stretched her neck.

Isn't it true, Balestri said, that this Red Cross is some kind of secret French society of utopian socialists, determined to undermine the capitalist system in this country?

Mr. Balestri, Rabbi Cohen said, I must object!

Let her answer the question, Craine said.

Diana stood up, her chair scraping the floor. She ground her teeth for a moment, trying to regain control. They had met resistance before, though rarely so blatantly ignorant.

Gentlemen, Diana said, these questions are unfounded and insulting to our organization and to Miss Barton.

The commission members stared at her. Balestri cleared his throat.

Now, miss, you see—

We have come here of our own free will, Diana said, with our own financial backing, asking for *nothing* other than to be allowed to help the people of this afflicted city. Especially the children.

But, ma'am, there are things that a lady just shouldn't see. We've had a great loss of life—

Perhaps you've heard of the Siege of Paris? The Franco-Prussian War? Strasbourg? Or maybe you've heard of the Battle of Antietam?

Miss, please—

Thousands, dead and dying! And this woman tended to them with nothing but a rag to stanch the blood and a bucket of water to slake the thirst of suffering men. How *dare* you, sir! You will *not* speak to Miss Barton in this manner!

For the moment, the room was silent but for the furiously scratching pencil of Miss Williams, the stenographer. The committee members looked at each other. Diana felt Clara's hand around her wrist, gently pulling. She sat down and dabbed at her face and neck with a handkerchief.

Ma'am, Balestri said, I don't know how things go up north, but this is Texas. We have a different set of rules.

Switzerland, Clara said.

I'm sorry?

Diana looked at Clara, and her face had a strange, distant look, as if she were looking through the men of the commission and the wall of the building, out past the horizon. Diana's righteous indignation and rage plummeted. She recognized this look, but not on Clara. It was the unfocused gaze of the venerable wandering in the shadowy twilight. Clara was lost and alone, in some dim realm that no one could reach.

Switzerland, she said again in barely more than a whisper.

Diana put an arm around her. She gave the old woman's shoulders a squeeze, and Clara turned to her, the unfocused look clearing for a moment as she recognized Diana. Her eyes brightened and she smiled.

The Red Cross is a Swiss organization, Diana said. But now it is an American one, too.

Diana eased Clara up till she was standing. Would she be able to walk out of here?

Of course, Rabbi Cohen said. And we will work together with the American Red Cross.

We have informed you of our intentions, Diana said. Good day.

Clara placed her steps slowly and carefully, and they made it out the door and down the hall to where Mr. Lowry was waiting for them.

Miss Barton is tired, Diana said. She needs rest.

***

The next evening after supper, Diana was up in their room making out lists when Cordelia came in carrying a stack of folded laundry. Diana watched her sister as she went to the pitcher and basin and rolling up her sleeves began to wash her hands. Cordelia's fair skin was blotched and her blond-red hair in a tangled bun, but somehow she seemed even more enchanting, her raw beauty enhanced by her distracted state. Oh, if only Delia's gentlemen callers could see her now! The pile of desperate amorous verses on the parlor mantel would fill the room!

From the floor below she could hear the murmuring voices of children as they readied for bed and the window coverings rippling in the westerly breeze. On the beach in the distance the fires smoked, filling the air with particulate matter and turning the sunset into a dizzying spectacle of mawkish pinks and purples. The children were more numerous than they expected and it was proving difficult to coax some of them out of the wreckage. The children they convinced to come into the warehouse were usually catatonic or so emotionally distraught they wouldn't eat. It was a trying task to console a young boy weeping over the loss of his entire family. The ladies often resorted to speaking of God's plan for them, that this was a trial that would someday bring rewards, in this life or the next.

The children seem restless, Diana said.

They'll sleep, Cordelia said. They just don't want to go to bed, like any child.

How many do we have?

Sixteen so far. I was thinking Mr. Lowry could get a crew together to repair the carriage house in the back garden, and we can house a few more there.

I will ask him to start first thing tomorrow, Diana said.

Cordelia dried her face with a towel, took out her hairpins, then loosened her apron and stepped out of her skirts.

She's a full-figured woman, not an old broomstick like me, Diana thought. Her beauty was ageless, like something you'd see in oils on a twelve-foot canvas hanging in the gallery of a European museum. When she walked down the street in Washington men staggered in her wake, declaring their love-drunk proclamations, gathering like hungry crows outside her door, bearing gifts purchased with their last dime. Cordelia swiped her underarms with a rag then sat on the cot to take off her boots. She put her feet in a small wooden bucket filled with water and lavender oil. They had all taken to putting oils and scents into anything they could in an effort to mask the hideous stench of rot. Cordelia glanced up at the picture on Diana's desk, frowned, and scrubbed her toes with a horse-hair brush.

Something the matter? Diana asked.

I just wish . . . I had someone to think about, I guess. Some-one in another place, better than here.

Diana looked at the picture. The memory of that whiskery mustache brushing her cheek and neck. It was distant but still there. She still thought of him that way, but not often. His hands on her waist. His lips . . .

I wish I had someone to write to, Cordelia said. About all this.

You could write a friend back in Washington.

That's not what I mean. A friend wouldn't understand. How could you explain it?

I don't know, Diana said. I wish I had someone to write to as well.

Cordelia's face twisted up and she rushed to her sister.

Oh, Diana. I'm so sorry. So thoughtless.

Diana stood up and embraced her sister.

I can't think straight, Cordelia said. It's like I've been picked up and shaken and all the pieces are bumping around in there.

Diana squeezed her tighter and Cordelia sighed into her ear.

You'll be all right, Diana said. You're strong.

**

Diana walked downstairs and through the main hall, which was lined with cots where children slept or wrestled with their blankets. A boy in linen pants and shirt cried bitterly as he sat on his bed clutching a tattered peacoat, a lady in white kneeling beside him, her eyes closed in prayer. Diana took two cups of tea, some honey, and a small pitcher of milk from the cart and put them on a tray. In a small room in the front of the building was a makeshift parlor where Clara received guests and wrote letters. Diana found her there, wrapped in a horse blanket and napping on a water-stained couch.

Here, Diana said, setting down the tea tray. A drop of honey, no more.

Clara sat up and massaged her neck.

Thank you, dear.

Diana tipped in some milk. Clara held the saucer under the cup while she sipped. Upstairs, something banged on the ceiling and they heard the nervous laughter of children. The two women smiled at each other, and Clara stood up and moved to the window. A group of Red Cross ladies ladled soup out of a steaming copper pot by the doorway and a line of people stretched off down Market Street. Through the smoke, the sun was a ball of molten lead falling fast toward the water. Fine wrinkles gathered in delicate labyrinths around Clara's eyes as she squinted into the hazy light.

The second day at Antietam, she said. A horrible situation. This was September 1862. The badly wounded were laid in an apple orchard. It was late in the afternoon and I remember how the trees were lit by the setting sun—a lot like this one. It gave the orchard a look of something carefully put together, like a detailed model, lined with patterns of golden light.

Diana sipped her tea and found it hard to swallow. Even with milk and honey, the tea seemed fouled with the smell of death. She didn't understand where this story was coming from or where it was going. It was unlike Clara to reminisce like this. She was an entirely unsentimental woman.

The company moved out of the valley, Clara said. They said they would be back for the wounded. We knew they wouldn't. We crawled about on our hands and knees because there were still rebel snipers in the trees. There was a young cavalry officer. His legs . . . nearly shredded by grapeshot. There was color in his face. His voice was still vigorous. I was holding his hand and he was talking about the apples on his farm back in New York. How crisp and delicious they were. As a boy he used to perch in those trees like a falcon. He still thought he was going home.

Clara held out her hand, palm up. She moved it slightly up and down as if balancing some invisible weight.

I was supporting his head, she said, giving him a drink of water. There was a small *snap*, like breaking a green stick with your fingers. I felt a tug on my wrist. The bullet passed through my sleeve and hit him in the temple. Just inches from my hand. And the next second he was dead. I saw his eyes just . . . fade out, like something disappearing into the dark. I suppose I'm grateful that he passed over with this moment of his childhood playing out in his mind. Better than the agony of his wounds.

Clara took hold of Diana's hand as if she was suddenly embarrassed. Her eyes were shining and she took a deep breath. The two women had worked together closely for more than a decade, but Clara never confided on personal matters.

This memory was always, Clara said, another passing tragedy in the long, cruel narrative of civilization. A loss, a waste. But today it fills me with a powerful feeling . . . of regret. About my life. Regret for all that I have let slip by.

The two women stood looking out over the wretched remains of the city. Long shadows were falling and it would be night soon.

This mask that I wear, Clara said. You have to promise me that you won't make the same mistakes that I've made.

Diana didn't know what to say. Clara was someone who did *not* make mistakes. Who could possibly walk this earth with a clearer conscience and lack of regret than someone who had dedicated her entire life to easing the suffering of others? Clara released her hand and turned away from the window.

The children and the ladies are at risk, she said. I'm counting on you to hold them together. To keep them safe.

Yes, ma'am.

Please take the remaining tea and honey and give it to the children. I've had more than enough.

***

Though Mr. Lowry warned her against it, Diana began taking her break in the evening to walk the various neighborhoods and wards of the city alone. She thought that if she encountered orphaned children by herself, without her Red Cross dress and sash, they might be more willing to communicate with her. She wanted to explore the eastern part of the island, low-lying areas like the twelfth ward, where the destruction was greatest. These were also the poorest neighborhoods in Galveston, where blacks, Mexicans, Italians, and a dozen other immigrant communities lived. The committee expressly warned the Red Cross against venturing into this area, where there were reports of unrecovered bodies half buried in the wreckage and a general lack of potable water.

Before venturing to the east side, Diana first visited the area near the beach where the St. Mary's Orphanage had stood. All the children and the sisters were missing and presumed dead. How the children must have despaired, Diana thought, praying to God in their final moments, the sisters of the holy order unable to save them. She didn't blame the survivors, if there were any, for hiding in the wreckage and avoiding adults, who only brought more false promises.

The first few blocks off the beach were almost wiped clean. The storm had pushed all the debris into a wall halfway across the island, smashing through the city and scraping buildings off at the root. Only some scattered bricks and shattered timbers indicated that the orphanage had ever stood here. Diana walked around the ruins, carrying a basket with tinned biscuits, apples, and a small bag of hard candy. On the beach, teams of men were excavating large sections of sand. A cold wind blew from the north and pushed the waves into sheer faces that crunched down with a foamy roar. A man was standing on a pile of concrete block looking over the beach, and Diana recognized him as the Englishman from the Central Relief Committee, Rabbi Henry Cohen. He was watching the digging crew, hands clasped behind his back, rocking slightly, a cigarette in the center of his lips. A bicycle lay on the sand behind him. Diana climbed the small pile of rubble to where he stood.

Rabbi Cohen?

Cohen spun around and tossed away his cigarette.

Diana Longstreet, he said. Of the American Red Cross. That was quite a meeting.

I want to thank you, Diana said. I am glad to know that we have a friend on the committee.

My privilege, Cohen said. What brings you out here today?

I was told that many children went missing in this area. From the St. Mary's Orphanage.

Cohen put his hands in his pockets and jingled some coins. He took a deep breath.

Two days ago, a corpse was found on this beach. A young girl. Half submerged in the sand, with a length of rope tied around her waist. They eventually uncovered fourteen girls and one of the nuns. They were all bound together.

Diana put her face in her hands, trying to stop the image of a long strand of drowning girls, tethered together and spinning through the murky water with their mouths frozen in silent screams. Doubly cursed—betrayed yet again by the adults in their lives.

It appears the nuns thought the line might save them, Cohen said. It seems unlikely that any of the poor creatures survived.

They watched the work crew for a few minutes, Diana's dress snapping in the crisp wind that blew at their backs. The men were digging a long series of trenches marked with stakes.

I'm sorry to have told you, Cohen said.

No, Diana said. It is important to know.

Of course, sorry.

You are a polite man, Mr. Cohen. I appreciate your kindness. Please stop apologizing.

Understood, Cohen said. Right, I presume you have plenty to attend to, so I'll take my leave. I'd offer you a ride on the handlebars of my Arnold and Schwinn, but I suppose that would be out of the question.

I'll have you know, Diana said, that I have pedaled a penny-farthing through the streets of Washington for years.

I beg your pardon! A penny-farthing high wheeler! I am humbled by your athletic courage! There is a place not too far from here where they do a demitasse of coffee and butter rolls that rival anything on the Rive Gauche. We can have a cup and discuss the virtues of the velocipede! Do you love the theater, Miss Longstreet?

I have been to the theater if that's what you mean.

Do you have a passion for the theatrical arts?

I cannot say that I do. I rarely find the time for such things.

What do you do for entertainment then? When you do have the time?

I suppose I read.

Cohen crooked his arm and Diana took it. They stepped down off the pile of block.

Do you like Dickens?

I've read several of his books. They are well imagined.

I believe he's the master chronicler of the era, Cohen said. But what books or fine arts are you passionate about?

It was a question that Diana had never considered. The only things she cared about deeply were her work, her sister, and Clara. *And him. Do not forget him!* She had only one book with her on this trip. He gave it to her before he left for the sanatorium the last time. A thin volume in green cloth binding. She carried it everywhere she went, wrapped and tied in brown paper and tucked in a pocket in her traveling chest. She hadn't looked at it in over a year, as if she were afraid to open it again. But she remembered the inscription.

For my Diana—my friend, my companion, my love. These are only words but you can carry them with you. That way, I will be with you wherever you go. Love, M

Emily Dickinson, Diana said.

Ah, Cohen said, giving her an appraising glance. A romantic. Something sorely missing in this infected land. Here, grinding ignorance is fed and deployed for ill purpose.

What ill purpose?

You'll see soon enough. But we do have a theater, the Grand Opera House, which is reopening next week with a production of *Captain Brassbound's Conversion*, by the Irish writer George Bernard Shaw. You must sit in my box with me and my other guests. I'll also be hosting the celebrated Jewish boxer Joseph Choynski. From San Francisco. They call him Chrysanthemum Joe. Do you know of him?

I do not, Diana said. That seems like an odd name for a boxer.

When you meet him, you'll understand. Are you acquainted with the pugilistic arts?

You mean men thrashing each other with their bare fists? Hardly.

No, not bare fists, Cohen said. Three-ounce gloves. We are Texans, madam, not savages.

HESTER

She watched the ladies in white from across the street, hiding underneath a wagon piled with moldy sailcloth. In the afternoon the activity slowed as the ladies prepared supper, and Hester could smell onions simmering in oil. Then they came out in small groups in their crisp white dresses bearing baskets of food and began to spread out across the city. Hester watched a woman approach a group of black boys squatting on a pile of boards, picking at sores and slapping flies. She handed them metal plates heaped with rice and beans and the boys ate it gratefully with their hands. After talking with her for a few minutes they followed her back to the Red Cross building and went inside. Hester watched for the rest of the afternoon, but the boys did not come out again. The gentleladies of the Red Cross were not *bad*. She shouldn't be afraid of them. But where did the children who went into that building *go*? What if the gentleladies were gathering the children to put them back where they belonged? Would she go back to the island before the storm? Or to the second life? Or would she go to some other place?

Then she spotted Diana and another woman as they came out with baskets on their arms, heading east. Hester followed. They walked down Avenue E, sloshing through the ankle-deep water that flowed swiftly toward the harbor as the island continued to drain. After a few blocks, the hems of their dresses were soaked. There was something about the way Diana carried her head—the angle of her chin, the way she cast her eyes over everything—that reminded Hester of someone. All the ladies seemed to go about their days with a sense of righteous purpose, much like the sisters, as if they were bound by something powerful and unseen.

What doth the Lord require of thee, but to do justly, to love mercy, and to walk humbly with thy God.

Hester wondered if their God was the same God as the sisters'. Was it the God who reached down with a blunt finger to crush out the life of the unrepentant or the unworthy? Was it like the God she saw in her dreams—the massive, glistening holy eye that watched unsleeping and unblinking as we crawled about the earth like ants on hot sand?

At the corner of Eleventh and Avenue E, a crowd of people clothed in dirty rags gathered around the listing front porch of a mercantile store. Water gurgled down the street in a shallow river. They were watching two men in front of the store yelling in Italian, a language that several of the girls at St. Mary's spoke but that Hester didn't understand. One man was wearing a suit with a torn and ragged sleeve. An older man in a nightshirt was yelling at him, making urgent gestures. A woman in a shift dress sat on the steps with her head in her hands, moaning loudly. Several families were heating food over campfires in the alley beside the mercantile, sleepy-eyed children sitting in the mud. Diana waved to them, gesturing to the children. She pulled cloth bundles of bread and apples out of her basket.

Then the man in the suit reached in his hip pocket and stepped forward, taking a jerking swing at the old man's face. Several women screamed as the old man staggered back up against the wall, holding his mouth. His nightshirt turned crimson as the blood ran down his chest. By this time other people had noticed the Red Cross ladies standing in the street with water rushing around their ankles and they began to crowd around them, pleading and gesticulating with open hands. Behind them the old man rolled around on the sidewalk, croaking and gibbering with bloody lips.

Per favore stai calmo, Diana said, *c'è il cibo per i bambini.*

They passed out all the food in their baskets in a matter of seconds, giving the baskets away as well. Then a woman in a mud-caked dress tried to press a baby into Diana's arms.

Aiuta mio figlio, the woman said. *È malato e ha bisogno di medicine! Hai una medicina?*

The other Red Cross lady was frightened and tried to back away from the press of people. She was young, maybe just a teenager. Her hair was the color of the sunset over the dunes but she had Diana's dark eyes, filled with tears.

What is she saying? What does she want?

The child is sick, Diana said.

It began to rain—a hard, vertical rain that made the muddy street erupt around their feet. The woman held the baby boy out to Diana again. Hester could see that his color was all wrong and his dangling feet were swollen like fat little sausages. Another woman came out of the crowd with a young boy who limped badly. He had a long festering wound along his calf, puckered and exuding a yellowish fluid. Everyone was shouting in Italian, and Diana was holding her hands up, trying to explain something. Hester could see in her face that she was afraid. Diana wasn't afraid for herself; she was afraid of making the wrong decision. I can help her, Hester thought. There are no wrong decisions for me anymore.

Wait, Diana said. Just please give me a moment.

Hester darted across the intersection and into the crowd. She stepped in front of Diana and held out her arms for the sick baby. They all looked at her in that familiar way, wondering at this strange, dwarfish child with the sullen mouth and wise eyes. The mother hesitated only for a moment and then gave the baby to Hester. In her years at the orphanage Hester had held many babies, but this one was lighter and smaller than any of them. He was almost purple, like an unripe plum, and Hester could feel his chest rattle as he breathed. The cold rain increased into a driving downpour.

A dozen women were now pressed around them, shouting in Italian, and people had started to run back into the wreckage to bring out more sick and wounded. An old woman leaning on a stick tottered off, muttering in some ancient tongue. Diana turned around and gestured for the mother to place the boy with the injured leg on her back. The other Red Cross lady was already holding a toddler with red blotches on her skin and a hacking cough.

We will be back, Diana said. *Noi torneremo.* I promise.

They began walking back the way they came, Hester leading

with the baby, Diana with the boy piggyback, and the other lady cradling the toddler. Nobody said anything as they trudged through the mud, the rain drowning out all sound. Diana let Hester lead the way and she took them through alleys and blasted lots of rubble until they hit Market Street. Hester tried to lean over the baby to block the rain, but the poor thing sputtered and moaned in the deluge. Hester's arms began to ache and when she stopped and turned around, Diana nodded her head and got down on one knee in the street, her head bowed, her eyes closed. Her white dress was coated in black mud up to her waist. The boy on her back was asleep. The other Red Cross lady sat down in a puddle and sobbed with an open mouth as she shifted the child in her arms. Diana raised her head.

Delia, she said. We're almost there. You can make it.

They rested there for a few minutes, the dog whining pitifully. He wanted to be back in their hiding spot by the beach, warm and dry. Diana is not crying, Hester thought. I am small, but I am strong, too. Even through the rain, Hester could feel the unblinking eye of God on her like warm afternoon sun. She hoisted the infant high around her neck and pushed out her hips for balance. The way the baby cried out made her think of Little Cora, who she had held and comforted so many nights, and something splintered inside her chest and she felt the gaze of God shift away.

They kept walking. People rushed by them in the darkening evening and Hester saw the faces of a group of women in a shop window, watching them with blank expressions, candles flickering behind them. A block away from the Red Cross building she could see ladies in white hustling in and out and a group came toward them across the intersection with umbrellas and blankets. A woman took the baby from Hester, looking at her with large dark eyes. She also had a familiar face. The shape of her mouth and olive skin reminded her of someone she knew.

Little Cora? Is it you?

I've got her, dear, the woman said. Come inside now. Come.

Diana and the other woman sat down in the street, shaking with exhaustion. More women in white gathered around, shielding them from the rain with umbrellas. Hester backed away, rubbing her sore arms. What if they discovered she was one of the children who were supposed to be dead? Would they pile her with the others on the beach? Would she be put under the ground, her mouth filled with sand? A couple of men put the other two children on a stretcher, covered them with a blanket, and jogged through the front door of the warehouse. Hester kept backing away as the ladies huddled about Diana, helping her to her feet. The dog licked Hester's hand and whined, swinging his big head around toward the beach.

Hester turned and ran. She heard the ladies calling after her. Still feeling the baby like a ghost child in her aching arms, she ran. She ran through the rain until she reached her hiding place by the beach and rolled herself up in the scraps of carpet and blankets. The dog curled his length around her as the charnel mounds on the beach steamed and hissed in the rain.

After she warmed up she opened the book to her marked page and considered the cloudy abstractions of mottled ink, sliding her finger down the edge and silently moving her lips the way she saw the sisters do with their Bibles, willing the story of her second life to appear. But she was tired and the story remained obscured, so she tucked the book away and closed her eyes. A solitary rat, roused by her presence, emerged from her bedding and moved along a shattered windowsill, stretching each leg in turn before moving out into the evening.

As she drifted off to sleep Hester decided that the gentleladies who wore white and bore the sign of the Red Cross were some kind of angels come down from heaven, like in the stories the sisters told them from the Bible. They were made from the souls of all the girls at the orphanage, grown and matured into the women they would have become, then sent back to Earth to clean up the mess God had made. Perhaps she could help them, and then perhaps Diana would not let them put her with the rest of the dead girls who swam under the sand. The girls with rolling black eyes who called to her in her dreams, singing "Queen of the Waves" as the dark sea churned overhead.

The next night Hester sat in her hiding spot watching the moon dip into the smooth, oily water. The line of fire pits down the beach glowed with pulsing red coals. The dog rested his chin in her lap, groaning and lurching in his restless sleep. The tide was going out and the bodies were stacking up again, rolling in the shallows. There was a ripple of movement and suddenly a young man rose up from the water, jerking and awkward as if waking from sleep. He stood there in the waist-deep water, looking for a moment at the bodies that floated around him, then began working his way around the humped and bloated shapes, pushing between them, moving toward shore.

I am not the only one, Hester thought. Others that are supposed to be dead are waking up.

The young man stopped to bend over and peer at a body, then another. Sometimes he rolled them over to see their face. Each time he stopped he would take their hands and hold them for a moment. Was he looking for someone? Was he searching for his family among the floating dead? He was so silent and patient that Hester figured he must be praying with them, the way the sisters sometimes would when the girls were troubled. When Little Cora couldn't sleep, Sister Lucy would sit by her bed, holding her hand and praying. She let Little Cora recite her favorite prayer out loud in her tiny lisping voice before she went to sleep.

> *Angel of God,*
> *my guardian dear,*
> *to whom God's love*
> *commits me here,*
> *Ever this day,*
> *be at my side,*
> *to light and guard,*
> *rule and guide.*

God be with you, Little Cora.

I love you, Sister Lucy.

After Sister Lucy left the room, Hester would put out her arm and Little Cora would roll into her, nestling under her arm, her breath quickly becoming steady and her body warming with the onset of sleep.

I am with you, Little Cora, Hester whispered.

After Little Cora went to sleep, Hester would lie awake watching the moisture gather on the pipes that hung from the ceiling and listening to the quiet exhalations of the other sleeping girls. She used this time to imagine the second life—not the second life that the sisters spoke of, the eternal life with God the Father, but a second life here on Earth, with a family.

Hester's second life would be spent in the green backyard of a wood-frame house, somewhere with rolling hills and fruit trees in a row bending over the horizon. Inside the kitchen a dark-haired woman in a long dress was making fried potatoes and meat gravy, and a man with golden hair was watching Hester through the window, a book on his lap, a slight smile on his face. She was sitting on the grass, waiting to come in for supper, relishing the expectation of the way the man would pick her up with his big hands and the woman would nuzzle her cheek. After dinner there would be stories in a soft bed and the gentle creak of the house in the wind at night, and she would sleep long and dreamless.

This woman in the second life had always been somewhat faceless, a vague impression of neck and cheek and hands, sweet-smelling hair. As she imagined it now, lying in bed with the woman reading stories, the rustling of the pages, the warmth of the blankets, she could see the woman clearly; it was Diana. It was always her. But how was that possible?

The young man came splashing out of the water and up the beach and from the shadow of a pile of debris, a boy emerged. Another one, Hester thought. They hunched together on the wet sand and a match flared, illuminating the two of them, the young man kneeling and the boy, also black and maybe fourteen years old, looking closely at something in his hands. Hester could see the flash of reflective objects, something sparkling in the flickering light. The match went out and the boy sat down in the sand, and over the slow rumble of the waves Hester could hear him sobbing. The man tried to pull him up but he wouldn't go. He sat there and cried while the man pleaded with him. Something was wrong.

Hester stood up. The dog stretched and rolled over onto his side, snoring. She had seen many things since the storm. But the sight of this boy, a younger brother to the other—she could tell by the resemblance and the way they touched each other—awoke some aspect of her that wanted to remain apart. She thought of the sick baby on the east side of the island, and how Diana and the ladies went out looking to find those who needed help. It struck her then that the only way to survive this life was to be more kind. These boys didn't understand. They had just woken up from death and didn't know yet that they didn't belong here. *What doth the Lord require of thee, but to do justly, to love mercy, and to walk humbly with thy God.*

All of us, Hester thought—we have to be more kind.

She climbed down from her perch, dropped onto the sand, and began walking toward them. Low clouds moved across the disk of the moon and the beach turned dark. When Hester was about a hundred feet away the older boy suddenly stiffened and looked around and Hester felt something like a distant echo in the ground, a vibration under her feet. The unmistakable thumping cadence of running horses. Looking back over her shoulder she saw a kind of moving smear in the dark, topped with bobbing points of light—a group of figures becoming clearer as they rode toward Hester and the two boys. It was a group of men on horseback, maybe six or eight, holding torches high and coming at a hard gallop. Hester dropped and lay flat on the sand. The horsemen had rifles across their saddles and pistols in their hands. One slapped his horse's hindquarters with a coiled bullwhip. They all wore sacks over their heads with ragged eyeholes.

The boys took off, the older one running toward the water

and the younger one circling around the pile of debris and heading toward the dunes. The men on horseback rode by, passing within fifty feet of where Hester lay. The young man was running through ankle-high surf when they ran him down. They wheeled around as he tried to crawl back up the beach, dragging his crushed legs and when they rode over him again his body arched like a fish and Hester covered her face with her hands. She heard the crack of the bullwhip, followed by several gunshots. Then all she heard was her beating heart and the wind and waves and then low voices of men talking. Then a guttural baying sound, coming from her building. It was the dog, wailing into the night, wondering where she was. Hester lay still.

When she looked up the riders had dismounted and were standing around the body of the young man in the water. The other boy lay facedown up the beach and one of the men was searching through his pockets. Several of the men had taken off their masks. Their torches sent flickering tongues of red across the water, broken up by the rolling lines of low surf. The dog went quiet. The clouds shifted, and the moon emerged briefly like an open mouth in the surprised face of the sky.

A voice cried out, coming from the ruined buildings. A girl running out of the dark and onto the beach, heading for the circle of men. A black girl a few years older than Hester, barefoot in a calico dress, running hard, calling out a name. When she entered the circle of light from the torches, the man with the bullwhip raised his pistol and fired. The girl was yanked off her feet and tumbled backward on the sand like a puppet tossed in the corner. Hester covered her eyes again and screamed. Another pistol shot, then silence.

When Hester looked up, three of the men were coming

up the beach on foot with torches, swinging them from side to side, moving in her direction. The man with the bullwhip was in front. He had a burlap feed sack over his head with two misshapen eyeholes, and a sash across his chest that bore a red cross and some words that Hester could not read. The red cross? Were they helping the ladies in white? Had they come for her and the boys because they were supposed to be dead? Were these the men who put the dead who wandered this place back where they belonged? She kept her hands in front of her face, peeking through the cracks between her fingers. Maybe they would think she was just another body and let her be. She began to pray in the manner of the sisters, but instead of everlasting life she prayed for darkness and silence.

The man in the mask kept coming, his torch dripping thick sparks. Slowing his pace, he stopped about thirty feet away. He called over his shoulder to the others.

Over here!

The others came toward him, torches held high. I don't want to be tossed into the fires, Hester thought. I don't want to roll in the waves with the others. The sand in front of her hands began to lighten as they came closer, and she could see that the man was wearing ill-fitting coveralls and mud-crusted boots. He held out the bullwhip, the tip sliding through the sand like a rodent's tail. His eyes glittered with torchlight in the tattered holes of his mask. When he spoke his voice crackled and squeaked like broken glass.

I see you, he said.

There was a blur of fur and sand as the dog blasted by Hester and came roaring into the circle of light. The man stumbled backward, cursing, dropping the torch as the dog sprang at his face. Hester leaped to her feet and ran. She was only about two hundred feet from a water-blasted concrete shell of a building with empty windows. The torchlight behind her swayed and bounced; she knew they were chasing her, and they were close. The whip sang through the air by her ear, snapping on her shoulder and down her chest like the tendril of a wandering vine. Hester stumbled but kept running and threw herself through an open window, rolling into a pile of shattered furniture. She got to her feet and ran down the hall, heading for the door along what used to be Shoreline Boulevard. Men were shouting behind her, and she heard the drum of horse hooves as she flew out the door and across the street, slipping between the crushed hulk of the Emporium Hotel and an apartment building with one side sheared off. The dog was bounding along beside her, tongue flapping out the side of his mouth as if this were some kind of game. She came through the alley and entered the Austin Schoolhouse on Avenue M, crawling in the pitch-black up the skeletal remains of stairs to the second floor. She found a room with a door and closed it silently behind her. In the street below she could hear the horses smacking through the mud and the men yelling to one another, the man with the whip shouting instructions, the strange pitch of his voice. The moon shone through the empty windows. In a corner of the room a man was sitting up on a bed, staring at her. He was young, maybe twenty years old, with a mop of dark hair. His face was gray with some kind of sickness, and his eyes and mouth were surrounded by open sores. Hester held a finger to her lips. He lay back down, covering his face with his blanket. The dog was panting in her face, tongue lolling. His jowls were stained with blood and he was missing a front tooth. He sniffed her and began to lick the wound on her shoulder and chest. Hester sat with her back to the door and held the dog, clutching folds of his fur, one hand around his muzzle. Light from the torches on the street below flickered across the ceiling, and she heard men cursing and the scream of a horse as it stumbled through wreckage. With a finger she lightly traced the burning line of ruptured skin that ran from her collarbone across her chest, soaking the front of her dress with blood.

In the darkness Hester saw the glistening eye in the sky looking down on her, yellow and clouded with just a pinpoint of black in the center that quivered and jerked, taking in everything.

God sees me. He must.

She reached for the doll she kept tied to her belt and found only the frayed ends of the cotton rope. The doll was gone; she had lost it on the beach. Still holding the dog's jaws shut, Hester clamped her other hand over her own mouth, her body shaking as she sobbed.

She waited until the sound of hooves receded, then slipped out of the building. The city was veiled in darkness—small cook fires burning in empty windows, shapes passing in the streets. Echoing gunshots in the distance. Tired and weak, Hester stumbled past the refuse piles that clogged the streets, orienting herself by a large bonfire burning in the distance. The dog trotted alongside her. She thought it was the same charnel fire that burned just a few blocks from Twenty-Fifth Street and the Strand, where Diana and the ladies in white lived. But when she reached the bonfire where a ring of shirtless men were burning animal carcasses, she realized that she had gone the wrong direction. She was back on the east side of the city.

She stopped at a rain barrel on the corner, drinking deeply then immersing her head in the cool, metallic-tasting water. She didn't know if the ladies in white would save her or take her to some other place, but she was so exhausted and scared, she didn't care anymore. Anything was better than this.

The cold water opened her eyes for a while, but after a few blocks she felt her knees folding on their own, and then she was down on the street, crawling. A pair of men carrying a body between them shuffled by in the dark. Hester crawled into a doorway and curled up. The dog licked her face.

Just a few minutes, she thought, then I'll get moving.

She could feel the spreading puddle of blood forming around her. Lights flickered, red shapes dancing up and down her eyelids. Her body relaxed, not cold, no longer hurting.

She had tried to be more kind, *to love mercy.*

I am with *you,* Hester, Little Cora said.

We are all with you, the girls chanted together, their black eyes spinning and their voices clotted with sand.

She felt the earth roll underneath her body and in the distance she saw the house and the field and the orchard as it spun away from her, the fruit trees bending over the hill, the fair-haired man with his book, the warm bed with Diana, stories in the flickering light—all of it disappearing into shadow. Something warm settled against her, and she clutched at it. It felt like a small child, a little girl like herself. She heard a voice calling to her. It was Little Cora. Sister Lucy was with her and some others. She could hear them singing "Queen of the Waves."

I'm here, Hester said. But I'm not dead! I'm not dead yet!

JOE

On a gray November morning Joe and Salazar went to Curley's office to go over the terms of the fight. The color of the sky matched the plaster of sea mud and sand that still coated everything in Galveston, creating a landscape that seemed all of one element. Joe was dressed in a tweed suit made in London with a mustard-yellow waistcoat and bow tie, his golden hair combed straight back with a gentle curl turned up at his collar. He wore rubber boots and carried his bespoke leather button shoes in a paper bag.

Jack Curley sat at a table made from an old door and sawhorses, the surface covered with stacked playbills, telephones, and an iron money box. A tangle of telephone wires ran across the floor. It was a cool fifty degrees outside but the windows were nailed shut to keep out the fetid odors and Curley was sweating through his suit, his cheek packed tight with leaf tobacco.

He had three crank phones and as soon as he laid one down his assistant would hand him another. An ashtray shaped like a horseshoe was festooned with a half dozen unlit cigars, and every few minutes Curley would pick one up and roll it around in his mouth as he yelled at someone in San Antonio about the gate or receipts. Another man sat in the corner reading a newspaper with an ivory pipe clamped between his fat jowls and one ear taped over with a wad of bloodstained gauze. Like everywhere in Galveston, the floor and walls were saturated, putrid water squeezing from the boards like glistening fat whenever you took a step.

Joe sat on a stool and put on his shoes. There was a mirror on the wall and he admired the keenness of his shave, turning his head back and forth, tracing his fingertips along his jawline. Salazar was some kind of genius with a straight razor. The Spaniard stood by at attention, holding his valise as if it contained something much more auspicious than an old towel, a flask of mineral water, a hunk of Jarlsberg cheese, a tin of rosemary oil, and spare tights for his afternoon workout.

Curley knew Joe from his early years in San Francisco, when Joe was the top amateur on the West Coast. It was Curley who arranged the legendary fight with James Corbett that would define Joe's boxing reputation and launch him onto the international fight scene.

When Joe left high school as a teenager he was already working two jobs. At daybreak he was in the blackened shed of the dockyard smithy with his buddy Eddie Graney ankle-deep in cinders and working the bellows while Joe used a dead blow hammer to work out creases in copper sheeting. In the afternoon he worked at the Roberts candy factory on Polk Street, wrestling three-hundred-pound sugar barrels up the ship stairs from the dank basement storeroom. The San Francisco of Joe's youth was the rich scent of stewed meat, potatoes, broiled clams, gashouse and factory smoke, wash on the line strung between canted buildings, a pair of bright-eyed men arm in arm weaving down the wet street toting a pail of steam beer, women clustered on the stoops with babies tucked in packing crates, the evening air thick with Irish brogue—Yiddish, Polish, Dutch, Chinese. In the evenings Joe hung around the docks of the Mission District with his crew, watching the brawny dockworkers and sailors batter each other bloody, then setting up their own bouts with rival gangs. Joe was faster and could hit harder than the other boys and he found that he could bear down and keep swinging long after the others quit. By the time he was fifteen he was the champion of his crew, notorious around the docks as the skinny hard-boiled kid with quick hands and feet, the kid who fought like he wanted to hurt someone with every punch.

His father, a writer and scholar who appreciated vigorous sport, didn't endorse his fighting directly. He wanted Joe to continue his education, to become a public intellectual, to make a difference in the New World. But he knew that Joe couldn't stand the confinement of the lecture hall any longer. This boy needed to *move*.

Despite their differences nobody was shocked that Isador was so unabashedly proud of his brutal son, so unlike his brothers and everyone else in the family. Isador's dream for Joe was that of the poet, the dreamer, and the warrior all compact—a Jewish Renaissance man who could speak the truth, do it beautifully, and defend it with his own hands. *It is decreed that some must fight in the streets for the honor of our people*, he said, grasping his sixteen-year-old son by the shoulder one evening when Joe came home with a bruised face and scabbed knuckles. *Who is like you among the heavenly powers, Lord!*

Every day, Isador fought with ideas and wrestled the abstract into submission through strenuous mental exertion. He would explode out of his study, any time of day or night, vigorously declaiming on Herodotus or Milton or Epictetus in his rich, rolling tenor, and when Joe and his brothers heard Isador pounding down the hall reading aloud from Emerson's lectures at six in the morning they leaped out of bed while the cook locked herself in the pantry, everyone readying themselves for the inevitable impromptu Socratic interrogation. Joe understood at least one aspect of his father's maniacal urges, couched in the philosophy of the ancient Stoics: to take what is chaotic and unruly and make it serve your purposes. What did he have control over? What could he *not* control? On every page of his training journal, he copied a mantra:

> *I have this body, this physical self that I can bend to my will. I can make it go on, to continue when others cannot, and that is the essential difference.*

Like every kid in San Francisco, Joe idolized John L. Sullivan, the Boston Strong Boy, the last great bare-knuckle champion. Sullivan was a braggart and a bully who promoted his reputation as a man who would beat you senseless at the slightest provocation. There was nothing abstract or subtle about him. Unlike Sullivan, Joe was an attractive, quiet lad who loved the theater and generally carried himself with an aloof confidence. Other kids teased him about his attention to personal grooming and his dreamy, often effeminate manner. He disliked wearing a hat, and so his golden hair was a constant source of attention. Joe was also goaded with anti-Semitic taunts. The Irish, Germans, Swedes, Italians—everybody down at the docks wanted a piece of the Jews. *Hey, Jew-boy! Get a load of this skinny Yid!*

Joe gave them what they wanted. He began to enter amateur tournaments and won several city and regional heavyweight championships. Naturally averse to alcohol, tobacco, and other vices, Joe established a regimen of harrowing fitness practices and a disciplined diet. He ate porterhouse steaks, calf's-foot jelly, pan-fried cod loins, and piles of boiled greens to pack muscle on his expanding frame. The Chinese coolies down on the docks taught him the secret of soaking his hands and face in pickle brine to toughen the skin. Joe studied Jewish mystics, the orations of Cicero, Kantian ethics, Cervantes. For a full year he carried a battered, dog-eared copy of Matthew Arnold's *Culture & Anarchy* and fashioned a personal philosophy that guided his athletic pursuits. He was honing himself into a keen blade, the ancient Greek ideal of human perfection.

When nineteen-year-old Joe won the Golden Gate Athletic Club championship in 1887 by knocking out thirty-two-year-old Joe Connelly in three rounds, the club gave him a gold pin studded with diamonds. His father wrote in *The American Israelite* that "The Jews, who take little stock in slugging, are glad there is one Maccabee among them, and that the Irish will no longer boast that there is not a Jew who can stand up to the racket and receive punishment according to the rules of Queensberry." It was mandated that if he wore the pin in public he had to defend it against any challenger—and Joe wore it every day.

I want to show them that I am capable of something, Joe wrote in his training journal. *Something great and terrifying and diffi-cult. Something that stretches to the pale of physical endurance and basic human dignity.*

There was only one other man on the West Coast who outstripped Joe's growing reputation, and that was Corbett. They grew up less than a mile from each other and as youngsters belonged to rival gangs, Joe to the Golden Gate Avenue Boys and Corbett to the Hayes Valley Gang. James Corbett grew up to be the first true scientific boxer, and he had all the physical tools: fast hands and feet, a geometric jawline, horsey buttocks, and a calculating fighter's mind. Corbett was trained by the legendary instructor Walter Watson at the exclusive Olympic Club, then went on to replace Watson as the "Instructor of Scientific Boxing." His classes sold out quickly, and a special women's class had a waiting list of ladies yearning to be near the dashing instructor.

One spring, Corbett was set to fight Joe McAuliffe in an amateur match at the Olympic Club. When McAuliffe had to pull out, Corbett sent word to Joe, asking him to fill in. Joe said sure, but since he had never fought in an actual ring he didn't have any tights or gloves. Corbett loaned him some, but the tights were about two sizes too small and the gloves two sizes too big. Joe also didn't have a "second" in his corner, so he was alone while Corbett had three guys fanning him and spong-ing him down between rounds. Corbett outweighed him by at least twenty-five pounds and was several inches taller, and he battered Joe, mystifying him with boxing techniques he had never seen before. Joe never trained under a learned instructor. He had learned to fight standing in oily puddles behind shipping warehouses by the light of barrel fires and he was humiliated in front of the swell crowd. So Joe did what he could and that was to stand in the pocket and swing deep and hard. Corbett felt it. There was no referee, but after five rounds Joe agreed that Corbett outpointed him for the win, and the fancies stood and applauded as he limped out of the ring. As Joe was sitting on a bench in the shower room trying to catch his breath, a jowly man in a gabardine suit poked his head in and pitched a pair of five-dollar coins at his feet. *Nice work, Yid.*

Joe's continued exploits on the docks increased his growing reputation as the toughest nut on the West Coast and Corbett knew he would have to settle things in a more dramatic fashion. Joe made no secret that he also wanted another shot at Gentleman Jim and the next year, in 1888, the two men would meet in one of the most storied bouts in the history of boxing, when Joe fought James Corbett on a barge in Benicia Harbor off the California coast. Curley chose the location to avoid the police, who tried to break up illegal finish fights, and to keep the crowds down. But it was a hot ticket and despite the secrecy, hundreds of men set out in the early morning darkness in skiffs, rowboats, canoes, steam launches, and sailboats to try to wangle a spot on the barge. At the last minute Corbett changed his mind and decided he didn't want to go bare knuckle, opting for three-ounce gloves. Joe had shown up without gloves according to the agreement, but rather than cancel he borrowed a pair of leather riding gloves from a spectator. There was no prize for this fight other than the unofficial title of best amateur on the West Coast.

The match began a few hours after sunrise, and the two men battered each other under a blazing morning sun, the sea glassy and rolling, the air unusually still. As the barge heaved, Corbett repeatedly smashed Joe's nose with his left jab, splitting a nostril which bled freely, and for most the fight Joe was choking on his own blood, spitting out mouthfuls between blows. The seams on the driving gloves cut Corbett's face badly, and both men fought paralyzing muscle cramps.

After ten rounds the deck of the barge was awash with blood and nearly everyone was seasick from the rolling motion of the boat. A chunk of Joe's lip was hanging by a thread of skin until Eddie Graney snipped it away with a pair of scissors. Seagulls gathered in shrieking clouds overhead, diving after the cigar stubs and bloody wads of cotton that were pitched overboard. By the fifteenth round most of the spectators turned away or took refuge in the cabin to avoid looking at the hideous carnage. Joe's mind had gone reptilian by this point, unable to think of anything but surviving the next terrifying moment. Their gloves, saturated with blood, made terrible smacking sounds as they struck each other with reckless fury. After each round Joe watched Corbett rise up on unsteady feet, towering like a gore-spattered god, and so he cranked himself upright yet again, believing that he still had more to give.

I have this body, this physical self that I can bend to my will. I can make it go on, to continue when others cannot, and that is the essential difference.

Eddie Graney wanted to end the fight in the twentieth round. Joe's face was a hideous smear of blood and contusions but he grabbed Eddie's hand and fixed him with his swollen eyes, squinting in the hard sunlight.

Don't throw in the sponge, Joe said. I'm not licked yet. Let him kill me, but don't say I quit!

Corbett mercifully knocked Joe out with a left hook in the twenty-seventh round. Joe was physically spent, weak from blood loss, heat-stroked, and dehydrated, his face so bloody and swollen he couldn't see the punch coming—a shot to the side of his head that felt like a spear going through his skull. His already overtaxed muscles let go and he folded up, sitting cross-legged with his head down like a battered yogi, then face-first into the deck, arms limp at his sides. Joe was carried off the barge on a piece of sailcloth. He wept bitterly the entire boat ride back to shore.

Corbett had broken both hands and fractured his wrists and when he came home his wife was hysterical over the damage to her husband's face—the only time in his career that he sustained such injury. Gentleman Jim took to bed and couldn't move for three days. Joe lay in the Hammam Baths overnight, barely conscious, and a rumor circulated that he was dying. But Joe rose up again. A few weeks later he was back at the docks with his crew, his lustrous hair combed back from his noble forehead, his face unmarked but for his scarred lip. No amateur, including Corbett, wanted any part of Joe after that.

But it was Corbett who would trade on his skills and "gentle-manly" personality to turn professional and in 1892, after just *seven* professional wins, he got the chance that every heavyweight wanted: a match with the undefeated heavyweight champion, John L. Sullivan. The younger, quicker Corbett pummeled the aging, potbellied Sullivan, ending thirteen years of dominance and launching Gentleman Jim onto the world stage. It was Corbett who went on to star in a dozen popular theatrical revues that enjoyed standing-room-only crowds, and it was Corbett who became one of the first American movie stars, featured in the very first film Thomas Edison made for the public. In his entire career as a boxer, Corbett fought only *nine* different men, a total of only twenty fights recorded, including the Olympic Club bout and the "Battle of the Barge." In his career Joe would fight at least eighty-six times as a professional. He never got a chance to fight for the heavyweight championship of the world.

***

The man in the corner of Curley's office folded up his newspaper and crossed his arms, scrutinizing Joe. He was unshaven with a deep sunburn across his jowly cheeks and small porcine eyes. He wore a high-collar shirt and his shoes were muddy and untied. Curley hung up the phone and snatched one of his cigars from the ashtray, clamping it in his teeth while laying out some papers for Joe to sign.

A standard exhibition bout, he said, fundraiser for the rebuilding efforts. You're officially here to do your scientific boxing show.

Joe signed the contract and they shook hands. The man in the corner spoke around the pipe still clenched in his teeth.

Folks say you're about the toughest nail in the bucket, he said. Sure as hell don't look like it. My mama always said never trust a man with long hair or low shoes, and be dammed if you don't got both.

His voice was odd, raspy and cracking around his words. He scratched the bandage on his ear with his fingertips. His hand was bandaged as well, his thumb and first finger wrapped in bloody gauze.

Joe looked at Curley.

Who is this man and what is his role here?

Curley swung around, looking at both of them as if he couldn't remember who was who. His assistant was reaching with a shaking hand for the phone Curley had pinned in the crook of his neck.

Mr. Craine is a former state senator, Curley said, and a member of the Central Relief Committee, which is one of our principal sponsors.

You put that darkie down hard, Craine said, and you'll be doing all of us a favor.

Now, hold on, Curley said. We got notices in every paper in Texas and cables going out all over the country. We want a good fight.

Craine snickered and drew hard on his pipe, spitting a jet of smoke out of the side of his mouth.

People say you're a man who's known to get aggressive in exhibitions. Get after people so hard that fighters don't want to get in the ring with you. So you make it look pretty if you want, but not *too* pretty.

Joe knew then that this was the man who had sent for him. This was the man who wanted this Jack Johnson fellow beat down and silenced. He looked at Curley, who just rolled his eyes and shrugged.

We was thinking, Craine said, about calling this thing the Texas Nigger versus the California Yid. Whaddya think about that, Mr. *Ko-in-ski*?

Salazar exhaled dramatically and handed Joe the bag containing his boots.

I will bear it with a patient shrug, Joe said. As will Mr. Johnson, I assume. For sufferance is the badge of both our tribes.

Joe sat down, unbuttoned his shoes, and slipped on his boots. Craine looked at him with his head cocked like a golden retriever listening for footsteps. The assistant cleared his throat and hung up the phone he'd been holding. Joe placed his shoes in the paper bag and handed it to Salazar. He wanted to go for a long run down the beach.

Listen, Craine said, you gonna put this big smoke down, or what?

Why don't you tell me, Joe said, what this Johnson fellow did to you?

Craine took the pipe out of his mouth. His red cheeks were quivering slightly.

These Negroes down here need a lesson, he said. You weren't here after the storm. Like a pack of animals. Ain't that right, Curley?

Curley turned his head and spat a long stream of tobacco juice into a tin bucket on the floor.

I don't know anything about all that. I just got here a week ago.

And now, Craine said, they getting behind this Johnson. They see him as some kind of hero! Soon they'll *all* be acting like him.

Joe stood up and took another look in the mirror, smoothing his hair back with both hands. The sea air made it wavier than usual and he liked the way it curled around his ears.

You've contracted me to do a job, Joe said. But my justification to beat the man comes from a very different place.

Oh, yeah? Where's that?

Salazar opened the door to the hall.

You wouldn't know it, Joe said. I'm afraid it's too far for you to travel.

Joe walked out and Salazar followed, shutting the door so that Craine's response was only a muffled bark. Walking down the hall, Joe squeezed the back of Salazar's neck while the Spaniard smiled and shyly ducked his head. Joe admired a solid sense of the theatrical, and Salazar always knew how to stage an effective exit.

***

After his afternoon workout, Joe returned to the Tremont Hotel and did the shameful act, whimpering through gritted teeth until he was through. He did the shameful act only while standing behind locked doors, in darkened water closets and bathrooms, and always in the same manner. A sheet of newspaper laid on the floor, his pants hung on a hook or draped over his shoulder, seizing himself with shaking hands, his mouth in a rictus of pain, eyes screwed shut. Sometimes it was clipped memory reels of women he had known, mostly in his youth, dresses hitched with one hand and a knee over his shoulder, a scalloped neckline under his groping fingers, the pained expression in her eyes when he pushed into her. Sometimes the fury of a fight intruded—flashes of moments in the ring, the collision of flesh, the taut muscles of a man's arm around his neck, rippled torsos slick with perspiration. A wet tongue trailing down his stomach.

It was all horrible. Joe didn't know why he imagined what he did, but afterward he could rest, read, work out, sleep, and eat with the ease and comfort of a man in balance with the world. How he had come to this point, he did not know. During the first year of his courtship and marriage with Louise they had enjoyed a fresh and vigorous relationship. His Lutie, as he called her, was shapely in a natural way that blossomed on the stage. In her corseted dresses with her hair in curls she was impossible not to watch as she stepped through her dances in her delicate, springing manner. She was shy when naked but Joe worshiped her form in the dark, putting his mouth to every part of her.

Joe and Louise were married on a windy fall afternoon in Louise's parents' backyard in Cincinnati in 1895, just two days after he knocked out Dick Wilson in Louisville, notching twenty-six victories in a row in less than three years. Back then Joe was still gunning for the heavyweight championship of the world. He also wanted another shot at Corbett, who had already become the most famous man in America. After they said their vows, Joe and Louise kissed under a towering maple tree as their families clapped and cheered, red and gold leaves drifting down on the party like snowfall. Joe smiled and toasted the small group with a glass of ice water while Lutie ran her hands through his hair, picking out the leaves and laughing in his ear.

Oh, you Joe.

It's easy to fall in love when you have a dream in your heart.

It came to sour for Joe at about the time he stopped getting good fight offers and it became clear they would not have children. He couldn't say which came first. Louise wanted him to quit the fight game so they could put together a vaudeville-style show and go on the road. So he tried. Charlie Murphy helped them write a thirty-minute play called *The Sketch Factory* filled with some of Joe's rapid-fire erudition and Louise's song-and-dance numbers. Joe played a college student athlete and Louise was a gentlelady's maid with a wicked uncle who tried to lock her away in a convent. They patched it into a vaudeville routine and booked seven weeks through the Pacific Northwest, starring the Killer Chrysanthemum. In the third act Joe sparred with the villain, an old punchy named Tom Mitchell, to win Louise's hand. Mitchell was drunk most of the time but it didn't matter. Most top boxers in the game had a theatrical show, and they all involved a character and story that allowed them to get into a ring in the third act. Even John L. Sullivan had a touring gig, and every night the aging Boston Strong Boy waddled out in his knickers, bloated to the eyes with whiskey, and fake-pummeled some poor sap who was paid to take some shots and go down in a dramatic fashion.

After a week it was clear *The Sketch Factory* wasn't going to draw the crowds they needed. Joe was already tired of the fakery, and Mitchell was getting progressively drunker and turning their boxing scene into even more of a farce. Joe wanted real drama, but who wanted to see a pug like him putting on literary airs? *Absolutely nobody*, the producers and theater bookers told him. Louise still came out each night dancing and singing with a buoyant, optimistic urgency. When she knelt in the footlights at the end of the second act, crooning a love song to Joe as he brooded in a locker room with a towel around his neck, he could see the real tears of anguish springing from her eyes. But it wasn't enough.

Their last performance in Yakima ended prematurely when Joe hit Mitchell in the liver and the rummy puked his clam chowder all over the stage. The producers pulled out and left them with stack of playhouse contracts and an array of debts. But Louise still believed. Even when she began to faint dead away and couldn't work at the milliner's shop anymore, even when she took to her bed in North Beach with the Victrola by the window. Her principle remaining desire was to get Joe to quit the fight game. They would revise the show; they could still make it work. She begged him to let her go into a common ward rather than bear the expense of private care at home, but Joe wouldn't have it. Then she no longer had the strength to stand, and she begged Joe to leave her. To go on, to live another life. He refused.

Soon, Lutie became so weak she couldn't speak and she lapsed into a semiconscious state, no longer registering any reaction to external stimuli. Joe stayed by her bed and read aloud from Wordsworth, Keats, and Longfellow, cranking the Victrola, and cleaning her pale, slack body with a pan of hot water and a rag in the smoky light of the fish-oil lamp. The doctors were baffled and saw no remedy or end to her descent into darkness. Joe waited, vibrating with anxiety, his body aching for some kind of expression or contest, the long days stretching into longer nights, pacing the room and muttering virulent oaths to the dusty corners, to the steamed windows, to the seabirds that banked across the steel waters of the bay. Months went by and the money evaporated, so Joe put together the scientific boxing revue and went on the road. For almost a year he had been writing letters and received nothing in reply. His life telescoped inward on itself as he retreated into his workouts, his scientific boxing, his solitary dark pursuits. His only friend was a melancholy Spanish trombonist with extraordinary culinary skills. He hadn't lain with his wife or any woman in more than three years and had no inclination to do so again.

After Joe burned the newspaper in the fireplace grate he sat in his armchair and read from a collection of lectures by R. W. Emerson until around four o'clock, when Salazar knocked to announce that Rabbi Cohen was waiting for him down in the lobby. Joe washed his face and hands and put on a white oxford shirt with wool trousers. When he came downstairs, he found Cohen waiting out on the sidewalk holding his bicycle, his pant cuffs tied tight around his ankles with twine and his face slick with sweat.

You don't mind? Cohen said. It's only about twelve blocks to my offices.

I can keep up, Joe said.

Cohen mounted the bicycle and tottered down the sidewalk, then rolled onto the street, dodging the wide puddles and piles of splintered boards, Joe jogging along behind him.

Dearest Lutie,

There is a Rabbi here who has taken me under his wing. He is an Englishman named Henry Cohen and he is quite an eccentric fellow. Before the storm Rabbi Cohen devoted himself to bringing Jewish immigrants to Texas from Bohemia and other places in Europe. There are many on this island who do not appreciate his work.

The Rabbi has invited me to sit in his box at the grand reopening of the Opera House theater to see something called Captain Brassbound's Conversion and I have accepted. It was written by an Irish novelist by the name of Shaw, but I know nothing about it. Cohen is not the sort of Rabbi I am used to. He has a scar that runs across the crown of his head, given to him by a Zulu war party when he was in South Africa. They surprised him and took his gun and hit him in the head with it, then tied him up by the neck before they left. He said that when he woke up his biggest fear was that he had shot one of the natives who attacked him. He is confident he did not.

I am getting two fine workouts a day and Salazar continues to surprise with his cooking and body-cleansing treatments. I believe he is also composing a symphony for solo trombone, but he remains tight-lipped as always.

This city demonstrates every day how cruel and unjust the world can be. Everything seems out of balance. Tonight I am thinking of all the suffering I have caused. Like that unfortunate man at the lumber camp in Australia, when I met Salazar for the first time. It was like I was designated as a kind of emissary of pain, traveling thousands of miles to bring destruction upon him. I was just twenty-two years old, the same age as the young Negro I'm here to fight. Why did I do it? Why am I doing this now, again? What is this rage that I feel in the ring that pulls me onward? Why are you stricken with this strange ailment?

> *"Like as the waves make towards the pebbled shore,*
> *So do our minutes hasten to their end;*
> *Each changing place with that which goes before,*
> *In sequent toil all forwards do contend."*

I want to say to Patrice that I remain grateful for her care. I imagine you tucked under the heavy rug on the sleeping couch by the window, watching the rain come in off the bay as she reads these letters aloud. I have to believe that you hear these words.

I will be here at the Tremont Hotel in Galveston for

the next two weeks, and then when I'm done with this
business I'll be on the next train to San Francisco.

Yours,

Joe

***

In 1890, Joe was invited to Australia for a chance to take on Joe Goddard, the Australian heavyweight boxing champion. The Aussies had heard about Joe after the barge fight with Corbett and a widely reported contest with a tough Chicago pug named Glover. The crowd for the Glover fight was liquored up and salty to Joe, this undersize fighter with his spangled locks and indifferent manner, and they jeered and whistled every time Joe took a shot, calling him *Molly* or *Nancy-boy,* mixed with anti-Semitic slurs. Between rounds, someone threw a bouquet of purple flowers into the ring at Joe's feet. Joe responded by befuddling the gritty brawler with lightning footwork and stiff jabs. Finally in the fourteenth, Joe loaded up with a terrific right hook and sent Glover sailing through the ropes, landing head-first on the concrete floor. He remained unconscious for half an hour in a gruesome state, nose flattened, both eyes swollen shut, missing half his teeth. As they attended to Glover on the ground, Joe promenaded around the ring with a purple flower tucked behind his ear.

The *San Francisco Call* headline the next day: CHICAGO TOUGH BRUTALLY BEATEN BY CALIFORNIA'S "CHRYSANTHEMUM." Joe was quoted in the newspaper: "I can lick anybody, and I will think so until somebody licks me."

Joe arrived in Sydney twenty-two years old and raw, anxious

to take on anyone. The Aussies put him up against a quality fighter named Fogarty to see if he was authentic and Joe outpointed him in ten rounds for the win. The Aussies told him that if he could beat Mick Dooley in three weeks he'd get a shot at Goddard and the Australian heavyweight title.

Joe asked the boxing commissioner to please stop introducing him as "the Jabbing Jew."

The boys in California, he said, call me Chrysanthemum Joe.

The next morning a Spaniard with a trombone tied to his back came knocking on Joe's hotel door. Salazar was carrying a jug of unfiltered cider and a pail of boiled eggs. He told Joe he had a lucrative fight lined up and they needed to leave immediately.

But I'm fighting Dooley in three weeks, Joe said.

Salazar assured him that this would have no impact on that fight, handed Joe a hundred dollars, and hustled him out the door and down to the docks of the Nepean River, where a small steamer packed to the waterline with dusty sheep was waiting. Joe and Salazar sat on the tar paper roof of the pilothouse as they steamed into the vast wilderness of the Burragorang, passing through heavy forests of bottlebrush and black wattle, wandering thickets of Guinea vine climbing the soaring bluffs. The sun was brutal, and Salazar rigged up a shade out of his waxed coat and sheets he had taken from Joe's hotel. After lunch Salazar squatted behind the pilothouse and meticulously waxed his trombone with vinegar and duck fat. When he finished, he played a few jaunty bars of Barbieri's "Jugar con fuego" as the sheepherders muttered to their flock, averting their eyes from the instrument's spangled glare.

That evening the heat was even more punishing and the

mass of sheep on the deck bleated and broke wind, waves of hot, reeking gas blurring the sun setting over the western hills. The pilot shut down the boiler and went to sleep, letting the boat drift sideways down the river, easing itself along the muddy banks. Insects screamed in the dark trees, and a blue-white swatch of stars floated overhead like a river of diamonds. Joe drank coffee and gnawed on a boiled egg as Salazar blew a contemplative melody on his gleaming trombone.

It took two days to reach the lumber camp. By this time Joe was sick of boiled eggs and rightly piqued, but Salazar hustled him into a canteen where they had big steaming bowls of mutton stew with black bread and tankards of frothy sheep's milk. Salazar borrowed five dollars from Joe to pay for the meal and they sat at the table for an hour, drowsing in the afternoon sun through the open-sided building, picking their teeth with matchsticks. Joe appreciated the Spaniard's intrepid and unwavering nature. He was a man with singular vision and drive.

The next morning they hitched a ride on a mule team to a remote lumber camp on the banks of a creek without a name. Some unlettered ruffian named Irish Mike was flattening men far and wide and the camp got together a thousand-dollar purse for a professional to take on their man in a bare-knuckle bout. The lumberjacks eyed Joe with disbelief, grinning at his white ankle-length tights and glossy blond hair.

Looks a bit of the dandy, they said.

But Salazar had Joe take off his shirt and then showed them his contract from the Fogarty and Dooley fight and so they agreed to terms, with Salazar putting a side bet of an additional hundred dollars at three to one that Joe would knock him out in the first five minutes. Joe took him aside.

That seems a bit ambitious, old boy, he said. We haven't even seen this man yet.

Salazar started kneading Joe's shoulders and arms, working the muscles with curious skill. A crowd began to gather under an ancient yellow box gum tree, the lumberjacks hollering and kicking up a storm of dust. The Spaniard had borrowed money from Joe again for breakfast and coffee, so Joe was quite certain he couldn't cover the purse *or* the side bet.

Salazar expertly wrapped Joe's hands with torn strips of canvas and they walked over to the tree. In the center of the ring of lumberjacks stood some kind of bearded titan, stripped to the waist and sweating rivers, a wild-eyed bushman with a humped back and bouldery gut. Irish Mike did a series of looping haymakers for the crowd—punches that would have killed a horse. Joe could see that the lumberjack was without skill but possessed of great strength and an obscene lust for violence. Joe looked at Salazar but the Spaniard just gave him a wink, holding out his pocket watch for the official timekeeping.

Somebody smacked a stew pot with a ladle and Joe circled while the big man grinned at him like a mad zealot, flexing his shoulders and smacking his belly. Joe put his left foot forward and extended his left hand, coming at the man conventional style, and the giant lunged into a couple of punches, Joe ducking and circling away. Thirty seconds in and already sweat fell off them in curtains as they circled and feinted. Then Joe centered his stance and put his left jab into the lumberjack's snout two, three times, then followed with a straight right, his fists making crisp smacking sounds and opening up Irish Mike's face under the eye. He stumbled backward, confused by the speed and combinations. When Joe advanced Irish Mike lunged forward and tied him up, clutching and leaning on him, breathing hard and hot in his ear. Then the lumberjack clinched his hands behind Joe's back and lifted him in a cross-buttock throw, slamming him to the ground at the base of the tree. Joe lost his air in a single *whuff* and the world got very small for a moment, the size of a pinhole he was breathing through. He twisted in the dirt, trying to catch his breath while the mob of men surged around him, whistling and howling. He had the sudden sensation of being alone on the far side of the world, surrounded by men who wanted to hurt him.

Joe got his wind back and crawled to his knees. Salazar was holding the watch, looking at him with an arched eyebrow. He held up one finger. Joe got up and circled out of range, trying to relax, shaking out his hands. Irish Mike was wiping the blood off his face with his forearms, mouthing something with his rubbery lips. Joe knew he would try to clinch again, so when the lumberjack charged with his head down, Joe came up with a hard uppercut under the chin, the sound like an axe chopping into a femur, and Irish Mike stumbled back, spitting a wad of blood and feeling in his mouth with his fingers. Joe moved in on him with hooks to the body and Irish Mike covered up, but Joe switched the angle and hammered his ear and neck with a couple lefts. The lumberjack tried to twist away but Joe moved with him and popped his liver and the big man flopped to the ground, his bloody face moaning into the dirt.

They should have let him quit. But the lumberjacks hoisted Irish Mike up and pushed him forward, a stumbling, senseless sack of flesh. For a brief second, he peered out at Joe from under his hideously swollen brows, his eyes brown and soft, and Joe could see an ageless light radiating from the man, a sense of innocence and regret in one illuminating moment. Joe's heart throbbed with rage and he battered the swaying, bloody hulk until Irish Mike stumbled back into the gum tree, turning and hugging the trunk as he slid to his knees then fell sideways to the ground, pink snot bubbles swelling from his nose, and his fingers twitching in the dirt. The livid crowd of lumberjacks began shouting the filthiest curses Joe had ever heard, most of them incomprehensible to him. *You fookin' bandy drongo!*

Salazar collected the money and hustled Joe onto the wagon for their departure while the lumberjacks rolled the unconscious man into the creek to revive him. As they rattled out of the camp Joe saw them poking Irish Mike's humped back with sticks as he floated facedown in the brown water.

They went back to Sydney that night on the same steamer, this time minus the sheep; instead the decks were stacked deep with fresh-cut lumber. Salazar fried up lamb chops with onions and after dinner that evening Joe offered to take the Spaniard on as his fight trainer and second in his corner. They shook hands on the deal and then Joe tried unsuccessfully to sleep while Salazar sat on the gunwale with a bottle of bush wine, playing his golden trombone to the sluggish turtles that bobbed in their wake.

In three weeks, Joe would knock out Dooley in the twentieth round and get the fight with Goddard for the Australian championship. He would hurt Goddard badly in the tenth, putting him down hard. But in Australia the referees were outside the ring and by the time the referee got around to the side where Goddard lay and started the count, the boxer had been on the ground for a good ten seconds already. The Australian champ would come back and in the seventeenth he would catch Joe flush on the chin with a hard right, putting him on the canvas. Joe would crawl to the ropes and try to pull himself up but his legs would not answer. He would be counted out as the home-town crowd roared with joy, relieved that their man had stopped this dangerous Californian with the golden hair and sleepy eyes.

A week later he would journey back to San Francisco, sharing a berth with Salazar and his trombone. He would take on all the great boxers of his era and fall in love with a stage actress named Louise. But he didn't know any of this as he drifted down the river that night, just twenty-two years old, wide-awake to the world, the boat sliding through the river grass while Salazar played a song that an illiterate farmer composed in 1566 to honor the beauty of the queen of Spain. Joe wasn't thinking about the future, about anything except that flash of innocence he saw in the eyes of that unfortunate lumberjack— the same bright gasp of life he saw in every man who suffered under his hands.

DIANA

Diana was lying on her cot with a blanket up to her chin when they brought in the girl. It was late, after breakfast, and the room was still cold. The iron pipes of her cot were slick with condensation and the backs of Diana's legs and arms were damp. It had rained the night before and she knew the streets would be a nightmare of muck. There were dozens of newly arrived freight cars at the railyard and off-loading was going to be a trying business.

Clara had not left her room for three days. *Just tired from the travel*, she said, but Diana knew it was more than that. The morning before, she found Clara lying on the floor by the window, dazed and white-faced, half finished letters scattered about her. She refused to talk about it and grew angry with Diana's entreaties, her hands trembling as she pawed at the letters, trying to gather them in a pile on her desk.

I suggest that you focus on the tasks that lie at hand and let me be! Have I made myself clear, Miss Longstreet?

Yes, ma'am.

Then be on with you!

Though she was always a stern taskmaster and unsympathetic to incompetence, in all their years together Clara had never lashed out emotionally at Diana, even in their most trying situations. Clara still insisted that the daily reports be brought to her while she lay in bed, but it was merely for appearances, a facade. Diana was guiding the Red Cross in Galveston. The other ladies would be devastated to know the truth, that Clara was drifting away to some distant place where they could not follow.

Diana was half listening to Cordelia downstairs leading the children in a chorus of "Camptown Races" when her assistant Judith knocked on the door. She swung her feet off the cot and quickly folded her blanket, tucking it under her pillow. She splashed her face with water from the basin and smoothed her braid.

They found a girl, Judith said. We think it's the same little girl that carried the baby back from the east side? She's badly hurt.

The girl was lying on a pallet made of blankets in a small room on the second level. Ladies were kneeling around her with bowls of steaming water and cotton towels. Her dirty blue dress was ripped down the front and one of the ladies was trying to clean a festering wound that ran over her collarbone and across her chest. The girl's face was blanched white and her lips were purple, and Diana's first thought was *this child is dead!* She knelt down and took the thin wrist in her hand and felt a feeble pulse murmuring through her fingertips. Despite her ashen color, the girl was hot to the touch.

A man brought her in a wheelbarrow, Judith said. He said he found her curled up in a doorway.

We've got to get that wound covered, Diana said. Get the big shears from the kitchen and a fresh smock.

Liverwright tried to set up his camera in the doorway for an exposure of the little girl and the crowd of women around her, but Diana demanded he leave the floor immediately. The ladies cut the dress off the girl and wiped her down with sponges and wood-ash soap, her emaciated body covered with mosquito bites, fresh scars, and open sores. She was oddly small and compact, like a miniature version of a much older girl. Diana could tell that she had been malnourished, living on the streets since the storm, maybe even before. They got her wrapped up in cool towels, but her fever persisted. There was no response even when Diana pricked her toes with a darning needle. When the doctor arrived he examined the girl and came out of the room shaking his head.

The wound across her clavicle is infected, he said. Keep the bandage soaked with carbolic acid. She's lost a tremendous amount of blood.

Dr. Mountcastle was in his undershirt and suspenders, his glasses smeared with fingerprints. He was sleeping in a house down the street when the Red Cross ladies burst in to fetch him. Near eighty years old, he was one of the few remaining local doctors who survived the storm, found the morning after perched in a lemon tree in the orchard west of town. He was often drunk but a good doctor, and Diana and the ladies had come to rely on him.

Her fever is very high, he said. Keep her cool. Is there any ice to be found?

Can you tell how she got this wound? Diana asked.

Dr. Mountcastle scratched his armpit and looked away for a moment.

I was working in New Orleans before the war, he said. I saw a lot like this in those days. This young lass has been bull-whipped, I'd say.

Bullwhipped?

It's a miracle she's alive.

Will she wake up? What can we do?

She's between worlds, he said. There's no medicine that can help her where she is now.

Diana instructed Judith and the other ladies to take care of Clara's needs and the off-loading of supplies. Mr. Lowry was waiting with the ledger, but she would do the inventory later.

Open the kitchen, she told Cordelia. Feed and clothe anyone you can find. We have train cars arriving all day and the storage rooms are already full.

There's a dog, Cordelia said. Outside. We tried to shoo him away but he won't budge.

Give it food and water and let it be.

Then Diana closed the door. She put cold rags under the girl's neck and across her forehead and used a large piece of woven rattan to fan her body from head to toe. She knew right then what she was going to do. It was as if all the other concerns and obligations she kept ordered in her mind just drifted away like sand. She was going to bring this child back.

Because this was *the same girl*, she was sure of it. This was the girl who emerged out of the dark fog of smoke that first night. This was the girl she had seen that day on the beach, perched in a ruined building, regarding her with a flinty eye. And this was the same girl who burst into that circle of people in the Italian quarter and took that sick baby into her arms when Diana and everyone else was paralyzed with indecision. Until the girl took the baby, Diana hadn't known what she was going to do. The baby had a bad case of thrush and was having an allergic reaction to something, probably bad water. The girl's quick action likely saved the baby's life.

Diana stayed in the room with the girl all day. At Cordelia's insistence she ate a bit of porridge and milk for dinner, but otherwise she kept the door closed and cared for the girl. She washed the girl's hair and brushed it out till it shone and pulled it back and tied it with a bright blue ribbon. She cleaned and trimmed her finger- and toenails, rubbed lanolin on her scars, and powdered the sheets. She massaged the girl's arms and legs to promote circulation and changed the dressing on her wound every few hours. As daylight faded she lay on the floor next to the pallet, watching the girl's profile—the small nose, the rise and fall of her chest.

After a few days the fever finally dropped and Dr. Mountcastle recommended they get her into a more upright position and try to feed her. They piled cotton sacks stuffed with rags under her upper back and head and Diana spooned broth between her lips, wiping her chin as it ran out the corner of her mouth. The girl remained completely insensible to the world. Diana knew that dozens of boys and girls in their makeshift orphanage and around the island needed her care. She knew that she ought to be spreading her attention around to ease the suffering of the most children possible. And yet she stayed.

On some days she knelt by the pallet and ground her teeth, her fists knotted in her skirts, thinking about this little girl being whipped like an animal. The storm exposed a malignant tumor here, she thought. The island of Galveston and everyone on it would be better off if they just surrendered to the ocean. It was a cursed strip of sand covered with mosquitoes, sand fleas, and a thousand other biting insects, stinking swamps, fetid brackish pools, the wreckage of hundreds of homes, searing winter sun, damp cold evenings, a constant fog of humidity. The inhabitants were a scrappy bunch of unwashed and unlettered immigrants and Negroes ruled over by a select sliver of elite society that parroted the latest fashions and mannerisms of New Orleans or Austin, the born-on-the-islanders a scornful batch of mostly German stock with abrasive personalities and blistering sunburns. Vigilante squads of mounted men roamed the streets, looking for an opportunity to use the broad concept of "law and order" to justify killing the undesirable. Just a few days ago they found three bodies—the children of a popular black preacher named Ponder from the Avenue L Missionary Baptist Church—murdered on the beach. A group of island preachers organized a large protest outside city hall to demand justice. The CRC promised to take up the matter and find who was responsible for the string of attacks, but Diana already knew they would do nothing. Instead, they used the rumors of anarchist gangs of blacks and immigrants setting fires and looting the dead to bolster their policies for martial law, quick adjudication, and brutal sentencing carried out from the back of a horse. And now men with cardboard suitcases were showing up at the depot, buying up decrepit lots for a fraction of their worth, accumulating property and any kind of business that was for sale. Then there was the ongoing presence, even months after the storm, of the decomposing corpses of cattle, men, women, and children. The makeshift morgues in the warehouses on the docks remained full, row upon row of bodies crusted with mud. And always the pervasive stench of festering rot and death.

No, Diana did not believe in the resurrection of Galveston. As soon as the local authorities could care for the orphaned children who lurked amid the rubble Diana would take Clara and Cordelia out of this nest of thieves, speculators, bigots, and confidence men preying on a doomed race of the unlucky and the destitute. Let the waters roll over this murderous ground and be done with it.

***

One afternoon a few days later, Henry Cohen came riding up to the warehouse on his bicycle. When the ladies showed him in Diana was just finishing washing and combing out the girl's hair. The wound across her collarbone was finally scabbing up and the rest of her sores had faded. Cohen was wearing a finely tailored suit and waistcoat with a silver pocket watch, and his trouser cuffs tied up with twine.

Hullo, he said. What's this?

Diana explained the whole story. Cohen shook his head and whistled a long, slow note. When Diana told him Dr. Mount-castle's theory about the girl being whipped, Cohen smoothed the thin swatch of hair across his pate and studied the ceiling for a moment. He seemed to be calculating something.

A new horror every day, he said. So are you about ready to go, then?

Go? Where?

Oh, my dear. The theater, Miss Diana. We are going to the theater tonight!

Diana looked at him blankly. Her hair was still in a rough braid and she was wearing a dingy white Red Cross shift and hadn't bathed in over a week.

Captain Brassbound's Conversion. The opening of the Grand Opera House. Surely you haven't forgotten?

I'm so sorry, Henry, Diana said. Things have changed; I haven't been doing my normal duties lately.

I see. What's the girl's name?

We don't know. We think she was from the St. Mary's Orphan Asylum.

Ah, a survivor, then! At least there's one. Has the doctor said when she will wake up?

He doesn't know. He says it's not up to us.

Right, Cohen said. Now, pop on up and sort out the hair and dress and we'll be off.

I'm sorry but I can't go with you tonight.

Why not?

Well, I can't *leave* her.

Nonsense, Cohen said. You literally have a house full of qualified nurses!

I'm not . . . I'm not prepared.

Miss Longstreet, Cohen said. I'm quite confident that a modern woman like yourself can be washed and dressed for nearly any situation in a quarter hour. Now let me sit and do a Mi Shebeirach for the girl. It's a prayer of healing. I daresay you'll be back in an elegant dress fitting for a woman of your station and comportment before I'm through.

Cohen knelt by the girl and took her hand, bowed his head,

and began to murmur in Hebrew. Diana had a green dress made of silk and crinoline packed in her trunk. It was the same dress she carried on every trip. It would serve.

She went upstairs where her sister was cutting clean swatches of cotton for bandages in the rectangle of light from the open window.

I will watch over her myself, Cordelia said. Go. You need a break.

Looking at her little sister in that moment, Diana seemed to see her for the first time in years. The fair-skinned flower was gone and now Cordelia's forearms were browned by the sun and her fingers chapped and nicked. She had her hair tied in a loose bun and there was a line of grit in the fold of her neck. Her eyes, normally glistening with emotion, were dry and flat, the eyes of a veteran. What have I done? Diana wondered. She embraced Cordelia, squeezing her until both their backbones cracked.

I will not leave her side till you return, Cordelia whispered into her ear.

They walked the eight blocks to the theater, following the flow of people winding their way along the network of boards laid across the wet street. Cohen offered his arm, and she took it to be polite and allowed him to make a great show of guiding her around mudholes and board gaps. The Grand Opera House on Post Office Street was one of the first buildings to begin extensive renovations after the storm. Cohen was the driving force behind the repairs and the push to reopen with a full season of plays and music. A functioning theater, he explained, brought a sense of a return to normality. He must really love this place, Diana thought. Fully committed to the resurrection of the island.

Rubble from the shattered buildings across the street was piled high in front of the theater, and sagging power lines hung from newly erected poles of green pine. Garish red oleanders, freshly planted in big clay pots, lined the sidewalk in front of the theater, their heavy blossoms perfuming the chill air. Cohen remarked how the oleander was brought to the island from Jamaica in the mid-nineteenth century and flourished thanks to its tolerance for subtropical weather and alkaline soils. "A city of colorful blooms, delightful scents, and friendly people," was how Cohen described it. Diana found it difficult to imagine the island before the storm, a scenic haven covered in the gaudy red, white, and pink flowers. Cohen told her that the ancient plants were referenced in the Talmud, that in the Mishnah it was said that animals that ate the oleander and then died were kosher. Then, in a disarmingly casual tone, he mentioned that oleanders were also famously popular in the gardens of Pompeii—another city capriciously destroyed by the terrifying dynamism of the earth.

They passed through the stone arch and the ticket exchange area, Cohen greeting and shaking hands with every other person they met. Diana was introduced ("the acting director of the American Red Cross while Miss Barton is indisposed due to exhaustion") to a dozen people whose names she promptly forgot. They made their way to Cohen's box in the first balcony, draped in velvet the color of cherries, fitted with gleaming silver rails. The painted stage backdrop was of a sylvan scene—a rushing brook, demure swans, and flowers bursting into streams of sunlight—and Diana had to admit it was a fine room, bright and airy and possessed of good acoustics. The wavering strains of the orchestra warming up in the pit rose through the air like an atmospheric change.

A man was already sitting in the box. His chair was pushed up to the rail and he was leaning forward, looking down into the crowd taking their seats. He wore a gray suit with an ascot and had a golden mane of hair swept back over his forehead and down to the tips of his brightly starched collar.

Ah, Cohen said. Joe!

The man rose and turned to greet them. He shook Cohen's hand and then Cohen introduced him to Diana.

Diana Longstreet, this is Joe Choynski.

Very nice to meet you, Diana said.

Joe is a professional boxer, Cohen said, known to fans around the world as Chrysanthemum Joe.

I'm grateful for the invitation, Joe said.

He did not look like a professional boxer, at least not the professional boxers Diana had read about in the newspapers. John L. Sullivan, the most famous boxer of the day and the only boxer she knew of, was a hulking, pot-bellied brute in a sleeping shirt with a mustache full of beer and the language skills of a twelve-year-old. Joe was trim and elegant in a snugly fitted suit with silver cuff links and several rings on each hand. His face was large and heavy-boned, his sharp blue eyes sleepy-lidded. The only giveaway was the mashed nose, slightly askew, and the curious notch in his lower lip. Joe met her gaze for a few moments as they shook hands and then his eyes drifted away to Cohen, lazily moving on to other things and people in the theater. He had a rich, heady bouquet about him—lilac, cinnamon, some kind of perfume. Must be happily settled, she thought. She took the seat next to him and Cohen sat on the other side of her. The theater manager appeared with a bottle of champagne on ice and Cohen poured her a glass. Joe demurred, waving it off and asking for a glass of cold water before returning to his rail like a child on a ship at sea. Diana sipped the champagne and savored the dry rush of bubbles. She crossed her legs and settled into her seat as the house lights dimmed and then rose again three times.

Do you spend a lot of time at the theater, Mr. Choynski? she asked.

Not as much as I'd like, Joe said.

Cohen leaned into her shoulder.

Joe is a stage performer himself.

Oh, really?

I think that Henry is referring to my career as a boxer, Joe said.

Yes, that, Cohen said. But Joe is also an actor, a veteran of boxing and the boards! And a playwright as well, right, Joe?

I wouldn't say I'm a playwright. I've written a few things.

A boxer and practitioner of the fine arts, Diana said. How very . . . modern.

Joe turned his heavy face to her, leaning back in his seat. His eyes are an indistinct shade of blue, she thought—changing and evolving, a hue one might find cradling a lonely coral atoll in the Pacific or reflected in a mossy bucket in Appalachia.

There are some people, Joe said, who would characterize boxing itself as a fine art.

Is that the way you feel?

I'm open to the idea.

I'm sure, Diana said. And for some the lobster is an exemplar of aesthetic perfection.

Joe shrugged, scanning the audience again. She meant it in jest, but he didn't smile. Diana sipped her champagne and was shocked to find the glass nearly empty. The lights blinked again and the tuning of the orchestra faded away as the musicians began to assume a ready position, the conductor shuffling his sheet music one last time.

Do you enjoy the theater, Miss Longstreet? Joe asked her, still watching the crowd.

My vocation keeps me quite busy. I don't have time for such entertainments.

Oh, the theater is not an *entertainment*, Joe said.

Then what would you call it?

A reflection of life, he said. Everything is laid bare on the stage. Tragedy, comedy, music, love.

He pinioned her again with those blue eyes.

It is a looking glass, positioned to show the deepest corners of the human condition.

She opened her mouth to reply, but Cohen was refilling her glass and the curtain opened to reveal an exotic setting with swooning palm trees, Moorish turrets, and men in billowing trousers striding across lurid carpets someplace in North Africa. An aging missionary was tending a fantastically overgrown garden while other men entered and began to speak in strong Scottish accents. The play seemed to pass quickly, with the titular Captain Brassbound as some kind of notorious pirate—a double cross—and a woman, Lady Cicely, involved in a trade for another man's freedom.

Throughout the play Diana stole glances at Joe, who remained rigidly still, leaning forward, his hands gripping the rail. She could see the emotional swings of the performance play out on the side of his face—a slight crinkling of the eyes when the audience laughed, the tightening around the mouth when a character demanded justice. In the last act, Lady Cicely delivered an impassioned monologue on behalf of the imprisoned Brassbound and effected his release. The shadow of a smile flashed over Joe's face. The dashing pirate then sailed offstage, leaving Lady Cicely in a state of disarray. *What an escape!* Lady Cicely wondered aloud to the audience, and the curtain dropped and the lights came up.

Joe stood up and began to hammer his meaty hands together. His face was shining with sweat and Diana could smell exertion on him, as if the play had been a physical contest—a clean, pure smell, like a lakeshore on a windy day. She joined Cohen and the rest of the audience in the ovation, all of them smiling and nodding to each other, her shoulder brushing against Joe's, and she couldn't help but imagine, just for a moment, the perspiration that must be coating the body under his clothes, a shimmering veil over his fair skin. She realized then that she had only the vaguest notion of what the play was about, or anything that had transpired over the past two hours.

They pushed through the lobby with the crowd and out into the brisk evening. The street and board sidewalks were crowded with people talking and smoking together in bunches, the puddles in the street reflecting a sliver of the pallid moon. Cohen stopped to talk to someone but Joe and Diana kept walking, Joe leading her across the street, where they stopped to look back at the theater, blazing with interior light.

I wanted to get clear of the crowd, Joe said. I hope you don't mind.

They watched the crowd beginning to disperse. In the upper windows of the theater Diana could see the complex lines and ropes of the backstage apparatus.

Henry told me about your efforts for the orphans, Joe said. I'd like to help if I can.

We welcome all kinds of assistance, Diana said.

There is the boxing match on Tuesday, Joe said. We're taking donations for the Red Cross. Will you be there?

Of course not.

Joe jammed his hands in his pockets and looked up at the night sky. Could he be surprised by this answer? Diana kept watching him, head cocked, a slight smirk on her lips.

Why do you think I would consider attending such a spectacle?

He smiled and looked into her eyes.

Because you strike me as a modern woman.

Cohen came jogging across the street toward them. Diana watched a group of children emerge out of the gloom and wind through the theater crowd, hands out and pleading looks on their faces. She realized that for the first time in a week, she had gone several hours without thinking of the girl waiting for her back at the warehouse.

Apologies, Miss Longstreet, Cohen said. I left you out in the cold.

It's all right, Diana said. Mr. Choynski and I were just enjoying the night air.

Please call me Joe.

Only if you call me Diana. Both of you.

Glad that's settled, Cohen said. Now, I know a café just a few blocks from here that does a nice slice of kugel with black tea—just the thing after a performance.

I'd better get back, Diana said. It's late.

Right, Cohen said. You've got the little lass waiting.

You have a daughter? Joe asked.

No. One of the orphans. She's not well.

Then I will wish you good night, Joe said.

Yes, Cohen said. The match is in two days! You need your rest.

Joe turned to Diana, and the streetlamp light fell on his face in such a way that she could see the lumps of scar tissue that rimmed his eyes, the heavy bones of his face and jaw, the nose that had been crushed by violence many times. It was the face of a man who was once beautiful.

Chrysanthemum Joe.

This was an enjoyable evening, Joe said. I'll leave a ticket for the match at the hall in case you change your mind.

He turned away and Diana watched him walk down Broadway with a long stride, his suit tight across his broad shoulders, his golden hair glowing in the dark.

PART 2

"I never asked anyone to let [the fight] go on," Johnson remembered. "I was darn glad it was over, but I didn't much like the trip to jail." He and Choynski were locked into the same cell and photographed there together, peering glumly out between the bars like stray dogs at the pound.
–Geoffrey C. Ward,
Unforgivable Blackness: The Rise and Fall of Jack Johnson

As the flood waters rose, the nuns took the children to the second floor of the girls' dormitory, where each sister used clothesline to connect a string of children to her waist . . .
The sisters were buried wherever they were found, with the children still attached to them. Two of the sisters were found together across the bay on the Mainland. One of them was tightly holding two small children in her arms. Even in death she had kept her promise not to let go.
–"Orphanage Tragedy Remembered,"
The 1900 Storm: Galveston, Texas,
Galveston County Daily News, 2014.

Don't throw in the sponge, Ed! I'm not licked yet. Let him kill me, but don't say I quit!
–Joe Choynski during the "Battle of the Barge"
fight with Jim Corbett, June 5, 1889

Wandering between two worlds, one dead,
The other powerless to be born
–Matthew Arnold,
"Stanzas from the Grand Chartreuse"

HESTER

The sound of a woman weeping.

She was on the beach again, some unknown stretch of white sand and blue water that could not be Texas or at least not the parts she had known. But instead of the sound of water and wind it was silent save for the faint, directionless, muffled sound of a woman crying. Hester walked the shoreline, scanning the horizon for anything she might recognize or some sign of habitation. The dunes topped with tufts of salt grass were an unending maze that she explored many times without result, so she ended up staying along the shore. There was nowhere to go. Everything just went on without end. She would wander for a while and then she would blink and be unable to tell if she was continuing or had started again. It was like this place was the meeting point of now and forever.

Hester was not afraid, or even uncomfortable. She was not

hungry or tired, and her blue dress was clean and she had no wounds or pains of any kind. Her body felt strong and pure. She marveled at the unblemished wonder of her skin, the softness of her palms, the fullness of her hair. There was no smell. That was odd but not unpleasant.

What was unsettling was the doll. It was always there in her hand when she looked down. Even after she dropped it. When she raised her hand again it would be there. But the doll was also different. It was new and clean just like she was, but covering the face of the doll was a small burlap sack with ragged eyeholes. It was horrible to look at but when she pulled the mask off there was always just another underneath. She tried throwing it into the water, burying it in the sand. It didn't matter. When she looked down again there it was in her hand. She could not be rid of the thing and so she tried to forget about it and kept walking.

The great unblinking eye in the heavens was not here. There was a limit to what He could do, Hester realized. Even He did not know this place. He was sitting in the audience and watching the story unfold, just like the rest of us.

The weeping was the first sound that she had heard since she got here. How long *had* she been here? She could pose this question yet she had no sense of the passage of time. It seemed like forever and perhaps just a moment. Where was the sound coming from? What did it mean? She crouched on the top of a high dune, looking out over the sparkling, silent sea. Then faintly, as if someone were slowly turning up the volume, Hester began to hear other sounds. She could hear the rushing of the wind and the crunch of the waves on the shore. She moved her feet in the sand and heard the slide and shift of the grains.

That's when she saw him coming out of the water. It was

the man she had seen on the beach, his pale body shining as he emerged from the waves. He walked out of the water and stood there looking at her. He was smiling, his blond hair slicked back over his forehead, and he raised a hand and waved. Why was he here? How did he get here? Hester waved to him and he grinned and put his hands on his hips. He was waiting for her.

The sound of the woman sobbing carried over it all, increasing in volume, and as Hester started down the dunes toward him, stepping through the deep drifts of sand, the sky suddenly cracked open and huge shafts of blinding white light enveloped her. Hester put up her arms to shield her eyes and then all the sounds seemed to come together and accelerate, rising to a howling point. And then silence.

She was lying on her back. It was dark except for one flickering light, an oil lamp at her feet. She was in a room, a place she didn't know. Beside her a basin of water, a pitcher, a pile of rags and dressings with rust-colored stains. On the other side of her a woman in a clean white dress was kneeling, covering her face with her hands, sobbing. Her long black hair was in a single thick braid and her shoulders shook as she cried and the name came to Hester like a shout over a distant horizon:

Diana.

But she was so tired. Hester closed her eyes and lay down in the sand and silence, the wind blowing her hair around her face like a wreath of fire.

JOE

It was a miserable night at the Galveston Athletic Club on the corner of Church and Twenty-Second Streets. Joe tried to stay warm and loose in the dressing room, shadowboxing with his overcoat on while Salazar fed wood scraps into the blackened pot stove. It had been raining all day and Joe's gloves were already damp when Salazar laced them up. The roof of the hall had been ripped off in the storm but Curley rigged a tarp over the ring to keep the fighters out of the intermittent drizzle. Admission was free and people had started lining up around noon to secure a space. They had to bar the doors to stop more people from pushing inside, the hall already packed deep with over nine hundred people on ascending wooden benches, the rising heat from the bodies creating a kind of salty fog that hovered over their heads. Donation buckets were passed around for the American Red Cross recovery effort, and every newspaper for five hundred miles was on hand to see "the storied veteran Chrysanthemum Joe Choynski take on Jack Johnson, the young Negro upstart they called the Galveston Giant."

Joe gave his copies of the contract to Salazar to file, and the Spaniard tucked a monocle into his eye socket and read the documents, his finger tracing the lines in rapid succession. As long as neither fighter was paid for the actual fight and there were no admission costs, it was considered an "exhibition" and not an illegal prizefight. Joe's forty-five hundred would be paid out by the committee for his role as a "scientific boxing instructor." Salazar stopped at one part of Johnson's section of the contract, tapped the paper, and whistled a long, slow note. Joe leaned over his shoulder to read. They were paying Jack Johnson a total of twenty-five dollars.

About an hour before the fight, Joe walked out to the ring with his coat and cap on. There were a variety of preceding acts, including Court P. Edwards and his Famous Bicycle Tricks, a troupe of minstrels from Houston in short red jackets with gold epaulettes, and a boxing match between two local black boys who had each lost a leg in the storm. Vendors in straw boaters with badges pinned to their lapels trundled crates of boiled clams and corn fritters wrapped in cones of newspaper. The crowd was already lively and a large section stomped their feet and cheered when Joe doffed his cap and bowed, interrupting the minstrels in the ring singing "Old Uncle Ned."

Five men sitting in the front row were not watching the minstrels. These men wore ten-gallon hats, long oilskin coats, and sun-creased, unreadable expressions. They were trying to appear nonchalant, a couple of them holding untouched bags of peanuts. Joe approached Curley and Craine, who were sitting at the timer's table. Curley told him the men were Texas Rangers.

Just to prevent trouble, Curley said. But don't worry about all that.

What kind of trouble?

If the Negro wins, Craine said, there'll be trouble.

He squinted at Joe with his porcine eyes and nodded as if they were compatriots in some kind of sacred pact. The bandage was off his ear, the lower half of his earlobe hideously shredded and crusted with dried scabs.

A few rounds, Craine said. Then you put that darkie *down*.

On his way back to the dressing room Joe saw Rabbi Cohen standing in the back of the hall having an intense conversation with some other men. Cohen held out one arm and moved his feet as if demonstrating a dance step and the other men laughed. Joe stretched his neck and got on his toes, searching for the face of Diana Longstreet. He didn't see her. Since the night at the theater he had been searching the face and body of every woman he saw for some resemblance. He hadn't seen anyone remotely like her.

He couldn't stop thinking about the frankness of her gaze, the way she raked it over him, as if she was considering his usefulness. Joe knew the naked look of desire, sometimes furtive, sometime blatant. This was different. She *appraised* him, was the best way he could put it. As a physical being she was confusing to him and his sensibilities. Though Diana was tall and slender, her hands were knuckled and veined like those of a tradesman. The way she held her chin up and slightly to one side, the crease of skin between her eyes when she looked at you. There was something inflexible about her, like a strap of fresh leather. So unlike the plump softness of Lutie and her rounded smiles and dimples. When they stood in the street under the gaslights he noticed that Diana was as tall as he was. When she was standing beside you her presence had weight, like she had her own gravity. He remembered how she looped her fingertips in the inside of his elbow for a few seconds as they navigated a muddy patch in the street and how that simple tug burned hot long after she let him go.

Why do you think I would consider attending such a spectacle?

She abhorred his vocation and found his artistic ambitions absurd and trivial. And his inane chatter about the theater, *the deepest corners of the human condition*—what pretentious twaddle! She must find him positively repellent.

And yet, the feel of her gaze during the play, the way she followed him across the street, how she seemed content to stand quietly beside him and watch the crowd, that touch on the inside of his elbow. The way she looked him straight in the eyes as they parted, her face receptive, open. Walking back to his hotel he could still see a kind of spirit image of her standing outside the theater, walking down the street, at the warehouse with orphan children, in her room at night framed by a dark window. It was as if he could see her in every place she inhabited. She walked here, he thought. She touched this. She was in this place.

Later that night Joe tried to read R. W. Emerson but couldn't relax, so he stripped down and did sets of calisthenics until he collapsed, panting in a pool of sweat on the floor, but he finally came to it: Diana was a woman who seemed shaped by strife and tragedy, and in this crucible she emerged forged like something unalterable and beautiful. And she positively hated boxing! Why would this woman direct the luminous cone of her attention his way at all?

Dearest Louise,

I'm writing this on the eve of the match, as it has been my custom to do in case I am knocked insensible. However, please do not concern yourself as I am confident that I will give this young man a lesson in scientific boxing.

I attended the grand opening of the theater this last Sunday evening for Captain Brassbound's Conversion at the invitation of Rabbi Cohen. It was wonderfully conceived and artfully acted. This writer Shaw renders the exchanges between people that illuminate and betray them.

I think the Rabbi sees me as a kind of brother and confidant even though I do not share his enthusiasm for our religion. It is true that my father provided a sterling model of the virtues of Judaism. But the long hours of prayer, the Hebrew, the rituals, always seemed like some kind of elaborate farce. As a young boy I found myself thinking that surely one of these intelligent gentlemen, like my father, would any minute now stand and interrupt the droning cantor and turn to his fellows and say: Why must we continue this charade? What is this game about?

My mother found the presence of the divine in the arts. Growing up we went to plays nearly every week, musicals, minstrel shows, comic acts, Shakespeare, Yiddish dramas. I remember walking down Harley Street after a play and my mother with her eyes on the sidewalk, a smile on her face. She was still living in the world of the performance.

My father did not share our enthusiasm. He respected

the theater as he respected all the fine arts, but Isador would rather spend the evening reading Richard III *in his study than going to a production. He found all the pageantry and stage art he needed at synagogue. For me it is the pure distillation of emotion that happens onstage. That's when I feel the ghostly fingers of G— in my chest.*

There is something else troubling me that I cannot name. Whenever I think about myself boxing I see it in my imagination in the third person, never from my own perspective. Is my mind unable to connect the man who does those things in the ring with the person I am? I am about to enter a new contest and I already feel the stirrings of desire, a powerful urge I cannot name. This Jack Johnson fellow, the man I am to fight tonight, what inexorable course of fate has brought me here to destroy him? Or has he come for me?

I hope that by the time you read this I'll be on my way back to you.

Yours,

Joe

With about a half hour to go Herman "the German" Bernau, a retired boxer and the referee for the fight, visited Joe in his dressing room. They had met years ago when Joe battered Bernau in an embarrassing exhibition. Bernau had gained weight since then and in his white collared shirt and apron he looked like an aging butcher counter clerk.

After all these years, Bernau said. Still at it! I heard you had Bob Fitzsimmons threatening to leave the country just to get away from you.

Salazar took off Joe's coat and started rubbing down his shoulders.

Nobody, Joe said, ever accused Bob of being charitable *or* forgiving.

Now, you can't wear this Negro fella down, Bernau said. I've seen his last three fights. He flattened Jack McCormick in sixteen. So start out quick. And remember you can't knock a Negro out by hitting 'em in the head.

He leered at Joe with a gap-toothed grin, his jowls quivering. Joe just gazed at him with sleepy eyes.

You gotta hit 'em in the heel!

Bernau laughed and slapped his globular gut. Joe turned away and threw some combinations in the cracked mirror leaning up against the wall. Bernau kept talking but Joe focused on his form. He was thinking about those Rangers in the front row, the stoic looks on their faces, the long pistols under their coats.

When they called his name Joe shook some rosemary oil on his hands and smoothed back his hair then walked out to the ring with Salazar trailing behind with the towel, water bottle, sponge, and bucket. The crowd was on its feet, roaring and waving their hats and tossing bunches of dried wildflowers that rained down on Joe as he snaked through the crowd. Hands slapped his shoulders and men cried out, Oh, you Joe! Salazar collected the flowers and by the time they got to the ring he'd arranged a festive bouquet in the spit bucket.

Jack Johnson was waiting in the ring, already stripped down to his tights. Joe had seen a range of physiques but Jack was something special—sleek and muscular, long arms, thighs bulging like hams in his short tights. But it wasn't the size of the man, though he was certainly big, several inches taller and at least twenty pounds heavier than Joe; rather it was the palpable *density* of Johnson. You could sense it in the way he moved, the way he carried his limbs. Sometimes, Joe thought, you simply cannot weigh a man with a scale.

The one-legged boys were crawling around picking up coins that the audience tossed in the ring. Their faces were swollen and bloody and one of the boys was tucking pennies into his cheek because his hands were full. The nine-piece band at ringside wheezed to a stop, the accordion bleating a final note, and then the announcer had the bullhorn tilted up into the smoky air, bellowing out, *Good evening, Galveston!*

Johnson grinned at him from across the ring—even rows of white teeth, a handsome jawline, and high cheekbones. His smooth, hairless head was slick with sweat.

The Galveston Giant . . . Jack . . . Johnson!

Johnson's second said something in his ear and Johnson waved him off. The length of his arms gave Joe some concern. Salazar slapped Joe on the back of the neck three times as he bobbed on his toes.

The man who fought Jim Jeffries and Bob Fitzsimmons to a draw! The California Terror! The pride of San Francisco! Chrysanthemum Joe . . . Choynski!

At the bell Johnson came out in a conventional stance, his lead hand stretched out, and they circled each other, feinting and jabbing for range. Johnson's footwork was smooth but he had almost no head movement. Joe knew he'd have to get past those long arms and put some jabs on that shining skull bone. He started with a few probing lefts and Johnson seemed content to counterpunch, swinging his left hook around the jab, and about a minute in he caught Joe with a solid shot to the neck.

Not a full-power hit but Joe felt the blow deep in his backbone. He danced inside with a combination and Johnson reached out and tied him up, the two men embracing each other. Joe leaned into him and drove with his legs but Johnson easily pushed him back across the ring and against the ropes. Dear G——, the man was *strong*!

How you doin', Mr. Joe? Johnson said in his ear. You having fun yet?

So he was a talker. This was not unusual, except that Johnson seemed genuinely relaxed, like he was having a good time.

Not quite, Joe said.

Johnson manhandled him on the ropes, pushing him toward the corner. Joe jerked an arm free and tried to slip out and Johnson used the opening to club him in the ribs. Joe gasped and regained his guard, clutching Johnson's arms.

How's that again, Mr. Joe?

Say, Jack, Joe said, how about we break nice and gentlemanly?

Sure.

They lifted their heads and pushed off and Joe set his toes and fired off a tight combination landing a straight right to the forehead that made Johnson's eyes flicker, a left hook to the body, then ducking under Johnson's swinging counterpunches. The combination went nearly perfectly and Joe felt as if he were rehearsing a choreographed scene. Johnson backed away, surprised but grinning, nodding. *So this is how it's going to go.*

Joe stood in the center of the ring, his eyes half closed, a slight smile on his lips. He beckoned to Johnson.

Come on.

The crowd roared. The bell rang and the round was over.

Salazar squeezed the sponge over the back of his neck and said something about the left hook, but Joe was focused only on the man across from him. Forget the fundraising, the Red Cross—all of that. This was no exhibition. Johnson was powerful enough and quick enough to put him down if he wasn't careful. He stared at Johnson sitting on his stool across from him and the ring seemed to tilt and constrict as if Johnson were at the narrow end of a long cone, the light fading away around the edges. Johnson's second rubbed his shoulders and dashed water on his blinking face. As the crowd quieted Joe could hear Johnson's cornermen talking to him. They wanted him to open up, to take more chances.

This ain't no Jack McCormick I'm fighting, Johnson said angrily. I'm going to be careful!

Joe fell into his pattern of deep breaths, timed with the flutter of Salazar's towel. Some in the audience muttered and hissed, impatient.

Hey, Choynski! someone yelled. You better *kill* that smoke!

Joe shut his eyes, took another breath, feeling the noxious air of the place in his lungs, the smoke, sweat, resin, stagnant water, crushed rock, muddy tide flats, and something sickly sweet underneath it all.

You *better* kill him, Yid, yelled another man, or we're gonna kill *you*!

Joe opened his eyes. From across the ring Johnson grinned and shrugged.

In the second round they stayed cautious, both men keeping their chin down and guard high. Johnson lunged in low, a hook in the wind, and Joe paid him with a straight left to the nose. Johnson straightened up and wiped his face, annoyed. He shifted his stance and circled left and caught Joe off balance, making him stumble backward. The crowd moaned with grudging acknowledgment. Joe's hair was soaked with sweat and he flung it back out of his eyes with a flick of his head. He watched Johnson's feet and hands. Joe did not want to get into an extended contest of hand speed or he'd be back on the road taking on drunk hayseeds for fifty cents a head.

Give them a show. Show them the true science.

The third round started off with Johnson again bending his knees and circling low, trying to turn Joe against his lead left. Joe knew he would have to impose himself to break up the rhythm; he would have to take a chance. They clinched and Johnson easily threw him off to the side, hooking him hard to the neck and temple. The concussion from the blow radiated through Joe's face and traveled down through his torso like fingers of lightning through a cloud. He stumbled and blinked; everything was framed with black shadows trailing smoke. He blinked again and now Johnson was stepping toward him, the crowd murmuring, and Salazar rattled off a string of Spanish curses. Joe felt like he was losing track of his own feet. He couldn't see anything but the dark man looming in front of him. Johnson didn't seem interested in drawing out the fight. Is this how it ends? For just a fleeting moment Joe was grateful that Diana wasn't there to see it.

Joe backpedaled and circled away to the left, retreating until his vision cleared. Forget about the crowd, he thought. The distance of the fight, my career—forget all that. Focus on technique. *Move your feet.*

Joe began working his feints and head shifts, trying to confuse Johnson, who responded with lightning-fast jabs. Joe stayed in the pocket, moving his head and slipping punches until he caught the timing and everything started slowing down until he could see Johnson's eyes widen the split second before he threw a punch, how the shoulder bunched and the glove dropped a fraction before rising up and coming at him like a surfacing whale. The crowd roared with every jab he bounced off Johnson's head. If Joe could just get him to bite on a fake. Get an opening for a good left. He could hurt him, change the fight. Joe raised his guard and opened up his hands wide, inviting Johnson in to his bared ribs. Johnson sidestepped, looked, dipped, looked again. Joe slipped a jab with a head shift, a fist whispering by his ear. Johnson's face seemed to shine with an unearthly light and Joe coiled himself. It was coming.

The next time they closed Johnson took the bait and looped a punch at his midsection and Joe stepped into it and launched himself into a left hook, torquing his whole body into the blow. Johnson could not get out of the way and Joe's fist crashed into his head below the right temple, the deep thud of brain and bone resonating down Joe's arm, and he knew the blow was true.

Jack Johnson fell forward into Joe's arms. He had one arm around his neck, and Joe embraced him for a moment, staggering to support his weight. Then Johnson let out a small sigh, a puff of breath, and as Joe stepped back Johnson briefly hugged his torso and waist before sliding face-first to the floor, both arms stretched over his head.

The building erupted, everyone on their feet. Johnson rolled over onto his back. His chin was slack and his eyes were closed. He looked peaceful, as if he had been released from some enormous burden. Bernau was leaning over him yelling the count and Joe shook out his hands, backing up, taking deep breaths.

He felt the familiar hot spike of adrenaline peak and falter, replaced by a gentle wash of relief that rolled through his body. The count reached ten and still Johnson didn't move, so Bernau waved him out and the auditorium exploded. Joe bounced on his toes, rolling his shoulders.

Craine, Curley, and other fight officials were clambering over the ropes when the five Texas Rangers jumped into the ring with their pistols drawn. One of the Rangers, a wizened older man with a heavy mustache, stood in the center of the ring and discharged his pistol into the air. Everyone froze, the crowd going quiet but for the scrape and groan of the bleachers, a few lone shrieks in the dark.

Everyone remain in your seats! the Ranger bellowed. I am Captain John Brooks of the Texas Rangers! By the power of the State of Texas these men are under arrest!

The other Rangers surrounded the prostrate form of Johnson. The crowd began to jeer and whistle and wadded newspaper and cigar butts began to rain down in the ring. Captain Brooks pointed at Joe.

You boys are going to the crossbar hotel!

DIANA

Cordelia brought up a small box that had been left by the front door with "Diana Longstreet, American Red Cross" scrawled across the top. Inside was a doll made of feed sacking, dyed dark brown and filled with tiny seashells. There was a note.

I found this on my run along the beach and thought of your orphan girl. I hope to see you at the match tonight.—Joe

Such a strange man, Diana thought. A confusing combination of the beastly and the baroque. Diana met hundreds of men in her work, including some who were handsome, accomplished, and dedicated to admirable causes. Many of them tried to gain her attention and she never had difficulty letting them pass. But here she was a few days later and Joe had not simply dissipated like the others. Instead he was lodged in the front of her mind, like a barb stuck fast in her imagination. Even walking down the hall of the warehouse she was thinking about the way his curiously disfigured lip worked around words, the calm placidity of his eyes, the way his hands grasped the brass rail of the balcony. The way he seemed to radiate a sense of his physical self beyond his skin. Joe had joined the small orbit of celestial objects in her head and as he gained light and expanded, others were diminishing and fading away.

Diana washed the doll and sewed up the hole in its side before tucking it beside the girl under the blanket. Her face was losing color again and the bones of her shoulders poked out of the neck of her dress. Dr. Mountcastle said if she did not wake soon they would have to try force-feeding her or she would die of starvation. Liverwright continued badgering Diana to let him take a series of portraits of the girl.

She could be the darling of this tragedy, he said. The orphan child-hero. Sell a hundred thousand papers.

Diana refused and made Liverwright swear he would not identify the girl or write about her situation until she was well and her background confirmed.

There are more than two dozen orphans in this building, she said. Pick one. Anyone but this one.

Dr. Mountcastle said it was quite possible she was sensible to at least part of the waking world. She may hear, feel, even smell things. Diana dug through her trunk and found the small copy of Emily Dickinson's poems and curling up beside the girl she began to read to her, going through the whole book a dozen times in an afternoon.

To fight aloud, is very brave–
But gallanter, I know
Who charge within the bosom
The Calvalry of Woe–

Diana did not fully understand what the poems were trying to say, but she was comforted by the rhythm and cadence of the language and the lingering sense of meaning. *Longing. Confusion. Courage.*

There once was a man, she whispered into the girl's ear.

***

He was young and kind and he worked as an attorney in Boston. He came from an old Rhode Island family and his parents were not fond of me. They distrusted my disposition and my work but it didn't matter because he loved me. We spent almost a year together before he grew ill. In another year he was gone. I was working in South America when he died. He was at a sanatorium in Colorado. His family sent him there believing he might be cured. I wrote so many letters. He was only able to reply when someone agreed to write for him. He was too weak. He had fair skin, like yours. An intellectual, a man of principles. He believed in the common good. We talked about marriage before he grew ill, but then not again after that. I was sure I would never love another man. They all seemed of one kind, like puppets of their own devising, putting on a show for the world. Instead I decided I would dedicate myself to my work. I don't know if that was the right decision. And I don't know if I can change it now. Maybe I'll never know that kind of love again. Maybe it's too late.

That night the city was quiet and Diana fell asleep with the girl in her arms.

***

She woke in the morning nestled against the girl's neck. They were both overwarm and sweaty as if a fever had broken. Diana's arm was over the girl's chest and she felt something brushing her skin and her first thought was one of the cats had gotten in the room. It was the girl's fingers, brushing over Diana's forearm.

Diana pushed herself up quickly. The girl's eyes were open, blinking. They were mottled brown like a split nutmeg, and Diana realized with a shock that she had never seen them before. She felt as though the world was falling away, a momentary weightlessness, leaving her body below, and rising up she could see the two of them huddled together on the mess of blankets and pillows, like the last two survivors on a ship at sea. Diana wanted to call out, to send Cordelia for Dr. Mountcastle, to get the canteen to bring up some soup, but she was still too stunned to speak. The girl fumbled with something under the blanket, her eyes growing bright, and Diana thought maybe she was going to say something. The girl brought the feed-sack doll out from under the blankets. She stared at it, her mouth working around several silent syllables. Then she looked at Diana, her eyes watery with tears. Diana stood there, helpless.

***

The girl would not speak. For the first couple of days she was too weak to get up and Diana fed her beef broth and slivers of hard-boiled eggs and hot tea. The girl's large eyes, luminous and wet, followed her across the room. Her face seemed to glow with a feverish intensity. She would not speak, but Diana was sure that she was aware of everything. She occasionally narrowed her eyes at some item of food Diana was trying to poke between her lips, but otherwise she had an inscrutable, flat demeanor, never smiling or indicating emotion.

Diana asked her again and again who did this to her. Who whipped her and left her for dead? The girl just shook her head or stared at her doll with a fearful expression. In a few days she was walking again and she began to collect small items from around the orphanage and store them in her pillowcase and under a loose board she found in the closet. A blanket, crusts of bread, a can of beans, tinned fish, a fork, the torn remnants of a burlap sack, needle and thread, a candle, Diana's ivory-handled hairbrush. Diana supposed she was trying to safeguard herself against want. Or she didn't feel safe. The thought of this made her heart ache and in the evenings Diana fell asleep clutching the girl to her as if she might be swept away in the night.

Cordelia and the other ladies brought Diana the daily reports and briefed her on all the news and activities while she sat with the girl. The city was sliding backward into confusion and violence. The boxing contest between Joe Choynski and Jack Johnson ended in controversy when the Texas Rangers arrested the fighters. Apparently Joe had knocked the young Negro fighter unconscious and the Rangers sprang into the ring, waving guns. The relief Diana felt to hear that Joe was not otherwise injured surprised her. She found herself in odd moments imagining what the boxing match might have been like, picturing a kind of gothic fever dream: Joe with his flopping blond hair, his sweaty arms swinging in the lights, battering a dark giant of a man, the two of them surrounded by hundreds of silent, rapt faces. No, it couldn't really be like that, she decided.

The newspapers reported that the three children murdered on the beach were the children of the Reverend Ponder, preacher at the Avenue L Missionary Baptist Church. By this time the summary executions, mob violence, and lynchings had become almost commonplace, but this was different. Reverend Ponder was the senior preacher on the island for all the black churches. He had the ear of the mayor, and a legion of blacks and immigrants would rise at his command. Even as he mourned in private at least two hundred black men and women gathered to sing hymns in the street outside the committee offices for two days until an army unit dispersed them at bayonet point. The paper also reported that Reverend Ponder released a plea for witnesses to come forward and identify these masked vigilantes, and a solemn vow that justice would be served by whatever means necessary.

The ladies of the Red Cross stopped their evening visits to the east side and the beach areas where shadowy gangs prowled the sands at night. The orphaned children, some of whom had encountered these men before they found sanctuary with the Red Cross, started speaking of the masked men on horseback like some kind of predatory devils out of a morality play, hunting down the weak and the doubting, punishing the sinners among them.

Clara remained in her room and slept most of the time. She was vague in her responses to these troubling events. Just a few weeks ago Diana would have expected Clara to have a troop of Red Cross ladies in the streets marching for justice and peace.

Clara Barton never ran away from tragedy; she charged directly into the gaping maw of whatever horror God or man spawned. This was the very attribute that first drew Diana into her world.

Diana grew up just west of Evansville, Kentucky, in a hewn-log farmhouse built by her grandfather in the early nineteenth century. In the back field that stretched down to the Howell Wetlands and the Ohio River her father and brothers ran four hundred head of cattle and farmed a dozen acres of beans and corn. On that strangely warm day in February, she was awakened by a heavy crunching sound echoing up from the river, like a troop of giants trudging down the valley. When she ran outside her mother stood in the back field by the fence line, hands on her hips, staring down at the massive floes of ice that smashed over the banks of the river, the icy water swelling up the sides of the valley and engulfing farms and whole villages. They were lucky; their farm was on higher ground, but most of their neighbors lost everything. The Johansen family down the valley lost three sons when they tried to save their cattle. For two days the raging flood was choked with dead cows, horses, mules, sheep, and pigs. Thousands of animals clustered on thin strips of raised levees until they starved and collapsed. Military boats fought the waters to rescue survivors, but they had no provisions for the hungry or medicine for the wounded and sick. The acrid stench of mass death rose up the valley and Diana was wrenched out of sleep at night by the searing reek, sitting bolt upright in the darkness of her small room, shuddering with revulsion and wonder as her parents murmured in the kitchen, the faint lamplight spilling under the door.

A few days later, the steamer *Josh V. Throp* came down the valley from Cincinnati, flying the Red Cross flag, a high-toned silver bell ringing on the masthead. Fourteen-year-old Diana stood on the levee as the steamer unloaded corn, oats, and meal for cattle; clothing, cooking utensils, tea, coffee, rice, sugar, and crates of medicine for the sick and dying. And directing the whole operation from the deck of the steamer, men springing at her command, a severe, composed older woman in a black dress with a lace collar, her long dark hair in a tight braid.

Diana knew she would have to appeal to the committee herself. When the girl was sleeping Diana slipped out of her dress, unwound her braid, and knelt in front of a bucket of hot water, scrubbing her body with a rag and a hunk of soap. Her underarms, groin, and neck were chafed raw and her feet laced with blisters. The grit on the floor bit into her bare knees and she balled her fists and pressed them into her thighs, her eyes clouding with angry tears. Why was she here? What was the point of it all when each day brought new suffering? But where would she go? Her permanent residence in Washington, D.C., was a brick row house that stood along the canal, dusty and shuttered, sparsely appointed with items from her parents' farmhouse after they passed. Her bedroom consisted of her great-aunt's bed with a lumpy mattress that smelled like moss and an old chifforobe that traveled across the Atlantic some-time in the previous century. A wasted garden in the back full of clover and onion grass. There was nothing there for her. Her life was with Clara and the Red Cross.

The old dog had been on the warehouse porch for a week. The ladies put out bowls of scraps for him in the evening and at night when the sky was clear the dog would send his guttural howls of lamentation over the city. Eventually they let him in and he followed his nose up the stairs to the girl's room and flopped on the floor next to her pallet.

Then one morning to everyone's surprise the girl came downstairs to the breakfast table and took a place among the other orphans with their tin bowls and spoons. She still did not speak, but something about her demeanor had changed. She seemed relaxed, more at peace, and she ate three bowls of buttered grits and drank a pint of milk. The doll was tied to her waist with a cord, and it wasn't until she got up to carry her dishes to the scullery that Diana noticed the girl had fashioned a small hood of burlap to cover the doll's head and had used charcoal to draw black eyeholes and a crude smiling mouth.

PART 3

Jeffries number one? No, sir. Give me Joe Choynski anytime.
I faced both and should know. Jeffries had a powerful wallop,
but Choynski had a paralyzing punch. His left hand was a
corker. He was the hardest puncher in the last fifty years, with
Joe Walcott a close second.
–Jack Johnson, when asked if Jim Jeffries
was the hardest puncher he ever faced.

Little Joe (Choynski) was the hardest hitter I ever tangled
with. To this day I can't figure out how a runt like him could
hurt so damned bad.
–Gentleman Jim Corbett

While it's true . . . that some people just don't like oleanders,
the resilient, flowering evergreen shrubs have special status
in Galveston and occupy a special place in the hearts of many
islanders. They are the city's official flower, for example, and
for some they embody in plant form those things that make
islanders different: they are tough, flourishing here when
others have failed; they are stately and colorful in bloom; and
they can be dangerous if handled incorrectly.
–"International Oleander Society Galveston Turns 50
Years Old" Valeri Wells, Texarkana Gazette,
May 16, 2017

For hope is always born at the same time as love.
–Miguel de Cervantes,
Don Quixote

HESTER

There were too many visitors. Men in suits with sweaty faces crowded around, wanting to shake her hand or take her on their knees. They wanted to talk about her recovery and the baby she carried from the east side and the other orphans, St. Mary's, the Sisters of the Incarnate Word, the Red Cross ladies. Hester said nothing. A fat man with a bowler hat bounced her on his lap and when he tried to pinch her cheek she clamped down on his forefinger with her incisors until blood ran down her chin. There was a lot of yelling and swearing and after that Diana made sure that no one touched her. When she heard the next group coming in the hall Hester hid in the closet under a pile of linens.

She kept the doll tied to her waist. She would not let anyone touch it or let it be taken from her, for she had brought it back from the place in between worlds. Her bond with Diana felt like a living connection, something created before she was born. She would spend the rest of her life at her side, no matter what happened, for it was Diana who brought her into this second life. It was Diana who sent the shining blond man from the water to save her from the in-between place. It was Diana who saved her with her tears.

The other kids staying at the Red Cross warehouse moved about her warily. Hester looked for girls from St. Mary's but didn't see a single familiar face. At night when Diana slept Hester crouched by the window and clutching the doll she thought about the sisters and the orphanage girls and Little Cora. Sometimes she thought about the place between worlds, which was the absence of all things, including the God of the sisters. Were any of the girls trapped there as well? Would any of them make it here, to this life? Were they all gone? God wouldn't leave her the *only* one!

Last to come to the room was a group of men who were more important than the others. They shouldered their way in holding their hats, a half dozen of them, looking awkwardly around with their red cheeks and big teeth. They grinned at Hester and ran their eyes over Diana's body as she knelt on the floor.

These gentlemen are from the Central Relief Committee, Diana said to her.

Diana had told her about the committee but it didn't make much sense to Hester. They were supposed to be in charge of helping people but it seemed that only the Red Cross ladies did anything useful. Hester sat in the corner, the dog's head in her lap, playing with his floppy ears. She felt sort of foggy ever since she woke up with Diana. The sharpness of life, the edges of things, had softened. She thought it was probably the food. A full belly could do strange things to one's thinking. The men from the Central Relief Committee talked about her in awed tones as if she were something in a museum while Diana stood there with a worried look on her face. She didn't want these men here either, but for some reason she felt she had to appease them. Hester didn't want her to worry so she tried to sit quietly and endure it. The windows were cracked open and a fresh gust of chilled air and a bar of sunlight ran across the dog's head in her lap. Hester could hear the murmur of the ladies outside stocking the mobile kitchen and the cries of the children as they played in the street. One of the committee men got to one knee, leaning toward her. Hester did not want to look at this man's face so she looked past him at the chipped plaster of the wall.

We've been looking forward to meeting you, he said.

The odd intonation of his words, how they crackled and sparked around the edges. His left ear was raw like a piece of beef jerky and he smelled of liniment and pipe tobacco. When he adjusted his tie, glancing warily at the dog, she could see there was something wrong about the shape of his neck, the way it moved when he talked. His collar shifted and Hester saw a white rope of scar tissue on his throat. She gripped the dog and closed her eyes, thinking of the doll, the mask with the jagged eyeholes. The beach in the flickering torchlight, the face bending toward her as she lay in the sand.

I see you.

She was trapped in the corner, the men all looming around her. The dog stirred and raised its head, growling, hackles stiffening. Hester was squeezing folds of his skin in her fists, her body rigid with fear. Then Diana said something quietly but firmly and the men murmured and left the room and Hester felt Diana's arms encircling her.

What is the matter? What is it?

Hester leaned into her, rubbing her tears on the sleeve of Diana's dress. Why would Diana bring them here? Why couldn't they go on to the second life with the house and the blond man reading in the chair and the orchard bending over the hills? Was there something else she had to do? What else did God require?

***

That afternoon they had an early supper of fried sausages and potatoes and afterward Hester combed out Diana's hair and expertly rebraided it, tying it off with a bow of white linen. At the orphanage she had braided hair daily since she was three years old. They were going to see a friend, Diana told her. She wrinkled her mouth in a funny way when she said it. She was wearing her white Red Cross dress with the freshly starched sash and a heavy scarf of bleached wool. Hester hung on to the doorframe, swinging her body back and forth, watching as Diana squinted at the mirror that hung by a nail on the door, dipping her finger into a tiny pot of rouge and rubbing it in her cheeks. Then Diana bundled Hester up in a wool sweater and matching red mittens and toboggan. Ladies' groups around the country were knitting children's items and sending them by the boxcar load. The motif on the hat and mittens was a line of heavy-antlered reindeer prancing through a shower of snowflakes.

The sun had swept away the film of clouds and the sky was deep blue and the wind cold. After they walked a few blocks Hester's cheeks were already numb, but the air was from the north so it smelled of the salt marshes and grass for a change. A group of men were gathered around the doorway of the dance hall across the street from the Galveston jailhouse, teetering on their toes and craning their necks, angling for a view inside. There was a constant thumping noise coming from inside the building, a rhythmic triple-beat sound. Diana paused in the street, squeezing Hester's hand, as if she was trying to decide something. Then she sighed and picked up Hester and they mounted the steps to the dance hall. The men around the door parted for her and a small birdlike man in a tight suit came forward, beckoning to them with a smile. His face was familiar.

Henry, Diana said.

Hullo! So glad you are here!

They walked through the crowd of men, the thumping metronomic sound growing louder and louder. It was a large dark room with board floors that were warped and swollen and they made their way slowly as Henry parted the men with polite taps on their shoulders. Their collective breath gathered in steaming clouds among the rafter beams with the cigar, cigarette, and pipe smoke. Being so close to so many men terrified Hester and she clung to Diana, peering over her shoulder.

A tall window was uncovered and a bright rectangle of sunlight split the room like a golden wall. In the center of the room was a clearing ringed by a couple of rows of chairs and in the shaft of light from the window a man was toiling away at some kind of device, his gloved hands held up high and spinning. They were directed to a seat on one side next to two other ladies in fine, heavy dresses of silk and delicate boots. Hester sat on Diana's lap.

The man was wearing white tights that went to his ankles

and no shirt and his skin was so pale it glowed like the moon. He was covered in a glossy sheen of sweat and he snapped his head back when his hair flopped over his eyes, never pausing in the cycle of motion with his hands. His arms were corded with muscle and his side and back rippled, the sinews twitching just under the skin. He was hitting a small leather bag that hung by a short chain, and the noise was coming from the contact of his hands and the bag slapping against the wood. The rattle of the chain provided a third sound, an in-between clatter. The persistence and force of the sound vibrated in Hester's chest.

Tha-*thunk*-ah-tha-*thunk*-ah-tha-*thunk*-ah.

After a minute it seemed nothing else existed but the sound. It was like the coursing flow of blood that you heard in your ears after running a long distance. His golden hair swayed with the rhythm, rivulets of sweat trailing down his body, and Hester thought he had skin like something luminous that lived a solitary life deep under the sea. An enormous black man stood just out of the shaft of light, also shirtless and wearing short black tights, his arms crossed over his broad chest. Hester had never seen a man so massive and dark, his skin shimmering, spangled with flecks of reflected light. He was also wearing leather gloves and watching intently with a big incongruous smile on his face.

The man hitting the bag accelerated his pace, his hands a spinning blur that seemed like a thing disconnected from his body. The crowd murmured and shifted, everyone tensing; then suddenly he reared back and delivered a final strike, punching through the bag with a straight arm, twisting on his toes like a dancer. He put his hands on his hips and lowered his head as the men in the room clapped and whistled. The ladies sitting next to them whispered to each other as the man turned to acknowledge the small crowd, bowing at the waist, flipping back his hair with one glove. Hester twitched with excitement and Diana put both arms around her and squeezed her ribs.

It was *him*. From the in-between place. She could see him in that bright sunlight, standing with her toes in the sand, watching him come out of the water. The sleepy eyes and the slight smile. He looked directly at her and raised a glove.

Diana had brought her to him!

The black man and the white man began toweling off while other men tried to crowd around them, talking loudly. Sheriff's deputies started to usher people out.

Closing time, folks! Come again to see more scientific boxing from the great Chrysanthemum Joe and the Galveston Giant! This way, ladies and gents!

Henry Cohen sat beside them on a vacated chair. He was beaming and wringing his hands. Hester could see scratched notes in ink on his shirt cuffs.

Well? Cohen said. How about that?

Diana spoke slowly, as if in a trance.

It's really something, she said.

The speed bag, Cohen said, is a part of the boxer's training that develops timing and coordination. A compelling spectacle!

He made a move to poke Hester in the belly but Diana stiffened and made a slight motion with her head and he stopped. Hester was watching the two boxers who were conferring in low voices, a sheriff's deputy standing beside them swinging a set of keys on a chain. The white boxer put a hand on the black boxer's shoulder as the other tugged his glove off. They seemed like the reverse of something to Hester—not the opposite, but something turned inside out. Then the white boxer approached and Cohen leaped up to greet him. They shook hands and then he turned to Hester.

This is Joe Choynski. They call him Chrysanthemum Joe. A chrysanthemum is a type of flower, a bright, beautiful flower. Don't you think that's interesting? Why do you think they call him that?

Joe had a towel around his shoulders and he wiped his face. His hands were covered in white tape and the smell of him was strong, briny and vegetal like the sea. He knelt down in front of Hester. This close, she could see the faint scars around his eyes and forehead, the crooked nose, the mismatched lip. *Chrysanthemum Joe.*

Joe is the man who found your doll, Diana said. I thought you might like to thank him.

They were all watching her, waiting. The room was empty now but for a couple deputies smoking cigarettes by the door and the black boxer, who had put on a sweater and was drinking water from a glass bottle.

I'm sorry, Diana said. She still hasn't said a word. She keeps the doll hidden. But I know she's grateful.

That's okay, Joe said. Some things need to be kept hidden.

He held out his hand. Hester grasped his first two fingers, rubbing the tape with her fingertips. His hands were horny and callused, the knuckles swollen. Chrysanthemum Joe blinked his sleepy eyes, powder blue like the dress she found on the first day after the storm.

Joe is like me, she thought. He has been lost for a long time.

Something was building up inside her, pushing into her

chest and clogging her throat. Hester felt the smile breaking through on her face like a new skin.

He came from the in-between place. He came for *me*.

***

That night they were both exhausted but Diana made her wash her face, hands, and feet before they slipped into fresh night-gowns and wool socks. In bed Diana explained to her that Joe had to stay with the sheriff at the jailhouse along with the other boxer. He didn't do something wrong, not really, but they wanted him to stay there for a while. They would try to visit him again, soon. Diana promised. Then she read Emily Dickinson by the light of the oil lamp, Hester's head on her shoulder, watching the blur of words swim on the page. Hester liked the musical rhythm of the poems and the way Diana paused and emphasized certain words that seemed ordinary yet full of a kind of weight. *View. Slant. Snow. Host. Victory. Disappear.*

Diana put the book away and turned down the lamp and when they were twined together under the covers she showed Hester a picture of a man with a slight mustache and kind eyes, one hand tucked into his waistcoat, the other holding a pocket watch. As Hester was falling asleep Diana talked about how this man fell ill one day when they were rowing on a lake in Virginia. How he coughed and crawled through the woods because Diana could not carry him. How weeks later she said goodbye to him through a train window, his head leaning against the glass, too weak to do anything but smile.

Hester woke later in the night when the dog started whining in his sleep, his feet jerking as he ran through the grassy fields of his dreams. It was cold in the room and the window covering rippled with the draft. All the tea she drank strained her bladder and she got up carefully so she wouldn't wake Diana and crouched over the metal bowl in the corner by the window. She was pulling up her nightgown and gathering it in her hands when she heard something outside, down in the street. The clomping sound of horses standing impatiently. The creak of leather harnesses.

Hester went to the window and lifted the bottom of the canvas cover with one finger. It took a minute for her eyes to gather enough light to see the tops of the destroyed buildings across the street, fires burning in the distance. She peered down over the windowsill.

There was a line of men on horseback in the street. The men had their faces tilted up to the window and they wore masks with ragged holes for eyes.

The Calvalry of Woe.

Hester froze, uncertain whether they could see her. They can't get to me here, she thought. Diana will stop them. The ladies of the Red Cross will protect me!

One of the men pulled a bullwhip off his saddle. He held it out and it uncoiled, the tip falling into the street. Hester caught herself in a scream, biting down on her tongue, her hands gripping the windowsill. Urine ran down her leg and pooled around her feet. Then there was the scrabble of claws on the floor and the dog barked so loud that Hester squealed and ducked, covering her ears. The dog raged, butting the window cover with his snout, and then Diana was there, gathering Hester in her arms.

What is it? What's the matter?

Diana put her hand into the pool of urine on the floor and

held it up to the faint light. The dog kept barking, his front paws on the windowsill. Diana looked at her hand, smelled it, then hugged Hester to her. They heard a voice outside and the sound of horses wheeling about and the whistle and crack of a whip. Diana yanked the window covering up while Hester curled on the floor, covering her ears. She could still hear the pounding of the horses running and the whip singing through the air. Diana ran to the door, shouting down the hall for Mr. Lowry. Footsteps thumped downstairs, murmuring voices, and a light flickered in the hallway.

There's no one there! Mr. Lowry shouted up the stairs.

When Diana left the room Hester grabbed her doll and jumped back into bed and buried herself in the covers. A few minutes later Diana came back and peeled away the blankets and she held Hester and whispered in her ear that everything would be all right, that she was safe. But Hester knew it would not be all right, it would never be all right. They would never stop coming for her. She held the doll out to Diana. Diana shook her head, the skin between her eyebrows knotted. She didn't understand. Hester pointed to the window, then held up the doll again. She pulled down the front of her nightgown, tracing a finger along the scar that ran across her collarbone and down her chest like a pale worm. She pointed to the window again. Diana put her hand to her mouth. She nodded.

She understood. She knew.

JOE

When the Rangers led Joe out of the arena after the fight Jack Johnson was still lying on the canvas with his eyes closed, a young black boy fanning him with a towel while a couple Rangers looked on. They brought Joe to the Galveston County Jail in a horse-drawn wagon, seated between Captain John Brooks of the Rangers and Sheriff Henry Thomas. Joe was in his tights and shirtless so they gave him a heavy blanket for the ride. The night was raw and cold and Joe pulled the blanket over his head as they rattled through the streets.

Salazar was somehow already waiting for him at the jail with his valise and other supplies. Sheriff Thomas ushered Joe through the front room, pointing out his office and the other cells as if he were conducting a tour. The jail was full, and the men in the other dozen cells glowered at him through the bars, most of them wretchedly drunk but cowed into silence by this display of deference by the sheriff. The deputies took Joe down the hall to a washroom so he could wash and change. A deputy named Rogers stood just inside the door, sipping from a pint of gin as Joe stripped down and scrubbed himself under a nozzle fed by a rainwater barrel on the roof.

Joe moved through all this in a fog. He kept replaying the end of the fight in his mind. He shouldn't have loaded up on that left hook. He should have let the fight go longer, put on a true scientific boxing display for the crowd and promoters. It ended more like a scrap down on the wharves, the awkward feint to goad him and then that *hook*? More like a haymaker thrown by a drunk longshoreman. And the flash of recognition in Jack Johnson's eyes just before he connected. He knew it was coming and that Joe had put everything he had into it. Lack of control, Joe thought. And he gave that pig-faced bigot Craine exactly what he wanted in the process.

When he got back to his cell Salazar was setting out a stack of folded clothes. Joe put on a white oxford-cloth shirt, wool pants, and a heavy cable-knit sweater. He finished towel-drying his hair while he checked his face in the mirror. A few glove burns around his left eye, a bit of swelling around his ear where Johnson clubbed him in the first round. He still felt confused by the whole thing. Joe had been in plenty of fights that were broken up by the police. Normally they just sent everyone home and that was it. But there were other laws, some that weren't on the books. Like a white man fighting a black man in a state like Texas. As Joe was combing out his hair Sheriff Thomas came to the door of his cell.

You hungry, Joe?

Joe looked at the provisions that Salazar had laid out on the small table. A quart of milk in a bucket of ice, a loaf of French bread, a small wheel of hard cheese, six tins of anchovies, olives, pickles, relish, boiled eggs in a jar, a bag of apples, sauerkraut, radishes, a sack of pecans. There was a small shelf of books, magazines, a stack of the *Houston Chronicle*, an extra chair with a floor lamp, and two beds both made up smartly with wool blankets. His extra clothes were stacked along the wall, with two suits on hangers. His boxing gear including his spare tights, vest, towels, speed bag, clubs, ring boots, and three-, four-, and five-ounce gloves were arranged neatly in the corner.

I want to talk to Rabbi Henry Cohen, Joe said.

The rabbi? He a lawyer?

That's who I want. Where's Johnson?

Downstairs, Thomas said. He'll be more comfortable there.

I want to talk to Henry Cohen, Joe said.

Let's eat first, okay? Thomas said. We'll send for Cohen.

They walked him out of the jail a couple blocks to Broadway to a brick roadhouse with flagstone floors and a lean-to kitchen out back where black women in leather aprons stirred chicken parts in an enormous cauldron of boiling oil. The place was packed with men who had been at the fight and when Joe walked in they raised steins and crowded around him, shaking his hand and clapping him on the back. Their yawning red mouths shouted words at him but Joe didn't hear any of it. He was coming down from the adrenaline spike, and the lactic acid in his arms and legs made him feel leaden and sluggish and gave everything a dreamy, twilight feel. Sheriff Thomas and the deputies pushed through the crowd and walked Joe to the back where a table was marked off with rope. Craine's grinning red face showed up with several other men and joined their party and Sheriff Thomas ordered a couple of bottles of champagne and poured everyone a measure. Joe left his glass on the table while they toasted his victory but nobody seemed to notice. The proprietor came out with a tray of fried chicken, biscuits, beans, and pitchers of beer. Just looking at it made Joe tired. He nibbled on a salty wing while the men roared and toasted, sloshing beer foam onto the table. When they pressed him to have a celebratory drink Joe relented and turned to the proprietor.

I'll have an oloroso sherry in a cut-crystal glass, served on a white napkin, please.

The proprietor laughed as if he'd made a joke and walked away, slinging a dish towel over his shoulder. The gaslights on the walls flashed and the ceiling seemed pitched low and slanted in his direction. What the hell was this? Was he arrested or not? What was the matter with these people?

Cohen came to his cell in the morning with warm brioche and coffee. Joe was still in bed with the pillow over his head, trying to block out the morning sun that streamed through the high window. All night he had vivid, strange dreams, inhabited by the hulking form of Jack Johnson and some fleeting glimpses of a tall woman with a long dark braid of hair.

This is an unusual situation, Cohen said.

I shouldn't have knocked him out, Joe said.

They would've arrested you anyway.

Why?

It's complicated, Cohen said. But it has a lot to do with Mr. Johnson and his reputation.

They said he was downstairs.

There are some special cells in the basement. One cell actually. Not really a cell, more like a storage room. It's not nice. Damp.

Is he having brioche for breakfast?

Unlikely.

Joe threw back the covers and got out of bed. No real soreness or pain—the fight was too quick. He pulled on some trousers then bent over the washbasin and splashed water on his face.

Do you know they took me out to dinner last night? Paraded me around like some kind of prize. What the hell *is* this?

That's not all, Cohen said. Sheriff Thomas says he wants you two ready to spar tomorrow afternoon in the yard. And then a speed-bag exhibition at the dance hall. He's already sold tickets.

Tickets? Me and Johnson?

Welcome to Galveston, Cohen said. Pluggers, poachers, trimmers, always working their confidence schemes. You'll get your cut.

Joe stripped off his sleeping shirt and picked out a shirt and collar from the trim stack of folded clothes.

I'm not doing it unless they bring Johnson out of the basement.

I think the cells are full, Cohen said.

Then put him in here, Joe said. Why do I need two beds? And all this stuff. Hell, I need someone in here to help me eat all this food. Where's Salazar?

He's at the telegraph office, firing off cables to someone or other. He seems pretty upset. You sure about this, Joe?

Yeah. Why the hell not?

You keep saying *hell* a lot this morning.

Well, I'm a little upset, Henry. Can you get me out of here?

The bond stands at five thousand and the first hearing is Monday. I've got Marc McClemore coming in today, the best lawyer in south Texas. Sit tight for a couple days.

What's the committee doing about this? Did they know this was going to happen?

We're having a meeting this afternoon, Cohen said. But no, the Rangers are acting on the orders of Governor Sayers. We didn't know anything about it.

Joe spent the day napping and paging through the books and magazines that Salazar gathered from somewhere. In the afternoon he settled on a novel titled *The Monster* by Stephen Crane and read until supper when Salazar arrived with a hot pan of dumplings and gravy, roasted apples, and a bowl of salted cucumbers sliced with onions.

That night in the cell Joe lay on his back and let his body settle into the slack canvas of the cot, the thin wool blanket tucked tight around his body, like an Egyptian pharaoh in repose. He stared at the furrows in the ceiling plaster for a long time until he saw the dark form of Jack Johnson hovering above him. Since the fight Johnson had replaced Diana as the primary involuntary projection of his unconscious. When he fell asleep Johnson was there in the forefront of his fragmented dreams; he was there on the street corner wearing rags and a straw boater, tipping his hat to the fall of evening and the current of music that flowed under a beaten-brass door. Carrying ladies in their bright dresses in his long dark arms along the sidewalks, swinging them gently as they rode away to bed. His broad hand upon a slender white thigh. The quiver in her voice as she set the teaspoon down on the saucer, the windowpanes rattled by the wings of ghostly seabirds.

Joe started himself awake, sweating under the blanket, the blue-black square of the barred window above him pocked with a handful of stars. None of it made sense. He had fought men equally or even more physically imposing. Tommy Sharkey was a cunning and dangerous man in the form of a mutant bulldog. Jim Jeffries towered over all of them, a man inflexible as iron and powerful as a titan. But in Joe's dreams Jack Johnson was a towering black giant striding across the land, shouldering his way through clouds while the white crescent of the morning sun exploded on the blue waters of the Gulf. In dreams or in waking life, always there was the feeling of being adrift, outside of something. What is this thing that keeps me apart? Why am I on this island?

Ever since Joe was a child his manner, dress, and inclinations had separated him from his fellows, his family, the few lovers he had known. Even Lutie did not know the man who resided inside the body, the naked being behind the eyes, the one who found some kind of lurid satisfaction in the destruction of other men through physical violence. The man who did the shameful act in the dark of the closet, who set a match to the paper and watched the fire that erased the evidence. That man was kept in the dark.

Louise was a person who wanted every aspect of their life to be one shared thing that they could embrace together on the long slide to the final silence. There was something about it that drove Joe away and Lutie seemed to sense this widening distance and so she filled their time together with chatter, entreaties, and affection until the illness stilled her tongue. Then her face collapsed into a soft bag of skin stretched around bones, eyes that bore little light, the fragment of a song rolling around in her mouth.

She was dying.

The thought boomed through the night and Joe stretched his legs and strained against it, crushing his eyes shut. The blanket was twisted around his torso and his shoulders were exposed to the draft that came down the hall. He shivered and clenched his fists, squeezing until his knuckles crunched and popped. When he finally drifted off to sleep he was dreaming again of the tall woman with the long braid of hair down her back, walking down the beach in her white dress.

***

They brought Jack up the next afternoon. He was still in his tights and boots from the fight, his gloves hanging around his neck. His skin was ashen and crusted with dried sweat, his face swollen and his lips blue. At first Joe thought he'd really damaged the man, but as Jack shuffled down the hall in leg irons, gripping his arms as best he could in his handcuffs, Joe realized he was just chilled to the bone. When they opened the cell door Joe tossed him the wool blanket and Jack immediately wrapped it around his shivering body. Joe looked at Deputy Rogers.

Why don't you let the man get cleaned up?

Where? This is the jail.

He can take a shower the same place I did.

Naw, that's the deputy washroom, Rogers said. Not for prisoners. Certainly not for no darkies.

You need to tell Sheriff Thomas that this man can't spar this afternoon.

Oh, he can do it, Rogers said. He's a tough Negro.

Well, *I* won't, Joe said. So tell him that.

Joe picked up his washbasin and pushed it into Rogers's arms.

I'd like some fresh water. Hot, please.

Jack eased himself onto the empty cot and bent his head down almost to his knees. He rubbed his scalp and let out a long, lingering sigh. His head was fuzzy with stubble. Joe picked out a washrag, towel, and his largest pair of pants and shirt. He snapped his bar of soap in half and tossed it into a bowl, wiped his razor and dropped it in there, too. When Rogers brought the pan of hot water Joe placed it on the table and tapped Jack's shoulder. Jack stood up shakily, then stripped down and washed himself, reaching awkwardly over his head to wash his back. Joe sat with his legs crossed and flipped through a week-old newspaper. When Jack finished he stood with the towel around his waist and looked at the pants and shirt Joe laid out on the cot.

These your clothes?

Yes, Joe said. I have plenty more.

Jack slipped the shirt and pants on and lay down on the cot, pulling the blanket over him.

I need to sleep now, Mr. Joe, he said.

He fell asleep immediately, snoring in a wet, ragged rhythm. Joe rubbed his hands together and paced the cell for a few minutes, mumbling lines he half remembered from *Captain Brassbound's Conversion,* revising them to his liking. He wrote some out on a pad of paper. There was a scene he had in mind, between a man and a woman. But he didn't imagine Lutie on the stage. The female player was tall with a long black braid and she was filled with single-minded purpose and charitable acts. The man was a former athlete, once a popular attraction but now a washed-up hack. She would change him in some essential way, or perhaps illuminate something within him that was there all along—the usual tropes and dramatic arcs of character development. It was all terrible.

Joe began to shadowbox. He took off his shirt and did push-ups, leg lifts, and a double set of calisthenics, taking care to land quietly during his squat-leaps, to avoid waking Jack. When he finished he collapsed on the floor, gasping for air, and lay there awhile with his cheek on the cold concrete. How can I be a writer, he thought, when I can't even understand what *I* am feeling? How could I possibly understand another being beyond the physiological, past the cheap accumulation of physical traits and habits? Is that all that I am? Is it just this body? He closed his eyes and dozed in the thrall of uneasy dreams, wakened a while later by a plump rat tottering along the wall, dragging a ponderous hunk of Salazar's cheese-and-onion pie like a religious penitent.

Cohen and the lawyer McClemore showed up in the afternoon and Joe sat in the front room of the jailhouse with them to talk. McClemore would represent both him and Jack, and the committee would cover the fees. They would be held for up to thirty days while the district attorney tried to get a grand jury together. McClemore assured Joe that the DA would fail to get a true bill against them and the case would fall apart.

The sheriff likes you, Cohen said. He's quite the boxing fan. Keep him on your side and things will go well for you both.

In the cell Jack shuddered and moaned in his sleep. He was

clearly feverish and Sheriff Thomas agreed to postpone the sparring sessions. Joe covered him with extra blankets and kept a
cup of cold water by his head. He did his calisthenics and read
the papers and books Salazar brought and in the evening he
went to dinner again with Thomas and the deputies. The sheriff
brought a new round of men to the table, all of them eager for
a chance to talk about Joe's famous fights. Joe told them about
his rematch with Peter Maher, when the police commissioner, a
fellow named Theodore Roosevelt—now the governor of New
York—sat in the front row, roaring his approval of Joe's scientific boxing while masticating a cigar with his giant teeth. When
Joe had Maher stumbling around the ring, bleeding from the
ears, Roosevelt stood up, yelling, Don't stop the fight, don't stop
the fight! After Joe won the decision the police commissioner
insisted he shake Joe's hand, shouting, Cracking good show!
and blistering Joe's face with his savage halitosis.

The next morning Joe woke to find Jack sitting up on his
cot, stroking his fuzzy skull.

Morning, Mr. Joe.

Hullo, Jack.

When's breakfast?

The deputy will bring a bowl of mush around in about an
hour, but I've got cold bacon and biscuits right here and Salazar
ought to be here any minute with some fresh coffee.

Jack sat on the edge of the cot and took off his shirt and
tossed it on the floor. For such a large man he still carried the
languid slenderness of youth. His torso was muscular but sleek,
his skin unblemished. Joe was reminded that this man was only
twenty-two years old.

What kind of jail is this?

You don't know the half of it, Joe said.

When I woke up in the ring I had handcuffs on. First time that's ever happened.

Woke up with handcuffs?

I mean first time I been knocked out! What'd you hit me with?

An unorthodox variation of a left hook, you might call it.

I drop straight down?

Cold as a mackerel.

After that it gets a bit dreamy, Jack said. Mixed up. I was in another room for a bit, I know that. Someplace cold. And wet.

Joe watched Jack struggle to shave his head with the small mirror and razor.

You need some help?

Jack shrugged and tossed the razor in the pan.

You ever shave a black man's head before?

Shouldn't be any different than any other man's head.

You sure about that?

No, Joe said. I'm not.

First he wiped Jack's head clean and worked the skin with a hot towel to loosen the pores. Then he rubbed a stick of walnut-oil soap vigorously in his hands and applied a smooth layer of lather. He finished in twelve precise, sweeping strokes of the straight razor, then took out a shaker bottle of mineral spirits and oils that Salazar mixed up, shook some into his palm, and massaged it into Jack's gleaming black skull, marveling at how hypnotically smooth it was. Maybe there *was* something different. After he finished Jack stood in front of the mirror, turning his chin side to side, feeling his head with his fingertips.

You are a man of many skills, Joe.

The care and maintenance of the body is a vital discipline, Joe said. Personal hygiene. Especially for men in our profession.

I like that. Body maintenance. Vital discipline.

Joe piled a tin plate with biscuits and a slab of bacon and a couple of apples and handed it to Jack and they ate sitting on their beds.

You know what I was dreaming about, Jack said, sleeping there in the ring? I was in the storm again. I was up to my neck in that rushing water. There were people screaming and drowning and I couldn't do anything about it.

Jack stuck a piece of bacon between two halves of a biscuit and took a massive bite, chewing thoughtfully. The rest of the prisoners were rustling around in their cells and down the row someone was calling out to Deputy Rogers. The front door slammed shut and a chilling draft gusted down the block of cells.

All that water and wind, Jack said. I'll never forget that wind. Howled like all the devils in hell were coming for me.

Joe picked up Jack's shirt off the floor, folded it, and placed it on his cot.

This a damn fine biscuit, Jack said. Who made these?

As if in answer, Salazar appeared at the cell with a pot of hot coffee and a copy of the *Houston Chronicle* with a picture of the two boxers on the front page. The headline: JEW VS. NEGRO PRIZEFIGHT LEADS TO ARREST!

***

The next afternoon Joe and Jack put on their tights and laced on five-ounce gloves and Rogers led them out the back door of the jail to a muddy fenced yard. The deputies had laid down a square of folded tarpaulin for a ring and hammered bleachers together out of storm refuse. About forty men sat on the bleachers, and another couple dozen stood around smoking cigars with their hands jammed in their pockets. It was a clear day but windy and Joe and Jack immediately started jogging in place to get warmed up. Cohen stood beside the bleachers with Craine and Balestri. They all nodded at Joe as they jogged into the ring.

Gentlemen, Sheriff Thomas announced, I give you Chrysanthemum Joe Choynski and Jack Johnson, the Galveston Giant!

A dozen fellows slapped their hands together, a few whistles. Joe wondered what Thomas was charging for this little show.

What do you want to do? Jack asked.

Let's just move around a bit, Joe said. Get warmed up.

This like no jail time I've ever heard of, Jack said.

They shuffled around and shadowboxed. Jack's smooth head smoked in the cold air as they stepped around the tarpaulin, weaving, switching stances, circling each other. Joe noted Jack's easy foot speed, the way he cut off angles and placed his forward foot like a dancer. Natural skills, he thought. Something you can't learn.

Sheriff Thomas clapped his hands.

Say, Joe, let's see some of that scientific boxing!

The two men paused, looking at each other. Cohen was fingering his pocket watch and looking off over the fence to the east where the sun glowered behind a fog of clouds. Behind the fence someone drove a team of mules down the street with a whip, cursing furiously. Joe shrugged.

You ready to spar a bit?

Sure, Jack said. Just keep it light. My head may look good but it's still a little dusty from that last swing.

Three-quarter speed, Joe said. Hand-check them as they come, okay? Here's the jab.

He started pushing out his left and Jack tapped it away as they circled. After a minute they switched and Jack put out his long jab. Then they went through the straight right and some combinations. Jack's footwork was smooth, Joe thought, but he had no movement in his upper body. Would you move that beautiful black head!

At the end of their exhibition Jack did a little heel-toe shuffle then bowed dramatically to all four sides of the ring.

I hope all you good people enjoyed the show!

One of the men in the bleachers flicked a lit cigar at him and it bounced off his chest.

Shut your goddamn mouth! Balestri hissed. Nobody told you to say anything.

Jack looked at him, still holding his giant grin.

That's right nobody told me, he said. Nobody tells me to do *anything*.

I'm 'bout to put you back in the basement, Sheriff Thomas said. That'll shut your smart mouth!

After they put Jack back in the cell Sheriff Thomas took Joe into his office and counted out twelve dollars into his palm.

We'll do it again Tuesday, Thomas said. Then some of that speed-bag work.

If we're still here, said Joe.

Oh, you will be. Certainly *he* will. You better tell that Negro to watch himself.

After they washed and changed Jack lay on his bed drinking a quart of milk and gnawing on one of Salazar's lamb chops. Joe enjoyed Salazar's food, but Jack responded to it like a religious

supplicant reaching the promised land. Salazar met his enthusiasm with even more abundance, supplementing their larder
with roasted meats, steamed vegetables with rice, bowls of grits
fried in bacon grease, chicken wings smoked over hickory coals
and dressed with pepper sauce. Joe took the money Thomas gave
him, peeled off six dollars, and tossed it on Jack's bed.

Jack paused with a chop bone in his mouth, eyeing the
money.

That's your cut, Joe said.

Jack wiped his hands on one of the pressed cloth napkins
Salazar delivered each morning. He picked up the money and
tucked it in his shirt pocket.

Don't mind this little show, Jack said, if they keep paying
and feeding us like this. That second you got, that skinny guy
with the trombone? Where'd you find him?

Australia. But he's from Spain. And I'd say he found me.
It's a long story.

The man is talented with a skillet.

Jack wiped his mouth and reclined with his hands behind
his head, the plate of chops and a side of roasted red potatoes balanced on his broad chest. He had a strange, almost
theatrical way of speaking, of inhabiting space. Even small movements seemed blocked out and stylized. His large eyes, the clean
symmetry of his face, the tight knit of his body, the shape of
his head. Being in the room with him was like being part of a
scene onstage, and Jack was always the star. The man has a finely
structured skull bone, Joe thought. Like something phrenolo-
gists would keep in a locked case and revere like a golden calf.

I don't think I'm ever gonna get over that punch, Jack said.
Still thinking about it. Like my body was refusing the orders

from my brain. Like the seed inside the shell got shook free, just rattling around in there. You know what I mean?

I do, Joe said. I've always thought of it like your inside self gets knocked off the mooring. It's like you are set adrift in this strange mechanical flesh-box that is your body.

That's it, Jack said. That's what I'm saying. I can still feel it. Like a tattoo on my brain. And you were there, standing in front of me as the lights went out. But it wasn't you. It was like the ghost you. You were dark, like a hole in the sky, taking away all the light.

That's the black lights, Joe said. A glimpse of the void. You've been to the other side.

Joe told him how a solid shot can squeeze a bundle of nerves at the back of the jawbone that blinker you out so quick you don't have time to consider the floor rushing up at you. While the shock of the punch is still reverberating down your neck, your limbs are already too far away, your arms somewhere across the river, your legs in the next city.

The first time Joe saw the black lights he was seventeen years old, fighting in an oyster shed in India Basin. The stevedores got tired of getting thrashed by the skinny blond kid with precise diction and indifferent manner, so they put up a heavily tattooed Samoan who showed up wearing a seal-skin coat and stovepipe hat. This man had fought all over the Pacific and had a flat-footed, unorthodox style with extremely quick hands and Joe made the mistake of stretching out his jab too often. The Samoan knocked it down and followed with a straight right that caught Joe flat on his noble chin as he was stepping in, driving the lower half of his face into the back of his head like someone slapping back the drawer of a cash register. His brain slopped up against the back of his skull and the world went a dark color, shadows pouring over everything like a solar eclipse. The Samoan loomed in front of him, hooded in black and with glimmering eyes. A deep fear that was beyond mortal injury gripped Joe in those brief moments. If he had a soul, it froze up solid and dropped out of him. In the span of a single second Joe lost sensation in his feet, then his legs, then his back, each part of his body going silent, like riding a train down a long dark track and the lights ahead are blinking out, one by one. He woke up a minute later with his head resting on a frozen haddock, his buddy Eddie feeling his carotid artery with two fingers.

Since then Joe had seen the black lights another half dozen times, the last time just a year ago in New York when he was knocked out by the Barbados Demon, Joe Walcott. That time he was out for almost three minutes and when he woke Joe thought he was in his parents' house in San Francisco. He could even hear the turning of the Victrola on the highboy in the parlor, the squeaking handle that Isador kept forgetting to oil. The record playing was "Listen to the Mockingbird."

> *Listen to the mockingbird,*
> *Listen to the mockingbird.*
> *The mockingbird still singing o'er her grave . . .*

Then the pain in his face started to creep in and the sounds of the hall came rushing back and he realized he was lying on the canvas in front of nine hundred people, feeling naked as an oyster. A twisting pain gripped him like a living thing in his guts and he rolled over and vomited a gush of sour stomach fluid onto the canvas. The fight officials thought he'd suffered a brain injury and Salazar insisted he get to the hospital for an examination. Joe sat through two hours of tests rather than admit what he knew. It was the blood-hot humiliation of complete, unequivocal defeat that his body found unbearable.

The newspaper headline the next day: BARBADOS BESTS JERUSALEM.

That negative image of the Samoan sailor would still sometimes appear like a rancorous spirit while Joe was walking down the street, or having breakfast, or in the middle of a conversation with someone. Every knockout he had experienced stayed with him, chambered in his lost memory, occasionally floating free to remind him of that terrifying place where light disappeared and the darkness came like a hurricane wind. To depart from consciousness, to be severed from your body in this way against your will, was a kind of little death, and if philosophy was the study of preparing to die well, then Joe wondered why more boxers weren't more philosophical. Each encounter with the black lights was something like an anguished trial run—a brief, harrowing glimpse of the inevitable dull, cloistered end that awaits us all.

On other occasions Joe had taken massive blows straight on the chin, the punch snapping his head around so hard he could feel the muscle fibers in his neck tearing, and yet he just blinked it away. Some fights Joe would take dozens of huge shots, any one of which could have knocked him into a catatonic state. But he just shrugged them off. Most fighters believed it was just luck. Joe believed it was a matter of the slight displacement of a bit of flesh, bone, sinew, nerve. You tried to take the blows where *you* wanted them. Small adjustments to send the energy somewhere else rather than the direct route to the brain stem. Head movement.

Stand up for a minute, Joe said. I want to show you something.

Jack set his plate aside and stood up, dusting crumbs off his chest. Joe pushed the small end table across the cell to give them some space.

Watch me.

Joe took his stance and began to shift his head, bending at the knees. He worked his head and shoulders in a circular fashion, going a quarter turn left, then right.

Imagine there is a circle here, Joe said, tracing a circle about a foot in diameter in the air in front of Jack's face. Move your head along that circular path, upper half, bottom half, circle left, circle right. I'm going to throw some jabs and you slip them to either side.

Jack sighed and put up his hands. He began to move his head. Joe threw slow punches and Jack dipped and weaved.

Work the circle, Joe said. Always staying close to the center line. When you slip the right hand you should be ready to counter.

They circled around the narrow space between their beds. Jack paused to strip off his shirt, slinging it on his bed. Joe started to pick up the pace, going three-quarter speed.

Now counter, Joe said. Use the momentum you get from the head shift.

Jack slipped the jab and came back with a right which Joe slipped before throwing a left. After a few more throws Joe held up his hands and they paused. Jack bent over at the waist, hands on his hips.

You gonna give me a stomachache.

A man as quick as you are, Joe said, should never get hit.

You master some head movement and you'll never see the black lights again.

I'd like that, Jack said.

They started to circle and throw again. In the cell opposite, a leathery old codger stood with his chin resting on the bars, watching them with rheumy eyes. Sheriff Thomas told Joe the drunk hit his old lady with a fire poker and cracked her skull like an egg. He was up for a murder charge and due to be arraigned in a couple of days.

Deputy Rogers came down the hall carrying a wooden crate.

Back at it, Rogers said, and you boys just got done.

It's this'n, Jack said, motioning to Joe. He don't quit.

I got some bad news, Rogers said. The governor's office heard about this little arrangement here, all this fancy food and things. Now we got to clear it all out. From here on out its regular food and regulations. No more hot showers, suppers out on the town. No more visits from that Mexican with the trombone bringing fresh laundry.

Rogers started loading the food, drink, and extra clothing into the box.

Suppers out on the town? Jack said. And that Mexican is from Spain.

I'll just wrap these chops up for me and the boys, Rogers said, picking up the plate.

Jack snatched a chop and Rogers tried to smack it out of his hand but Jack was too quick. He tore off a big hunk of meat with his teeth then offered the chop to the deputy.

I always share, Jack said out the side of his mouth as he chewed. Even with a man as mean as yourself.

You are asking for it, boy, Rogers said. I swear it.

Oh, I'm not asking for it, Jack said. I'm *begging* for it.

Joe reached in the box and pulled out the stack of books and newspapers.

I'm sure the governor won't mind these. Did you send for Cohen? We want to talk to him.

Rogers snorted and gave him a two-fingered salute before closing the cell door and walking down the hall.

Why are you always causing trouble? Joe said to Jack.

Whaddya mean? I'm *angry*. Same as you.

I'm not angry.

Shit, Jack said. You angry as hell. The way you are in the ring. Peacocking around like you made of rosewater and caviar. You can see it from the back row.

I don't know what you're talking about.

That's why you hit so hard, Jack said. You angry at something. Every fighter is angry.

Well, you're still making life harder for yourself.

Jack flipped the clean chop bone through the cell bars and it clattered on the concrete floor.

Listen here, he said. You can wait around if you want. I'm going to live, right *now*.

Dearest Lutie,

You may have already heard through the wires of my current misfortune. The governor of Texas decided to enforce the prizefight law here and has incarcerated my opponent and myself. I do not want you to be concerned as I am in good health and well-taken care of. I prevailed in the contest and sustained no damage. Unfortunately the payment is held up by this legal proceeding but the lawyer assures me we will get the money.

The worst of it is being confined. I cannot get decent exercise and feel as if I'm about to burst. My opponent Jack Johnson is in here with me. Johnson is young and inexperienced but he is terribly quick and a mountain of a man with considerable strength. If he puts together his feet and head movement he will be impossible to hit cleanly. I wonder if he may be a new kind of boxer. All the great boxers of my day were great because of their ability to take punches. Bob Fitzsimmons, that balding beanpole, you can bounce your knuckles off his dome all day. They call him "Ruby Rob" not because of his red hair but because his face would be a bloody mess by round five yet he would go twenty more easy. Jeffries was like pounding a slab of beef. Even Corbett, with his technical skills and quickness—in the end the man had a face like iron. Where did it come from? Was it something they were born with? Or was it something learned or developed?

I knocked out Mr. Johnson in the third round and this was the first time he was rendered unconscious via the fistic arts. He still seems to like me well enough so perhaps I am forgiven for showing him the dark place that nobody forgets.

I feel old, Lutie. Almost twenty years of boxing. So much violence, given and received. Where did it all go? Is it stored up or saved somewhere? How many times have I been struck? I know I have been disfigured, transformed from my youthful visage to this swollen mask of scar *tissue and bone. With all my inane vanity, how could I let it go on?*

Last year in your letters you urged me to leave you behind, to go and live another life. How could I do such a thing? And where would I go?

Yours,

Joe

DIANA

Clara was still too tired to leave her room, so Diana brought Cordelia along for the meeting with the committee at the mayor's office. She assigned two ladies to stay with the girl and Mr. Lowry was stationed in the hallway with an old cavalry pistol in his jacket pocket. The front door was kept locked but the ladies still ran the kitchen out front while the orphans played card games and drank hot apple cider in the parlor.

They walked down Broadway after breakfast, Cordelia carrying the valise with the papers and the hard light of the winter sun putting a blinding glare on every surface. A work crew was rebuilding the stone edifice of city hall and teams of horses dragged sledges of block up the street. A group of women from the Civic League supervised the planting of red oleanders along the verge. Cohen was waiting for them on the front steps, talking aloud to himself while he jabbed the air with a cigarette.

At least one of the murdered Ponder children was whipped, he said. The medical examiner confirmed this. They found a few rings and a necklace in their pockets. One of the rings was still on a finger.

Oh dear God, Cordelia said.

We've heard reports, Cohen said, of people looting the dead. There certainly have been summary executions of the accused. The youngest of the Ponder children, the girl, was eight years old. Her mother said she'd gone out looking for her brothers. This was not simply some kind of vigilante justice. This was a deliberate murder.

Cohen looked strained and tired. His usual cheerful spirit was gone. He's finally wearing down, Diana thought.

I can't believe it, Cordelia said. I can't.

People are succumbing to rumor and emotion, Cohen said. I'm not even sure I trust the medical examiner anymore.

Who on the committee can we trust? Diana asked.

I don't know, he said. The mayor is a decent man but he is being manipulated.

Cohen gazed at the cracked edifice of city hall, rolling and unrolling a sheaf of papers in his hands.

They're waiting for us upstairs, he said, and pitched his cigarette into the street.

The committee had gathered in the mayor's study, a spacious room on the third floor with ornate furniture of polished oak and a bust of Stephen F. Austin on a brass stand. Oil portraits of Galveston mayors for the past hundred years lined the walls. The members of the committee were lounging around on various chairs, settees, and couches, smoking and chatting. Craine and Balestri stood by a window having a quiet conversation with the mayor. A teenage black girl in a cotton shift dress knelt by the fireplace, adding handfuls of pine chips to a small glowing fire. When Diana and Cordelia came in Craine rapped his ivory pipe on the windowsill and all the men in the room stopped talking and turned toward the two women. Diana handed over her copies of the railyard invoices, the records of the stores that arrived over the past two weeks: the pounds of cotton bandage cloth, bales of wire, stacks of lumber, gallons of antiseptic, sacks of beans, barrels of molasses, wheat, oats, cheese, milk, butter, apples from Maine, peaches from Georgia, bundles of dried buffalo jerky from Montana, boxcars of clothing, bedding, a gross of brass trumpets, a grand piano, a case of ladies' toilet water, a hundred machine-made straight razors, sacks of nails, wire transfers, personal checks, and stacks of silver and gold currency in locked iron boxes. The great heart of America and the world had opened up and poured its generosity upon the destitute city. Most of Diana's work was to get out from under the plenitude that arrived by ship and rail twenty-four hours a day.

She was also here to tell them that the Red Cross could no longer handle these tasks, that they would need to draw back into their more familiar realm of medical services and the orphanage. The committee agreed, and Mayor Jones described how they had already drawn up the papers for a new agency to be run out of the mayor's office. The CRC would officially disband and the members would take on an advisory role for the new agency that would oversee the rebuilding effort. The chairman of the new agency would be Floyd Craine.

Cohen paced about the room, fidgeting with nervous energy. Balestri poured out a round of brandies and passed them around on a tray. Diana declined but Cordelia accepted a glass and took a self-conscious sip and when she grimaced the men laughed, their eyes roving over her body. Diana took the glass from her sister's hand and placed it back on the tray.

A bit of good cheer never hurt anyone, Balestri said. We're celebrating.

I cannot see what there is to celebrate, Diana said. We have almost forty orphans with no surviving family members and the poorest citizens of this city remain in frightful conditions.

Galveston will be rebuilt, the mayor said.

And better than before, Craine said. We will outgun Houston and regain our standing as the top port of trade and commerce in the southern United States. We will make Galveston great again!

Hear, hear!

The men raised their glasses and drank their brandies while Diana and Cordelia stood in the center of the room, hands clasped behind their crisply laundered white dresses.

What will you do, Diana said, about Mr. Choynski and Mr. Johnson?

Regrettable situation, said Mayor Jones. But it's the governor's decision.

That Johnson was getting too high for his nut, Craine said. Let him stew for a bit.

Didn't you contract Mr. Choynski to come here?

He's lucky, Balestri said, that we'll still honor the agreement after what he did.

Nobody cares about that washed-up Yid, Craine said.

What did he do? Diana asked. Wasn't he supposed to fight the man?

He wasn't supposed to knock the Negro *out*, Balestri said. It was an exhibition of scientific boxing. He turned it into a brawl and settled his hash. Well, that's on him.

It was a hell of a shot, Craine said. But what we'd like to talk about is that orphan in your care, the hero everyone's talking about. We'd like to speak with her.

That is an absurd request, Cohen said in a pitched voice. What could we possibly want with this little girl?

Oh, I don't know, Craine said, easing himself into a leather wingback chair. He crossed his legs, pipe cantilevered on his lower lip, and unbuttoned his collar. Diana noticed that the lower half of his left ear had been mangled since she saw him at the first meeting.

We want to know what happened to her that night on the beach, he said. For the continued safety of our citizens.

Cohen was walking circles around the bronze bust, shaking his head.

The girl will not speak and therefore will have nothing to say!

Craine pulled his collar open with a finger and scratched his neck, his small eyes locked on Diana. There was a vertical white scar, just a few inches long, and it took Diana a few seconds to recognize that Craine didn't have a knotted bulge in his throat. *He didn't have an Adam's apple.*

I'm sure she could tell us something, Craine said. It's a miracle she survived, don't you think? Right at death's door. Then back among the living. Ha!

When he talked the effect was even more disconcerting. The normal movement, the undulation of the throat as words were pronounced, it was all off. It was like watching an animal speak.

I cannot allow that, Diana said. Her safety is a concern. A group of men on horseback came to the warehouse on Tuesday night to threaten her.

You saw these men?

I saw them riding away down the street.

So you saw a group of men riding horses down the street? This is Texas, ma'am. There are *always* men riding horses down the street.

The girl said it was the men who whipped her.

She *said*?

Not in words. But there is no doubt.

Well now, Craine said, what are we supposed to do with that?

These are the same masked men, Diana said, who murdered the Ponder children. But you already know this.

Craine smiled and folded his arms across his chest and everyone and everything else in the room became still and quiet. Diana stood with her hands clasped behind her back, her head cocked slightly. A faint tremor shook her shoulders and she repositioned her feet. I will not look away, she thought. Balestri dabbed his upper lip with a handkerchief. The mayor looked around as if he had just woken up and didn't know where he was. He's on the outside, Diana thought. They are just using him, too. Craine smirked and squinted at her.

You mean those darkies who were looting the dead? Defiling the bodies of decent white citizens?

Vigilante justice is not a solution, Cohen stammered. These children, their death—it has galvanized the population of the east side. There will be more violence!

And that violence will be dealt with, Balestri said. We will *not* let this matter distract from the reconstruction efforts. Law and order will reign!

Craine pointed a stubby finger at Cohen.

Outside agitators, that's *your* fault.

The rabbi fingered his shirt cuffs, shaking his head at the floor.

All those Yids you've been shipping, Craine said. If you could keep your people in line, keep them from throwing in with the Negroes, there wouldn't *be* any problem.

Wait, wait, Mayor Jones said. We're getting off track here.

The mayor sat on the couch and poked the coffee table with his forefinger. His forehead shone with sweat.

You must understand, Ms. Longstreet, that this visit by men on horseback to your offices isn't exactly compelling evidence. Of anything. We must be careful making these kinds of accusations.

Craine made a small movement with his hand and the mayor coughed into his fist and then picked up his empty brandy glass, looking into it as if something might appear.

Ms. Longstreet, Craine said, you know that you don't have official custody of the child. If she is under threat, then she will be safer in our care.

It doesn't matter, Diana said. She will remain with me.

We can have the sheriff retrieve her if needed.

Diana put her copies of the reports into the valise and handed it to Cordelia.

I think we are finished here.

Diana couldn't believe the staggering audacity of these men, lying right to her face. They had no fear of reprisal or accusation. Why would they? They had the city by the throat and everyone was afraid.

One more thing, Craine said. Is Ms. Barton in good health? We haven't seen her for several weeks. We'd like to talk with her.

I can speak for Ms. Barton.

Ms. Longstreet, Craine said, you're not exactly an *accommodating* woman, are you?

Balestri and a couple of other men snorted and turned away to conceal their amusement. Diana turned to him, lifting her chin. Oh, these men were tiresome.

Is that my obligation here? she said. To *accommodate* you? Is this delusion specific to yourself or would you say it is general among your peers?

Well, it seems clear, Craine said, that Ms. Barton's time here is over. When the handover is complete my committee will take control of all aspects of the reconstruction. Including your orphanage.

Are you saying that you want the American Red Cross to leave Galveston?

Don't you think it's time? Haven't you outlived your usefulness? We will not abide forever this intrusion by your socialist organization, however well-intentioned.

We won't abandon the children, Diana said. And we are not beholden to you or your committees. Good day, gentlemen.

Outside city hall a long mule team passed down the street pulling a fishing sloop, the masts lashed to the deck and a young black boy riding on the bowsprit. A steam pump squealed and clattered to life, the belts snaking through the spinning wheels in a cloud of white smoke. Diana went quickly down the stairs and started across the street on a narrow plank, one arm held out for balance, the other hand holding up the hem of her dress.

She was furious and wanted to be away from these men

and their cigars and pipes and raw-meat faces. Even after all this they still did not take her as a person to be reckoned with, someone with an estimable amount of grit and ability. The Red Cross was doing all the work as they sat in their parlors and acted like they stacked the bodies with their own hands, like they carried the weeping orphan children to bed each night, like they carried pots of soup into the shattered east end where a woman sustained her six surviving children for a month on rainwater and a sack of dried fish.

Diana, wait!

Cordelia started across the street, trying to catch up. She paused as some men on horseback trotted past and her boot slipped off the plank and she sank in the mud up to her ankle. Cordelia sighed, holding up her skirts as Cohen came up behind her and offered his hand. Diana made it halfway across the street before the board sank into the ooze and she had to jump to another. She stopped there, balanced on the flexing wood as it was trampled by passing horses, wagons, and men.

Diana! Please wait!

Diana stood frozen, one hand holding up her dress, the other held out for balance.

We want to know what happened to her that night on the beach.

The girl never said a word about what happened. How did Craine know she was attacked on the beach?

Diana!

She could see her reflection in the window of the mercantile store across the street: a tall form in white, her boots still clean and her dress spotless, balancing between lines of smudged figures that flowed around her like debris in a dirty river.

At the warehouse, Liverwright was camped at the bottom of the stairs, the photographer squatting on the floor with his tripod across his lap and a pint of whiskey in his hand. The ladies had refused to let them see Clara.

What does this mean? Liverwright asked Diana. Has she put you in charge?

It doesn't mean anything, Diana said. Now kindly leave us alone.

This is why I'm here. I'm here for the story.

There are plenty of stories out there. Why don't you start with the gangs of masked men terrorizing the city? Why don't you talk to the people whose children were murdered on the beach?

Yes, ma'am, Liverwright said, tipping his cap. But Clara Barton taken ill, too weak to do her work—that's a big story, too.

There are people on the east side, Diana said, who are living in the wreckage of their homes, who don't have clean drinking water. Take your camera out there and document that. Why don't you try to do some good for people and not just stir up trouble?

Yes, ma'am. But the trouble is more interesting, isn't it?

He snapped his fingers at the photographer and they slung on their coats and went out the front door into the bright morning, where ladies were carrying steaming soup pots and loading them in wagons. Cordelia stood by the hall window in her bare feet, holding her muddy boots in one hand. She watched the ladies carrying soup, idly scratching a streak of dried mud on her cheek.

You should get some rest, Diana said.

I'm tired of all of this, Cordelia said. I don't want to be here anymore.

It will be over soon. I promise.

I want to be where people are good and kind.

Diana put her arm around her sister and rested her cheek on her shoulder. Outside, men were stacking crates of chickens. A lady in a white dress sat on the steps of a ruined house across the street, elbows resting on her knees, smoking a cigarette.

These children, Cordelia said—it's like they each take a little piece of me. I love them all, but soon there will be nothing of me left.

***

Clara was asleep in her bed, lying on her back with her mouth gaping open. Diana closed the door and approached with quiet steps. The outline of Clara's body under the blankets seemed too thin and unsubstantial, as if the bed were water and she was floating with just her face, hands, and feet breaking the surface. Thin blue veins stood out on her sunken cheeks. She was as small as a child. It was after ten o'clock and Diana knew that Clara hated for anyone to know she slept past eight, so Diana raised the window coverings and tied them off. The room filled with light and Clara stirred and raised an arm over her eyes. The tea set was on the bedside table. Diana touched the pot and found it was cold.

Clara opened her eyes, stretched her legs.

Diana. It's good to see you.

She unearthed herself from the heavy blanket and sat up while Diana arranged pillows behind her. When she was settled Diana handed her the chipped china cup with a dollop of soda paste and a willow stick. The skin on Clara's face was pulled tight like tissue paper and her eyes hung heavy and bulbous in their bony cradles. She blinked as she brushed her teeth, her irises wet with light. Clara finished polishing her teeth and chewed a mint leaf to a pulp and spat it into the cup.

How do you feel?

Tired, Clara said. I'm tired of this bed, this room.

Diana quickly explained the situation with the girl, the men on horseback, the committee and their requests. She half expected Clara to toss aside the bedding and leap into her boots, shouting orders down the hall, writing letters to be mailed across the country. But Clara offered nothing as Diana talked—no consolation, no suggestions, no critique. When Diana finished they sat in silence for a few moments before Clara spoke.

I've asked Mr. Lowry to pack my things, she said. I'm heading back east, to Maryland.

A wave of nausea swept through Diana. How did she not know this was coming? And why would Clara keep this from her?

Then I will pack your things, Diana said.

It is already done, Clara said. My trunk is downstairs.

Diana glanced around the room. She hadn't noticed, but everything was gone except the black dress with the lace collar hanging from a hook on the back of the door and Clara's traveling boots beside the bed.

It's time, Clara said. I want to be back at Glen Echo. I want to rest and work on my book.

What about . . . What are we supposed to do?

The same thing you are doing now, Clara said. Lead these women. Finish the work.

I don't know if I can.

You are already doing it.

What about the girl? Diana said.

Clara smoothed the counterpane in a neat fold across her stomach.

If you cannot see the clear course of action, Clara said, then in all this time I've taught you nothing.

A child ran down the hall, flashing by the doorway, pursued by a lady in a white dress, hissing at her to *stop right now, young lady!* The hallway outside Clara's room was supposed to remain quiet at all hours. Clara smiled and fixed Diana with those dark, globular eyes.

I am at the stage in life where one begins to sort the hopes and regrets.

How could you possibly—

Diana! Will you stop talking and listen? I do not regret the actions I have taken on behalf of others. My dear girl. What I mean is . . . there is a shadow self that lives within us. Our true self, but we keep it hidden.

She lay back on the pillow and closed her eyes.

All the people, Clara whispered, who passed through my life. I let them all go.

Diana looked away from the old woman lying on the bed. The window coverings rattled in the breeze, bringing the earthy smell of the tidal flats to the north; Houston Bay, still choked with debris and shattered boats. What did it matter? Clara Barton, the most selfless, altruistic person she had ever known, was racked with guilt, here in the twilight of her blameless existence. And now she was leaving. She was leaving *me*. How could any of it matter?

I'm taking the four o'clock to New Orleans, Clara said. Please help me get dressed.

Diana stood her up and helped ease her out of her nightgown. Clara raised her arms and Diana wrung out a rag in the washbasin and wiped her down, passing the rag around her neck, under her arms, between her legs, rinsing and squeezing out the rag before starting again at her feet. Then she powdered Clara's body, smoothing it along her flank and thighs with her hands, kneeling to rub her calves and knees. She thought about the girl, having a snack in the kitchen with Cordelia and the others—biscuits and jam, orange currants, a crate of pears shipped from California.

Clara idly put her hand on Diana's head, playing with the thick braid. At her touch, all the strength seemed to go out of Diana and she gasped and clutched the old woman's midriff, pressing her face into Clara's slack stomach, shaking with sobs. Out the window a scattering of seagulls canted across the sky.

***

In their room the girl was sitting on the floor in the sunlight from the window wearing a sleeveless shift and wool socks. She was drawing a picture on the floor with a stub of chalk. When Diana came in the girl looked back over her shoulder and smiled before turning back to her picture. She was a different girl from the gaunt and dirty wastrel they carried in several weeks ago, her flesh stretched over her bones like a kite. It was as if she was getting younger by the day, returning to a childhood that she had before the storm. Watching her drawing a wavy line on the floor, pressing so hard with the nub of chalk that it disintegrated in her fingers, Diana was overwhelmed by the many things she didn't know.

But she knew her name. Diana was able to find a complete manifest filed at the courthouse by the orphanage last year—a list of ninety-three names. She didn't know if these names were given to them by the Sisters of the Incarnate Word or if they were birth names. She just hoped that the girl might recognize her own. So she held the girl's finger and traced it slowly down the list, reading the names aloud. She paused by several but stopped when she reached "Hester." There was no last name.

Cordelia was the only one who knew. Diana wouldn't tell anyone else, not until they were safe. Was this it? They would just leave everything and everyone else behind? She thought of Joe's glistening skin rippling in the dance hall, the metronomic thump of the bag, the spinning blur of his hands. The warmth of his shoulder in the theater, his face in the street after, the scars emerging in the starlight, a history of violence written on his face. The way Hester looked at him was unmistakable and she cherished the doll he found as if it was her last hope on earth. But how could Joe be so cultivated, sincere, and generous, yet so barbarically cruel to others as a vocation? How could he possibly balance such an equation? He must be a man who operated without regrets—no material accounting of his moral and ethical mistakes. He was, in this way, perfectly equipped for this island, and this world.

From the moment young Diana saw Clara on the deck of that steamer that morning, the clear silver bell ringing over the water, she saw the future, her life stretching out in front of her. It involved another, and she lost him and years passed and that part of her life closed. Then she watched Clara, the most powerful woman she knew, grind herself down to insensibility and despair. Alone. And now Clara was departing, and that future seemed long and desolate, empty and quiet as stone. Then came Joe.

The door that nobody else will go in seems always to swing open for me.

Here was a light, a warm hand, and a chance.

***

In the hall, Mr. Lowry drowsed in a chair, his bristled mustache sinking into his chest. Diana called down to the kitchen for more tea and he sat up, blinking, hand in his coat pocket where he kept the pistol wrapped in a handkerchief.

I am going out, she said. To the train yard and then other errands.

Shall I go with you, miss?

No, Diana said. Please stay here and watch over her.

Of course, miss.

Lock the front door. Keep her safe.

Yes, miss.

She took the tray of tea from the lady coming up the stairs and poured Mr. Lowry a brimming cup. He tucked the cup under his whiskers and slurped. Diana brushed the dusting of dandruff off the shoulders of his jacket.

You are a good man, Mr. Lowry. You are loyal and kind.

Thank you, miss.

Diana changed into a dark dress with black buttons up the front. She washed with cold water from the basin and looked at her face in the mirror. It seemed like a face she hadn't seen in a long time. She opened her eyes wide, stretched her mouth, smoothed her eyebrows with a finger before tightening her braid and covering her head with a wool scarf. There was still hope.

On the floor Hester was drawing a line of waves and the sun setting over the water. On the bed lay the small white dress with a sash that Cordelia and the ladies sewed for the girl to wear. Diana put her lips on her cheek, whispering into her warm skin—a sound like the wind pushing the rippled sand.

Hester. Hester. Hester.

***

The reconstructed railyard was choked with lines of boxcars that extended for several miles east and west. Diana knew that several more miles of trains were being held up in Houston, Port Arthur, Freeport, and Bay City, waiting for the jam to clear. The yard was bristling with gangs of men carrying picks, shovels, pry bars, and sledges, swarming over the boxcars like ants. So many cars were piling up that the yardmen were knocking together row after row of sidetracks and then completely dismantling the cars when they were empty. Mess kitchens were pitched right in the main yard with lines of men carrying pails of hot potatoes, steaming heads of cabbage, and casks of water and beer. The gangs worked around the clock and new men were lined up fifty deep at the tents to get their ration cards. A handful of Red Cross women in their crisp white dresses drifted amid the throng, carrying ledgers, trying to keep track of the avalanche of goods pouring into Galveston.

Blocks of ice and chests of dried flowers were carried to the rebuilt warehouse on the south end of the yard that served as the morgue, where the mortal remains of dozens still lay on the ground, awaiting identification and disposal. Lines of black men trooped in and out of the morgue carrying remains on stretchers, handcarts, and sacks. A sheet of plywood attached to a post fluttered with hundreds of tacked-up messages, drawings, entreaties from the living searching for those still lost. Nobody paid attention to Diana, one of many women in the dark clothes of mourning wandering the area near the morgue.

Diana kept her head covered and slipped into one of the long sheds that served as a dispersal point. The shed was for perishable goods and the men inside rushed down the long lines of stacked items with their trolleys and carts, the air sour with the tang of turning meat and rotting vegetables. She saw stacked chicken pens bristling with feathers, bricks of waxed butter, crates of fresh haddock and skate floating in pools of melting ice. A bearded man wearing pistols with a Central Relief Committee ribbon on his chest stood guard over a section cordoned off with rope where a team of men tossed shovelfuls of chipped ice onto a pile that reached the ceiling. A quarter ton of fresh beef from Colorado, boxes of smoked salmon from the Columbia River, glass jars of sturgeon roe from New York, crates of bananas from Chiapas, along with barrels of wine, beer, and whiskey. Men were tossing food in crates, shoveling ice on top, then nailing it up with a manifest and delivery point posted on the outside.

There is enough here to feed everyone a hundred times over, Diana thought.

Diana followed a twenty-gallon barrel of California sherry as two men carried it out of the shed. She passed in front of them to get a look at the delivery address, which was for the west side of the island, a neighborhood that she knew had survived relatively intact. She walked back to the shed to check on boxes of lobster tails, crates of champagne, barrels of aged scotch. They were all going to personal addresses on the west side.

A small contingent of U.S. Army soldiers created a compound on the edge of the railyard where they intercepted monetary donations. Money was pouring in, in a variety of forms: wires, vouchers, bank checks, gold bars wrapped in felt, antiques and heirlooms, rolled carpets, sets of silverware, lockboxes of diamonds and other jewels, as well as stacks of cash wrapped in paper bundles with the names of the donating entities: the Ladies' Auxiliary of Plattsburgh, the Alexandria Chamber of Commerce, Concerned Citizens of Tallahassee, the Royal Elks of Montreal. They used to come across Diana's desk where she marked them in the master ledger. In the early weeks after the storm she gave the ledger periodically to Clara, who wrote scores of thank-you letters: $12.25 from the Kansas State Insane Asylum; $24 from the Colored Eureka Brass Band of Thibodaux, Louisiana; $329.25 from the Ladies of the Maccabees of the World, Sacramento; $14,550 from the Cotton Association of Liverpool.

The soldiers set up fencing surrounding their compound, and when the horse carts were packed and covered for delivery they were accompanied by a squad of soldiers who galloped full tilt through the muck of the yard, forcing the snaking lines of men to stand aside as they thundered past. Diana circled the compound, watching the men with CRC ribbons locking strongboxes and safes, marking them with chalk before covering them with oilcloth. She watched a squad of soldiers pack up their gear for a delivery, taking along their bedding and a separate cart of provisions and tents. They were clearly going on a long journey. She stood up to her ankles in mud, feeling as though she was in the eye of a great storm of people and goods, rushing, spinning off into the city and far beyond. The men of the committee were right: the Red Cross couldn't handle this anymore. Their time *was* done. The new rebuilding agency would manage the influx of resources and money, and Craine would have unfettered control over all of it.

It was sixteen blocks to the jailhouse and when she arrived she was sweating through the bodice of her dress. On the front porch she removed her scarf and tied it around her waist and checked her face in the window. She was blotchy and flecked with mud and her braid had sprung a thousand tendrils that waved about her face.

The deputy inside launched out of his chair when she entered, patting his pockets and looking around as if she had caught him doing something. The sheriff's office was on one side, the door open, empty. Straight through another set of doors she could see the line of cells stretching back and heard the low murmur of voices.

I would like to speak with Mr. Choynski, please.

The deputy opened his mouth and pawed at the papers on his desk with one hand, staring at her. Then he put on his hat and bent low to look out the window, squinting.

Will you please take me to Mr. Choynski?

Uh, yes, ma'am, he said. Just one minute, please.

The deputy ducked his head and scuttled down the hallway. The jailhouse stank of unwashed men and a strain of mule shit so strong that Diana checked the bottom of her boots. The deputy returned a few minutes later with Joe trailing behind him. He was wearing a thin cotton shirt and tights, drenched in sweat, his face flushed and smiling.

Looks we've both been working on our fitness, he said.

Diana looked down at her dress, smoothed back her hair with her hand.

I don't know what you mean.

His heavy brows lifted, his eyes rounding.

I mean, Joe stammered, it's just that . . . Let me get changed. I'll meet you outside.

Outside?

Just give me a twitch.

He turned and jogged back down the cell block. The deputy shrugged.

Can I offer you some coffee, Miss Longstreet?

I would like a glass of water, thank you.

The deputy wiped out a filmy glass with his shirttail and filled it from a pitcher. She took a sip, the deputy watching her with a leering grin. The water was warm and salty. Diana drained the glass and placed it on the desk.

You seem at ease, Deputy.

Yep, the deputy said, things are pretty quiet around here.

Quiet? Is that how you would describe bands of masked vigilantes murdering people in cold blood?

Oh, well, the deputy said, you don't need to worry about *that*.

The deputy sat in his chair and put his feet on the desk and started rolling a cigarette. On the bottom of his left shoe was a dried hunk of green-black mule shit.

Unless you foolin' with things you shouldn't.

The deputy licked his cigarette and tucked it in the corner of his mouth. Diana was grinding her teeth and she closed her eyes for a moment and tried to relax her jaw. The deputy lit his cigarette and waved his hand through the smoke, motioning her out the door.

You better wait outside, miss.

Gladly, Diana said. This place stinks of excrement.

It's a jail, miss.

Yes, but I'm afraid it's you, Deputy. Good day.

The jailhouse faced a five-way intersection, a broad pentagon-shaped stretch of mud laced with board walkways and the deep furrows of cart wheels. The sun was bright and the ground steamed, releasing a lode of earthy scents. But the air was cold and the sun felt good on her face, so Diana stood on the bottom step and tilted her face to the sky. She wasn't sure what she was doing here. Maybe she just wanted to see him. That's fine, she thought. There is no harm in it.

A minute later Joe came out the door with the deputy trailing. He had put on wool pants, boots, and a heavy worsted sweater. His hair was wet and smoothed back from his forehead. The deputy grinned from the doorway.

Y'all have a good time, ya hear? You only have ten minutes, so don't go far now. The Mexican is bringing lunch at noon.

He winked at Joe.

They walked a board path around the side of the jail and along Twelfth Street.

Rogers there, Joe said, he's a bit of a lout.

Have you been released?

Well, no, Joe said. But I can step out for a bit.

Diana didn't understand how a man could just walk out of jail, but since Joe didn't seem to think it was unusual she didn't press. At the end of the block she glanced back and saw Rogers standing with another man to the side of the jailhouse, both of them watching. A squad of U.S. Army soldiers came through the intersection in a loose formation, marching out of step and carrying their rifles by the barrel. A small café in an alley across the street was serving up beans, tortillas, and beer. Men lounged in the shade, smoking and talking. Diana felt sure they were all watching. Joe was famous and everyone in the city knew he was being held in the jail.

I would like to ask you something, Diana said. In confidence.

Of course, Joe said.

The Central Relief Committee contracted you to come and do the match with Mr. Johnson, correct?

Yes.

Did they instruct you to knock the man down?

Not exactly.

What does that mean?

There's a system, Joe said. Certain unspoken agreements. We're supposed to entertain, to give a demonstration of scientific boxing.

Then why did you knock him down?

Things happened fast. There wasn't time for deliberation.

Were you afraid?

No. But I regret it.

For an actor you are quite unconvincing, Mr. Chrysanthemum Joe.

Please don't call me that.

Isn't that your stage name? Your sobriquet?

Joe was sweating again and had his hands jammed in his pockets. She wanted to make him furious, to enrage him. To cut through that sleepy-eyed calm, his languid way of negotiating the world as if he were only half in it.

The committee told me that you belong in jail because you violated the contract.

The committee said that?

They are also telling me that the masked men terrorizing the city are nothing to be concerned about.

Joe seemed genuinely confused.

I thought, maybe you wanted . . . something about the orphan girl. I don't know anything about masked men.

Hester would like to see you, Diana said. I don't know—

Her name is Hester?

Diana stopped walking and turned to him. He was responding with a sincerity that was unraveling her. He wasn't angry. Why wasn't he angry? She looked into his narrowed blue eyes. The wrenched nose, the notch on his lower lip.

The doll you found on the beach? That was *her* doll. You found it right where the Ponder children were murdered. They were whipped, just like she was. Then a couple nights ago a group of masked men came to our warehouse. They are trying to get to her, and I think it has to do with what happened to those children on the beach that night.

Good Lord, Joe said. Does the sheriff know this?

They all know! she said. That's what I'm trying to tell you. The sheriff, the committee—everyone. They want me to turn Hester over to *them*. Which of course I will not.

There was a hard knot in her throat and her vision began to shimmer. No, she thought, I will not cry here in the street in front of this man.

Hester knows who they are, Diana said. I think she saw them murder those children.

Joe closed his eyes and whispered through his teeth.

I am fortune's *fool*!

He took her hand. A couple of his fingers were bent at

such odd angles, she marveled that he could use them at all. But his skin was soft and she could smell sandalwood, maybe almond—some kind of lotion or oil he used. Such a pompous fop, she thought, such vanity. But she wanted to stay close, to continue breathing him in, because she could see something of that innocent young man in his weary eyes and battered face. What must it be like to travel through this world without regret, never hiding who you are.

I'm not asking for anything, she said. I don't want to get you in further trouble.

You can ask, Joe said. Please ask!

Across the street a loose group of people had begun to gather, watching them. The men sitting at the tables drinking beer all had their heads turned, nobody talking, the street going quiet.

Can you get away? Diana said quietly. Away from here, all these people?

I can talk to Henry. We can arrange something for tomorrow afternoon.

They started walking back to the jailhouse. A few horses were now tied up at the rail and Deputy Rogers was sitting on the side of the porch in a rocking chair. In one of the small high windows a pair of dark hands appeared, reaching up to grasp the bars.

HESTER

After lunch Diana began packing a basket in the kitchen. Hester watched her from the floor where she sat rubbing the dog's distended belly as he moaned and kicked his back legs. He was getting fat. The ladies kept his scrap pail full throughout the day and it seemed all he did was eat and sleep. Hester poked her own taut belly, full of milk and corn bread. Now that she didn't have to think about food there was so much else to think about.

Diana packed a roasted chicken with cabbage and onions, apples, a quart of milk, and a big wedge of rhubarb pie. She dressed Hester in a long wool skirt and a lined cloak over her white dress.

It's going to be cold on the water, Diana said.

They passed Liverwright sitting on the floor in the foyer paring his nails with a pocketknife. The photographer was stretched out along the wall using his coat for a pillow. Diana told him they were checking the inventory at the railyard and Liverwright grunted and pulled on a long hangnail with his hoary teeth and made no move to follow her.

Mr. Lowry took them in the horse cart to the western end of the city by Sydnor Bayou where they walked through the dry grass and weeds of the dunes toward the water. The beach was empty for half a mile until you reached the edge of the city where charnel fires still smoldered. The area of the beach to the west was marked with wooden stakes in a grid surrounding lines of deep trenches, now half full and dissolving in the water and wind. Diana and Mr. Lowry stood for a few minutes looking at the abandoned excavation site as Hester crouched and grabbed handfuls of the brown sand, letting it run slowly through her fingers. The finer parts were carried away by the wind, leaving behind a coarse mix in her palm. When she peered at it closely with one eye she could see the tiny whorls and complex ribs of shell fragments, like the bones of another world.

When Hester looked up a small sloop was cutting across the waves about a hundred yards from shore. A man sat in the stern, the main sheet held loosely in his hand, his forearm draped over the tiller. When the boat drew abreast of their position the sail slackened as the pilot brought the stern around in an easy jibe and pointed the bow toward the beach. At the last moment he heaved up the centerboard, sprang into the bow, and launched himself onto the dry sand as the boat beached and canted over. He was wearing a wool sweater and canvas pants rolled up to the knees. He waved to them, his blond hair flashing in the sun.

Joe!

Hester started pulling Diana's hand, trying to drag her to

the boat. Diana looked over her shoulder at Mr. Lowry as they stumbled down the dune toward the water.

We'll be back before dark, she called. You don't have to wait for us.

All the same, Mr. Lowry shouted back, I'll wait here for you, ma'am.

Hester pulled her hand free and began to run, Diana awkwardly following with the basket, her heavy skirts and cloak wrapping around her legs in the wind.

Joe is free! Hester thought. He's out of the jail and he's come for us. She squeezed the doll under her sweater, where she had it tied it to the waist of her skirt. They were finally going to the house with the orchards stretching over the hill, the grassy field, the kitchen, Joe in his chair with a book. They were going home!

The boat was painted deep blue with a white stripe at the waterline, the inside coffee-dark teak that was weathered smooth. Diana handed Joe the picnic basket and he tucked it under the middle bench. He grinned and winked at Hester. They all stood there for a moment, smiling at each other, unsure what to do.

Where did you get this boat? Diana asked.

Henry borrowed it for me, Joe said. Creaky old sloop but it'll do.

I didn't know you could sail.

I grew up on the docks of San Francisco. I could sail before I could walk.

I'm not sure if she's ever been on a boat before, Diana said. And I seriously doubt she can swim. I know that I can't.

There's a nice spot on the eastern point by Fort San Jacinto. We'll stay close to shore. I have to be back by sunset. I'll keep an eye on her. And you.

Joe jammed his hands in his pockets and rocked on his heels. Hester noticed how he moved his head as he looked at Diana—small, quick movements, like someone who was trying not to be caught. He looked at Hester.

Do you want to go sailing with me?

Hester nodded and held out her arms. Hold me, she thought. I want you to *hold me*.

Here we go then, Joe said and picked her up, cradling her to his chest. She put her arms around his neck. He was damp from sea spray and smelled like salt, seasoned wood, and something else, like an exotic fruit. Joe placed her in the bow of the boat then turned to Diana. He held out his hands.

May I?

Diana smirked and gathered up her skirts in one hand. She took a couple of steps and planting her other hand on the gunwale she vaulted into the boat, landing on the front bench with a clatter. When they got settled Joe began to push the boat into the sea. The wind was coming inshore and Joe had to wrestle the sloop in the surf to get it facing into the waves before he climbed in. Diana ducked as he steadied himself with the mast and stepped over her to drop the centerboard, his wet pants dripping on her shoulder and arm. Joe grabbed the sheet and heaved in the sail and they beat upwind for a bit, tacking again and again, the boom swinging back and forth. Hester had never been in a boat before but she immediately loved the creaking wood and raspy whisper of the ropes in the rigging. Salty spray doused her as they crashed through the surf break and Diana put a blanket around her shoulders.

When they made the turn east Joe cinched in the sails and asked them to sit on the high side of the boat. They settled into a long speedy reach, the sail crackling as the sloop skidded across the waves. Joe sat on the gunwale, leaning out over the water while holding the sheets in one hand and the tiller in the other, his hair trailing like a pennant. Diana closed her eyes, the sun bright on her face, her long braid swinging along her back. Hester saw Joe watching her, a faint, crooked smile on his lips. He caught Hester looking, and winking at her he yanked the sail in and heeled the boat up, the hull going almost vertical. Diana shrieked as she slid down the bench, clutching a cleat with both hands, her feet dangling over the water. Joe released the sheet and brought the boat down with a crash and he laughed, a wide-mouthed easy laugh, hidden behind the wind. Diana glared at him then reached in the picnic basket and whipped an apple at him, hitting him in the chest. Joe picked up the apple and stuck it in his mouth. He opened his eyes wide and waggled his head at Hester. Diana covered her mouth and ducked her head, trying to cover the laughter breaking across her face.

Diana's happy, Hester thought. She's happy we're finally going home.

They rounded the eastern tip of the island and came into the calmer waters of the bay and Joe eased the boat onto an empty beach, a stretch of dark sand fringed with a grove of live oak trees, their limbs bare and blasted gray-white from the storm. Diana led them to a small depression in the sand by the tree line that kept them out of the wind. Joe stacked a pile of drift-wood and got a fire going as Diana laid out the wool blanket and Hester explored. The dead forest reminded her of the morning after the storm, walking through the wretched wasteland by Offatts Bayou where the swollen bodies clustered in the trees. She found a large stick of driftwood, white with age and wind, and when she picked it up it was so light it seemed like a trick of the eye. She tossed it on the fire where it immediately caught and blazed with sparkling green flames. Diana gathered shells in a fold of her dress then placed them in a circular pattern on the sand. Joe was a few yards away, bent over at the waist with his legs spread, digging with both hands between his feet like a dog, pulling up handfuls of the insect-like sand crabs that burrowed at the water's edge.

They are like children, Hester thought. Like me. Each of us playing our own private game.

She crouched by Joe and watched him dig. He got a fat sand crab and held it out to her pinched between his thumb and forefinger, the crab like a translucent nut with a small forest of kicking legs. When she reached for it Joe dropped the crab on her head and took off running. Hester swatted at her hair and then chased him down the beach, scattering the sandpipers foraging along the waterline. Joe slowed and Hester plowed into his knees, knocking them both to the sand. He stood her up and held out his hand.

Come on, he said. Let's run!

They held hands and ran through the cold surges of surf, high-stepping through the water, staying just out of reach of the larger waves. Hester struggled to keep up and her dress was soaked, but she kept running. She never wanted this to end. Then Diana stepped in and intercepted her, wrapping her with a blanket.

She's still recovering, she said. We have to be careful.

Oh, she's all right, Joe said.

Hester stood next to him, panting for breath, gazing up at Joe, her face lit with pure ardor.

Diana got Hester settled by the fire before laying out the picnic. She piled plates with chicken and cabbage and they ate greedily, nobody saying anything, their fingers and faces slick with grease. Then Joe brought out a loaf of French bread and a metal tin.

Salazar made these for us special, he said.

A dozen large sardines packed in olive oil with garlic, peppers, and salt. Joe showed Hester how to take a sardine and run a wood skewer through the mouth and out the tail. Then they grilled the sardines over the fire and crunched on the crispy skin, pulling the delicate meat from the bones as gulls gathered in wheeling clouds overhead. Hester ate three then drank a cup of cold milk. Diana settled into the sand beside her, pulling the blanket over them. Joe sat across from them, warming his bare feet and tending the fire with a stick. Hester watched him through the flickering flames. She was suddenly so sleepy.

Henry told me that your wife is not well.

Joe tossed his stick into the fire and shook his head.

She's in a type of comatose state. It's a mystery. Nobody knows the ailment.

Hester could feel Diana's body shift, a tremor running through her legs.

I'm so sorry. Is she suffering?

We don't know. At first she just needed more rest, but then it worsened and she couldn't get out of bed. Lost the ability to speak. I haven't seen her in almost a year. I'll continue to provide for her care but . . . she doesn't know that I even exist.

Will you go back to her, after this is over?

I don't know. I'm not sure if there would be any good in it.

Joe picked up another stick. He seemed unable to stay still.

Did you marry? he asked.

No, Diana said.

Hester burrowed down deeper into the sand and held her tighter. She didn't want Diana to move. She wanted them to stop talking and for Joe to join them so they could pile together like dogs by the fire and sleep.

I was promised, Diana said. Years ago. But he became ill. Tuberculosis.

Joe nodded.

His parents sent him to a sanatorium in Colorado that had a very fine record of recovery. We wrote letters for a year; then he became too weak. He passed away while I was out of the country traveling with the Red Cross.

Hester began to drowse, the glow of the flames suffusing everything. Joe looked like he was sitting in the middle of the blaze, and their voices echoed like fragments from a deep and distant cave.

It's been more than four years, Diana said. I never should have entered into the arrangement. I was too involved with my work. His family didn't even notify me about the funeral.

Across the blowing sand to the west the sun was passing through scalloped lines of clouds, the sky going from pure corn-flower blue to a mottled purple. Small crabs emerged from hidden burrows, edging around the fire with their globed and stalked eyes, waving their mismatched claws at Hester. They looked like travelers on a departing train. *Goodbye! Goodbye!*

We have a nurse who stays with her, Joe said. She used to write but I haven't heard anything in months. I'm worried she's gotten worse and they don't want to tell me.

I'm sure there's some other reason, Diana said.

I don't know what to do, he said. I feel like I'm just tossing letters into the dark.

Hester's eyes were burning from watching Joe across the fire and she decided she would close her eyes and listen. For a while it was just the sound of wind and the hiss of sand running across the beach mixed with Diana's breathing and the garbled tones of their talk. Then Diana's body lurched as she spoke and Hester could hear the deep sounds bouncing around inside her ribs.

I can't stop thinking about that preacher, Diana said. His children. The justice he deserves. But it could endanger her. She has already gone through so much.

There has to be another way, Joe said, to bring them out of the dark.

It won't matter, Diana said. These people just repeat the lies until they become true.

Hester was falling into a deep, warm hole. The echoing quality of the sounds reminded her of the between world, where she wandered the dunes without direction or time. Pieces of their conversation came to her like swallows sweeping through a barn, darting in and out of the light with a whirr of wings.

I don't know who or what to blame, Diana said. I'm just so angry.

The other night in the cell, Joe said, Jack told me that rage is all we have when there is no one left to blame but God. You think that's true?

I don't know, Diana said. But I think I understand what he means.

The wind. The buzz and rattle of the grains rolling up against her wrist where it lay in the sand, like Diana saying her name.

Hester Hester Hester.

Hester heard the call of the gulls winging over the water, lost, seeking light. Another voice echoed deep within her ears, calling from the inside. Was it Joe or Diana? She couldn't tell.

Those who are capable of great rage are also capable of great tenderness. If you can reach one, you can reach the other.

Oh, I want to believe that. I want to believe that's true.

***

Hester felt herself being pulled upward and she clawed for Diana's body until her face was pressed against a neck and she could tell it was Joe and she relaxed. She could hear his feet rasping through the heavy sand, the crash of the waves growing louder. Then a bit later she awoke for a moment when a few drops of spray struck her cheek and dribbled across her lips. She tasted the salt and opened her eyes to see the bow of the boat rising and falling, bisecting a horizon lit with vermillion. Just a few points off the bow the sun was settling over the water, and Hester was wrapped in a nest of blankets, lying on an improvised pallet between the middle and bow benches. She worked her head free and looked toward the back of the boat, where Joe sat leaning against the stern. Diana was lying wrapped in a blanket with her head on the stern bench, her eyes closed. The light of the sunset filled the white sail and bathed them all in shimmering bronze. The whole world seemed to be dimming, slipping into twilight. Hester squeezed the doll under her sweater and a string of brief physical memories shot through her like a bolt: sharing her blankets with the warm body of Little Cora; the sisters lined up in chapel murmuring prayers on a warm morning and the black flies buzzing at the bright windows; a pack of girls in the yard hanging clothes on the line and singing "Queen of the Waves." The eye of God rolling over the seas, the heavy lid crunching shut like waves breaking on wet sand.

With her last glimmer of consciousness she saw Diana's hand emerge like a furtive animal from her blankets, reaching up by Joe's leg. Without taking his gaze off the horizon Joe took her hand in his. Diana's eyes were still closed, the light falling across her forehead and nose burnished by the wind and sun, the dark braid lying across her neck. Joe bent slowly at the waist, keeping his eyes forward, and pressed the back of her hand to his cheek. Diana smiled. The boat rose and fell as it rolled through the waves toward the coming dark.

This new life, Hester thought. There is so much to be amazed at.

***

When she awoke Hester immediately knew that she was not in the house with the long field and the orchard and the smells from the kitchen. The dog loomed over her in the dark, his foul breath hot on her face. Diana's arm was across her chest and they were sweating, the blankets wadded up around their feet, their bodies and bedding smelling like a campfire. The dog licked her cheek and she turned away and hid her face in the pillow. She was still in Galveston, in the warehouse room. What had gone wrong? Why was she still here? Was there something else that the God of the sisters required?

What doth the Lord require of thee?

Hester stared at the dark hole of the ceiling but couldn't see the eye of God in her mind. She couldn't tell if it was open, if it saw her, or if it cared at all.

The dog pawed at the door and whined. Hester eased herself out from under Diana's arm and put on the wool skirt and overcoat that lay over the back of a chair. In the hallway Mr. Lowry lay on a pallet across the doorway and the dog stepped over him, trotting down the hall to the stairs, tail wagging. Mr. Lowry had one hand in his pocket where he grasped the old cavalry pistol, the gray whiskers on his cheeks quivering as he shivered in the draft. Hester got her blanket and stretched it over him and he moaned and clutched it under his chin as she stepped over his body and into the hall.

The girl and the dog slipped out the back door by the garden, taking the boarded footpath around to the front of the warehouse. The streets were still and quiet, the sky moving with drifting clouds and the occasional faint blinking pinpoints of stars.

Why isn't this enough?

The dog raised his head and looked at her with his broad, sloppy smile. Hester listened for the sound of something, anything. She thought of Diana's hand on Joe's face in the rocking boat and the golden light washing over them. Yes. *Bring them out of the dark.*

The dog dropped his head and began to lope down the street and she hurried after him. He was on the trail of some secret scent and Hester followed his lead. They went west, toward the wealthier section of the city where the neighborhoods had decidedly less damage because they were built on a slightly higher elevation and with better materials. Just a few feet or a brick foundation made a significant difference between minor water damage and the entire house being ripped apart. They wandered down Broadway for a few blocks, the stone edifices of shipping barons and cotton kings looming in shadow. These neighborhoods were already cleaned and restored—no piles of debris, no bonfires, no stench of death. Clusters of freshly planted oleander lined the road, their thin leaves gray and withered-looking in the dark. Hester was looking for a building she remembered well: the massive pile of limestone and painted iron trim, broad front steps, and heavy doors that must have been twelve feet tall. She remembered the precise, timid sound of the girls padding across the carpet in the cavernous foyer, peeking about with reverent eyes. The sisters meekly filing into the study, the closed door, a reverence greater than at morning chapel. The old lady with the gnarled hand dangling a sweet in front of her face, the dry whisper in her ear.

Only thieves and poets truly exercise free will. But they often die young.

A horse-drawn carriage came down the street and Hester stepped behind some shrubs until they passed. The coachman was holding a lantern and humming to himself, the smoke from his cigar trailing behind him. The tower of St. Patrick's loomed, a ghostly outline in the dark. This part of the city was dead quiet. No gangs of masked men, no widows begging for food, no sickly children scavenging the debris. The dog turned right onto Twenty-Sixth Street, still following his nose. Now Hester could also smell roasting meat, as if someone was cooking beef over hot coals.

It was the limestone house with painted iron trim. Maybe. She was almost sure of it. A pair of men in long coats were standing by the front gate. The rooms on the bottom floor were lit and the tall oak trees in the back cast skeletal forms on the brick garden wall. She could hear men talking through the open patio doors. Hester stayed in the shadow of the garden wall and went down the alley that ran parallel to the house. There was a low side gate and she slipped inside the garden and walked between rows of freshly planted azaleas and rosebushes on a path lined with white pebbles. Men in suits stood on the back patio and smoke wreathed the garden in a gray fog. Through the wide back window she could see a table laden with food: platters of steaming meats, vegetables, colorful pyramids of fruits, tall decanters of dark-red wine—more food then Hester had ever seen before. A man in a white tunic jabbed a huge crusted round of beef with a fork and sawed thick red slabs, placing them on white plates. She didn't see the old crone with the rope of pearls. She didn't see any women at all. Was this the right house? If only she could see inside, a glimpse of the library. She could admit that she had stolen the book and they might help. These people could do anything they wanted. They made the world how it was.

Hester gripped the dog by the loose skin on the top of his neck as he pawed at the ground and shook his head, casting glistening arcs of saliva into the bushes. At the back of the garden a man was using a wire brush to clean the grill of a large brick barbecue. When he closed the metal lid and carried his basket of tools inside the house, Hester crept closer, dragging the dog along with her to the edge of the patio where she could peer into the back windows.

Inside, men were moving furniture and starting to clear away the food. It was a large room with electric lights, the walls painted a deep maroon, wooden furniture with legs carved to look like animal feet. The men on the porch filtered into the house, slapping each other on the back, laughing, the ice in their glasses clinking. When the men were all inside and they had shut the doors she knelt down and stroked the dog's cheeks. *Good boy. Good boy.* She released him and he loped down the path to the back of the garden and the barbecue. About thirty men were gathered inside, all dressed in fine suits with pocket handkerchiefs and oiled hair. They formed a semicircle around a short set of steps that led up to a landing and another large room. A table set up on the landing was covered with a shiny purple cloth embroidered with gold symbols that Hester didn't understand. Three men stood behind the table in an authoritative pose, hands behind their backs. The men stopped talking and it became quiet except for the smacking sound of the dog licking the barbecue in the garden.

Hester had seen the three men behind the table before, up in her room at the Red Cross warehouse. One had black hair with small oily ringlets, and she remembered the man in the middle who had tiny eyes set deep in a bristly, piglike face. He was the man with the voice that crackled like ice breaking in the water pail. These were the men who came for those who were in this life by mistake. They were the ones who killed the children that rose up among the dead, who cast the bodies in the big fires. These were the men who were coming for her. A light rain started to fall, pattering on the stone tiles of the patio.

See me.

But the eye of God was still shut tight.

Gentlemen, the man with the crackling voice said, I want to thank you for attending tonight's meeting of concerned citizens of Galveston. I hope everyone has eaten and drunk to your heart's content.

He paused, seeming to seek out the eyes of every man there. Hester fumbled for the doll tied to her waist.

This is a historic opportunity, he said. The tragedy of the storm must be balanced with what it has given us. The filth can finally be washed away, the undesirables removed or returned to their proper place. We can remake Galveston, return it to a time when it was the crown jewel of Texas and the nation.

He turned away and walked back into another part of the house. The remaining two men picked up a long sword and a leather Bible with gilt edges from the table, holding these items out in front of them like an offering.

Our faith in our Creator, the man with the oiled hair began, is what gives us strength! All who stand here today pledge their fealty to the noble cause of the white man in America!

The man returned to the table wearing a shimmering red robe with a white sash across the front bearing a red cross. There was something wrong with his face, something that Hester saw but couldn't process, as if her mind refused to see it. She looked away to the back of the garden where the dog stood on top of the barbecue, nosing at the latch to the lid. A breeze came from the north pushing the light rain sideways and rustling the bare branches of the garden—a raspy sound like grinding bones. Hester looked back at the man behind the table. He looked as if the flesh had been flayed from his head. It was a mask, a bright vermillion mask of a grinning skull.

The grand cyclops, someone shouted, has called the Klavern to session!

The red skull raised his arms, hands knotted into fists. He turned his head slowly, seeming to look out through the window at Hester where she crouched among the rosebushes.

I see you.

Hester turned and ran in a low crouch toward the gate, opening it quickly and slipping through. His voice continued to echo behind her in the dark garden.

Noble patriots! Kneel now to signify your allegiance to the invisible empire!

Hester just reached the other side of the street when the gate started clanging, the sound splitting the quiet. The dog was trapped in the garden. He started barking. She could hear voices, and the patio door swinging open. Hester sprinted back and unlatched the gate, the dog nearly knocking her over as he bounded out, his face smeared with grease. She reached out and gripped the dog by his sloppy jowls, staring hard into his eyes. *Please be quiet!*

The dog followed her as she made the back corner of the garden wall and broke into a sprint across the street behind the house. After a few blocks she reached the western harbor and jogged along the edge of the partially reconstructed cotton warehouses, her boots clattering on the board sidewalk. The rain began to pick up and the only lights visible were from a scattering of ships out in the harbor heading to Houston. The streets settled into the wet gloom, fading from view. Hester huddled under a tin awning over a recessed doorway and watched the street. The din of the rain hammering the metal roofs of the warehouses made it impossible to hear anything. The dog sat on her feet, licking his grease-smeared chops. After some time the downpour lessened to a fine mist, and the buildings and street around her began to take shape, the air now filled with the sounds of the waterlogged city struggling to drain. Hester didn't understand what she had seen, but the intent of the man with the red skull was unmistakable. They would find her and bring her down to death where she belonged.

She decided she would turn east and make her way back to the warehouse, staying off Broadway by a couple of blocks. She stepped out of the doorway as a gust of wind blew down the street, whipping up a sheet of spray. Lightning flashed along the horizon and in that momentary glimmer Hester saw a rider coming down the middle of the street, the horse at a slow walk, head down and drenched from the rain. She pressed herself back against the wall of the warehouse. The rider continued down the street at a languid pace, swaying in the saddle as if asleep, a rifle in a long scabbard along his leg. He wore a canvas coat and a sash emblazoned with a red cross. A ragged mask covered his face.

The dog was rooting in the gutter just in front of Hester and when the rider came closer the dog raised his head and began to snarl, the hackles on his back going up.

Don't, she thought. Please *don't*.

The dog faced the rider, planted his feet in the mud, and barked once, twice. The horse stopped and the rider turned his head to regard the dog, his hand now resting on the stock of the rifle. The dog snarled and began to creep forward, teeth bared. The rider pushed his long coat aside and slipped the rifle out of the scabbard, working the lever to chamber a bullet. The sky to the north strobed blue with heat lightning. The horse shivered and tossed its head, eyeballs large and white. The rider brought the rifle up to his shoulder and sighted on the dog.

This cannot be it, Hester thought. This cannot be the way.

She stepped away from the wall and clapped her hands, once, loud. The dog stopped and whipped his head around. Without looking at the rider Hester ran down the sidewalk. She heard the horse snort as the rider spurred him; then there was a hard snapping sound and something fluttered by her ear. A piece of the wall to her right exploded, shards of brick and mortar hitting her in the face, but she kept running. She took a right down the first alley and the dog was now racing alongside her, a stupid grin on his face. Across the intersection ahead Hester saw a store clerk in a long apron standing on the front porch of an Italian grocery, smoking a cigarette. Water streamed off the tin roof like a translucent curtain and the front door was ajar. Behind her she heard horses and a long, high whistle cut the air.

Hester ran across the intersection, splashing awkwardly through deep puddles. When she was halfway she glanced to her right and saw a group of men several blocks away coming at a full gallop, torches and pistols in their hands. They all wore masks. The clerk standing on the porch saw her coming and raised his hands as if he could ward her off. He was an old man with a long mustache, and he turned his head from Hester to the riders and back. The cigarette dropped out of his open mouth and he turned and scrambled around the corner. Hester covered her head with her arms and dived through the open door of the grocery, piling through a display of canned goods. She slammed the door shut, locked the dead bolt, and flipped off the light. Then she crawled backward into the shop, backing deep between rows of tall shelves filled with dry goods. She watched the door and the front window, gripping her knees to her chest. There was a clatter of hooves on the porch boards and men cursing, a confusion of shadow and light. The silhouette of a man on horseback holding a torch crossed the front window. The door rattled as someone tried the knob and more shadows gathered and mixed. The dog was not inside with her. Where did he go?

Then a gloved fist smashed through the door window and Hester could see the jagged eyeholes of a mask through the opening. The next second the door burst open and Hester scrambled to her feet, running to the stairs in the back corner. When she reached the dark upper hallway she started pounding on doors. She could hear the sounds of people moving in the apartments, the creak of bedding and floorboards, a quick confused murmur and a woman whispering harshly. The men were clomping up the stairs, the glow of their torches flashing on the ceiling. Nobody was opening the door; nobody was going to help her.

At the end of the hall was a window and Hester pushed it open and was straddling the sash when the first rider came up the stairs. He pulled a bullwhip from his belt and it whispered on the floor as he began to draw it back.

You.

Hester threw her other leg out the window and let herself fall. She landed in a pile of rotting garbage and rolled off into the alley. She ran another block and paused at the corner, breathing hard, her chest aching. She could hear the men back at the store yelling, more whistles, the pounding of hooves. But now she knew where she was. The jailhouse was only two blocks away to her left. She could see golden-yellow lamplight on the front steps.

Joe. He would bound out of the jail like a flash of lightning, overwhelming them all with his powerful fists.

Hester ran for the jail. When she glanced back a line of riders were coming around the corner, the horses creating a churning storm of mud. Someone was standing on the front steps of the jailhouse, a tall glowing figure, holding a lantern high in one hand. Beckoning to her.

Come to me.

Hester stumbled and fell in the mud just in front of the jail. The horsemen drew up as she crawled on her hands and knees toward the steps, their lathered horses stamping, blowing jets of foam from their nostrils. The circle of golden light fell over her as the figure on the jail steps came down and moved past her, walking toward the riders. Hester looked up to see the back of the tall figure in a long white dress, holding the lantern up high, a long braid of dark hair down her back.

Stop!

Diana's white dress was soaked through from the rain and Hester could see her shoulder blades and the lines of her hips. Several men had rifles and pistols out, pointing at her.

I am Diana Longstreet of the American Red Cross! I demand that you show yourselves!

The rider with the burlap mask let the end of the bullwhip fall into the street. He flicked his wrist and the whip snaked along the ground.

I am not alone, Diana said. There are others with me.

There was a light in the building across the street and a woman looked out the window, clutching a scarf around her neck. Then the woman turned away and the light went out. The dog came limping out of the dark, dragging his left leg, and came to where Hester sat in the mud, nuzzling her face.

You *are* alone, the man with the bullwhip said.

He spoke with a cracked, pitched voice, like someone whistling through a straw. Several dogs were barking now and Hester heard the sound of doors opening, people talking. Two men jogged around the corner by the Italian grocery and stopped when they saw the riders. They backed up, pulling their hats down, edging back into the darkness.

I know who you are, Diana said.

A rider slung his rifle into his scabbard, his horse stamping with frustration.

We got to go! he yelled.

Not yet, the man with the whip said. I ain't done with this one. And that goddamn *dog*!

He turned his horse toward Hester. Shadows moved in the background and voices murmured and several of the riders were wheeling their horses around. Someone was pounding on the door of the jail and Hester felt the sleeping lid of the eye of God crushing her with its iron weight.

Is there anyone there? Does anybody see?

The rider loomed over Hester as she squatted in the mud.

Now we can end things, he said. Properly.

He brought his whip hand back, rising up in his stirrups. As he swung Diana stepped in front of Hester with her arms up. The whip whistled invisibly, a sharp *crack*, and a splash of red appeared across the forearm of her dress. Diana gasped and clutched at her arm, dropping the lantern. The glass smashed and the flaming kerosene splashed on the forelegs of the horses, causing them to recoil in alarm. Several of the riders were trying to turn away from the burning oil and the horses bumped and nipped at each other and as he stood up in his stirrups to swing the whip again his horse stepped into the flames. The horse's lips rolled up and it reared, front hooves flailing in the air as the man cursed and hauled on the reins and the horse humped her back and threw him. He tumbled over the front, clutching at the horse's face and harness as he fell, landing on his back in the burning pool of oil. He rolled over and got to his hands and knees. His oilskin coat was soaked with rain, but his woolen trousers immediately sprouted faint, wispy curls of blue flame. He stood up and looked down at his legs as the faint ripple of fire flashed up the front of his shirt, sprouting around his neck and igniting the burlap mask. He turned and ran into the knot of remaining riders, shrieking and batting at his face, the translucent film of blue fire swarming over his head, before turning and coming at Hester with his arms stretched out. His body was now enveloped in flames, the mask blazing like a torch, and to Hester he looked like an enraged, burning doll made of fire come to life. His feet got tangled up in the whip and he fell, clawing at the burning mask, screaming in a high-pitched wail. Hester gripped the dog by the neck as the man thrashed about in the mud and the stink of burning hair and skin hit her nose—the familiar stench of the charnel fires on the beach. Two of the remaining horsemen dismounted and threw their jackets over him, slapping at the flames, and the man lay still. The rest of the horsemen all spurred their horses, galloping off in different directions.

Let's go, get him up!

The two men heaved him up and wrestled him over the saddle of his horse, his head hanging down on one side. His body smoked and raw red flesh shone through charred holes in his clothes. As they rode away, he groped with blackened hands at the remnants of the burned mask that shrouded his face.

The burning oil on the ground shrank to a few sprouts of blue then disappeared and Diana and Hester were alone in the dark. Diana was cradling her arm to her chest, her head down, her shoulders shaking. Then there were more lights behind them, the sound of footsteps in the jail, and Mr. Lowry came running around the corner, pistol in hand, a couple of Red Cross ladies behind him.

My God! Mr. Lowry said.

Then Diana got to her feet, her bloody arm hanging loose by her side like some lifeless thing, her face in the firelight blotchy and streaked with tears. She held out her hand to Hester, her white dress glowing like the rising moon. Blood dripped in a steady stream from her fingers. But Diana's face was shining, like something lit from within.

Hester, she said. It's okay. I'm here.

A powerful sensation washed over Hester, a feeling that she had never known even with the sisters, Little Cora, in any dim memory she ever had. At that moment she knew that Diana wasn't an angel, wasn't a walking spirit from the future. This wasn't the next life, or any new life at all. It wasn't fate or the hand of the God of the sisters that brought her here. Diana was a *real* woman, a living person, here, now, in this world, the same world that had ever been. Hester reached up and took her hand.

If there is only one world, she thought, then it is this one.

JOE

Joe woke up to blowing wind beating on the window. When he put his feet on the floor and stretched out his hand for the glass of water he found himself thinking, *she is a force for good.* He touched his scarred lip with his fingertips. At this very moment Diana is out there in the world. She is drinking tea, maybe. Holding Hester's hand, washing her face, reading a book. At this very moment she is alive and she is near.

They had been in the jail for eighteen days. Cohen assured them that they would be out within the week.

It's about damn time, Jack said. Joe has the run of the place but I can't set foot out the cell? People come by, want to take Joe out for dinner and the sheriff just lets him walk on out.

I'm sorry, Cohen said. I know that doesn't seem fair.

You're damn right, Jack said. I'm the one with the honeys

crying and wailing for him. I'm the one with people and friends who depend on me.

I'll see what I can do, Cohen said.

I'm the one who's dying for a spot of liquor and a good squeeze. Not *him*. He'll be fine just sticking around here by himself.

***

They sparred in the cell and did calisthenics and listened to music. Salazar brought in a Victrola and during their sparring sessions Joe played Franz Liszt's Hungarian Rhapsody no. 2 at a high volume, the barrage of piano crescendos echoing through the jail as the two men circled and feinted. The rest of the prisoners lined up at the doors of their cells, faces pressed to the bars.

Tone and tempo, Joe told him. Most boxers have one tempo. A good fighter will eventually pick up the timing of a consistent tempo, and that's when you get popped. Listen how Liszt changes things.

As the music swelled Joe jerked his upper body side to side, throwing punches from several angles, then rotating left, circling as the tempo eased into a moderate section.

That's tempo, Joe said. The *tone* is the mood you establish in the ring. Like the way the pianist pounds the notes with feeling.

Joe circled, jabbing, pausing, head bobbing.

Smooth and calm, then change. Quick and slow, hard and soft. Your opponent will always be behind you, trying to keep up.

As the music built into the final section the two men weaved and jabbed, matching the music and tapping each other with quick strikes. As the crescendo built, Joe backed up into the corner, Jack coming at him with an array of punches, pulling them up just short, Joe covering up, before they put their hands on their knees and gulped for air. In just under three weeks Joe could already see the transformation in Jack's body, the smooth, supple skin becoming rippled with muscle, his stomach ridged and his shoulders swelling. The man has all he needs, Joe thought. He lacks nothing.

The needle on the Victrola bumped and cracked as the record ended, and the men in the cells started yelling at them to play it again.

***

Every two days Jack would sit on the stool stripped to the waist while Joe shaved his head. The process took longer each time, Joe spending an hour or more, wrapping Jack's head in steaming hot towels, massaging his obsidian skull with his oils before applying the lather. Then after shaving, an invigorating splash of tonics, the scented moisturizers, working his hands in a circular pattern until Jack began to nod with a heavy head and Joe eased him down into his bed, tucking in his blanket around him.

Wake me for supper, Jack murmured.

After supper and washing up they lay in their bunks and talked long after lights-out. Joe tried to convince Jack to give up alcohol and tobacco.

Body maintenance is all about discipline, he said.

Well, while we're in here that's not a problem.

It'll make you a better fighter.

I love the fight game, Jack said, but I like *living*, too.

Just think about it.

I can't stop thinking about those black lights, Jack said. Day or night.

You'll get over it, Joe said.

No, I won't. You told me that yourself.

The more thou stir it, the worse it will be.

You quoting Shakespeare to me again?

Cervantes.

It'll never go away, Jack said. Those were your words.

Right.

That's all you got to say now?

What do you want? You think you ever get over anything in this life?

I don't know. Yes?

You don't, Joe said. You carry everything with you. You take it all with you to the end.

Well, that sure as hell doesn't help me any. Kinda makes it worse.

Then don't listen to me, Joe said. Who the hell am I anyway? I'm no philosopher. I don't even know what I'm doing here.

Why *are* you here?

I just said I don't know.

I mean the fight game, Jack said. You got a family full of educated folks, no need to get your hands dirty like this. You trying to get back at them, or something?

Joe shivered and pulled his blanket tight around him. A man in another cell cried out, shouting someone's name until a couple of others hissed and cursed him and he fell silent. Joe had thought about that question for a long time. There was no singular event or idea that turned him away from the intellectual life of his father and set him down on the docks in a ring of men, punching a drunk sailor for bragging rights. He often wished there were a simple catalyst, a clear reason. But all he could think of was the smoldering resentment that flashed into anger, a desire to lash out and hurt someone. To hurt them back. But why?

My family isn't to blame, Joe said. It was just something I was good at. I like being in fighting trim. I like to run and sweat and get the lungs burning. The feeling of soreness in your muscles. The way you can feel the extra spring when you recover. I like feeling strong.

Me too, Jack said. The need for deception comes from an imbalance. With strength comes honesty. You can speak the truth.

People saw me as this dandy, Joe said, a fancy lad from the intellectual family. I read books and went to plays and I was different. People noticed me. It gave me an edge. Since then I've fought every blacksmith, tugboat gaffer, iron puddler, boiler-maker, and gandy dancer from San Francisco to New Orleans. I've been knocked insensible, laid out cold, pissed myself in the ring. I've been to the other side and back. But every time I reach the bottom, I find there's more. It's like there's no end. I wanted to show my mastery of something difficult, that few people could do. My father understood this. He saw me for who I was. But now I've been doing it so long I don't know who I really am, or if I ever was anyone else.

I'll tell you what you are, Jack said. You're a man that hits too damn hard. How'd you learn to hit like that? You don't weigh enough to hurt that bad.

Everybody has a limit, Joe said. Some kind of barrier that stops us from acts of great violence against another person. Even our most primitive instincts find something abhorrent about doing terrible things to another of our kind. But in a fight . . . that just seems to go away for me. I stop thinking of my opponent as a man. They become something else.

That's damn scary, Joe.

Maybe that's it, Joe said. Maybe I am a creature of violence. A man born for this fistic carnival. Maybe it's fate. All of this.

All of this includes *me*, Jack said, so it better *not* be fate. Because I've got changes in mind.

After a few minutes Jack began to snore and Joe closed his eyes and thought about Diana and the girl. They seemed to be pure beings, making their way through this foul world of men and pain and blood and shit. The girl was one of the truly unfortunate, doomed to be helplessly borne along on this great tide of misery. Diana was trying to heal the world, to care for it, to nurse it back to life, the way she did the girl. And what was *he* doing? What was his part? A shadow in the empty doorway, the paper burning in the grate, the thing kept hidden. And Lutie, lying in her own prison in another world. No more traipsing in the footlights, the warm song in her mouth. The life had gone out of her but that life still burned inside him and he knew he would carry this for all his days. There was no way out.

Fate is a tricky jade, Joe whispered to the dark. She plays many strange pranks.

***

Their attorney, McClemore, put Joe on the stand for the bond hearing. The whole proceeding was a sham. Everybody knew the state attorney's office wouldn't be able to get a true bill.

Isn't forty-five hundred a lot of money for an exhibition? the judge asked him.

I've made many times more than that, Joe said.

Aren't you known as a top man in your line?

I was, Joe said. Now I'm just an old has-been.

Is it not a fact that you knocked Mr. Johnson down and out?

That blow wasn't hard enough to hurt a child. Jack could have gotten up if he wanted to. He just found himself a soft spot to lay down.

***

You make it so complicated, Jack said one night. I'm just looking to make some money. Be somebody. Keep the cakes and ale angled down my gullet at the same time.

Jack had a plate of Salazar's oysters fried with pickle and red chilies balanced on his chest.

Tell me about it, Joe said.

I grew up in the twelfth ward here, Jack said. East side. We were the Avenue K gang. Me and a bunch of white boys. There was a kid named Leo Posner who was the head of our gang. He's still around. I ate and played with these white boys; their mothers gave me cookies at their kitchen table. When I was twelve I hoboed all the way across the state to Dallas, worked in a bakery. Then I stowed away on a cotton steamer to Manhattan. You remember that man Steve Brodie, the guy who jumped from the Brooklyn Bridge and survived? I wanted to meet him. Someone famous, someone who'd done something special that caught people's attention. Brodie was running a saloon in the Bowery but I was just a kid and nobody would tell me who or where he was.

They'd say that's Brodie over there and I'd go over and it would be just some other bum sitting there drinking his beer and they'd all laugh. So then I figured I'd meet Joe Walcott. The Barbados Demon. He was up in Boston and I got a job at a stable, working horses. Afternoons I'd carry Walcott's bag to the gym for him. He took a liking to me and told me that boxing is a good game for a colored man. When I got back here to the island I told the rest of the gang that I met Joe Walcott but nobody believed me. Nobody believes my stories but they're all true. Then my buddy Leo helped me set up a couple fights. And then this happened. I want to be like Steve Brodie—you know, famous for something. So I figure the thing to do is get in the papers, get your picture all over the place. Like ol' Gentleman Jim Corbett, right?

Sure.

That fight on the barge in California, Jack said. I heard you were dead out for three days.

Not quite.

When Corbett beat Sullivan, Jack said, we had a party down in the ward. I think Corbett is one of the most beautiful boxers ever lived. Don't you think?

He's all right, Joe said.

Is he a gentleman like they say?

Joe exhaled and adjusted his pillow.

I suppose.

But if I'm being honest, Jack said, it's *women* that ruin me. I'm not just talking about the ol' slap and tickle. I mean all the joys and triumphs, the pain and disappointments, the money, all for women. Nothing else comes close. I can't *wait* to go see my girl Mary in the twelfth. Or maybe Darlene. You got you a woman somewhere?

My wife is in San Francisco.

I know that! I'm saying you been down here all this time and you haven't set yourself up with a local piece? Where you been going on all these little trips? What about that Red Cross gal with the long braid of hair?

It's not like that.

Right, Jack said. Man just walks out of jail whenever he feels like it. Like a hotel or something.

I'd sure like to walk out of here right now.

What's the biggest thing for you? Jack asked.

What?

The biggest thing you're carrying around, Jack said. The thing you'll carry to the end?

Joe turned his face to the wall. He tried to will the face of Diana to appear on the stained concrete.

I guess it's the thing that I face in the ring.

What's that?

It's that shadow you saw in the black lights, Joe said. The opposite of light.

Yeah, but what *is* that?

The door of the cell block shuddered as the wind gusted against the front of the jailhouse.

I don't know, Joe said.

I think it's you, Jack said. That's what you're fighting. The you behind those blue eyes. And you'll never beat *him*.

The drunks and the murderers slept in the thrall of their uneasy dreams. Joe put a hand out toward the ceiling, reaching into the dark. Diana had cracked him open, but she didn't know what was inside. He couldn't show her. He couldn't do that to someone like her.

The black lights.

Joe tucked his hand back under the blanket, squeezing his fist until his arm shook. The moon shone on the sable waters of the Gulf.

Boxing is not an art, Jack said. It's not a sport. It's goddamn survival.

***

After Joe returned the sailboat to the marina that evening he came back to the jail to find Jack asleep, sprawled across his cot like a fallen titan. Joe stripped out of his clothes and did sets of calisthenics until his legs trembled, then shadowboxed until he couldn't raise his arms. He sat on his bed dripping with sweat, holding his head in his hands. His face burned as if he had been branded and when he picked up the shaving mirror he fully expected to see a mark where he held her hand against his cheek.

Something terrible is happening to me, he thought.

Jack was still snoring when Cohen came by wearing a tweed suit and a pleated cape and told them to get dressed for dinner.

The sheriff has agreed to take both of you gentlemen out for a late *repas du soir* to celebrate the end of your stay here. I know the place well. They know how to treat a piece of beef.

About time, Jack said. I'm starving.

While Jack cleaned and perfumed himself Joe sat on his cot, cracking his knuckles and grimacing. He didn't bother to change, just throwing on an old Prince Albert coat over his sweaty shirt.

Now, uh, Jack, Cohen said. I promised the sheriff that you'd be on your best behavior. I don't mean to be presumptuous.

For you, my Hebrew friend, anything.

They walked through a light breezy rain with the sheriff and Deputy Rogers, everyone holding on to their hat except Joe, who was bareheaded, his hair uncombed and sticky with dried sweat. They entered a small storefront bistro on Broadway where waiters in long aprons carried crowns of beef with white paper frills, and glistening racks of fatty spareribs on silver trays. They were seated at a round table in the back with a pair of eager men who were picking up the tab for this chance to talk boxing with the famous Chrysanthemum Joe. Round, bald, ruddy-faced men with bowler hats and white-buttoned waistcoats, so alike in body and personality they could have been twins.

Tourists in the violent trades, Joe thought. *Savages.*

Joe and Jack sat on one side of the table by the wall. Jack was the only black man in the joint except the kitchen help. The waiter brought a round of whiskeys neat and Cohen ordered a glass of oloroso sherry for Joe.

No booze for the darkie, Rogers said.

This a classy joint, Deputy, Jack said. I'm surprised they let you in here.

Now you shut it, Sheriff Thomas said.

Say, Joe, one of the twins said, tell us about Gentleman Jim. Your great rival, right? The best fighter on the West Coast? Is it true you were unconscious for three days?

The waiter brought Joe his sherry in a cut-crystal glass, placed on a white napkin. Joe turned it carefully with both hands, letting the shards of light splay over his china plate. The two gentlemen wiped their shining foreheads with embroidered handkerchiefs. They looked like a pair of sweating eggs in a cup.

Is he a gentleman like they say?

I heard all the ladies come out for his fights.

They have to put aside the first six rows just for his admirers.

To beat Sullivan like that, it's truly a wonder!

What was it like to get hit by Gentleman Jim?

Joe rotated his sherry. He couldn't escape the feeling that he had done all this before, that this was part of some repetitive exercise, and when a man in a porkpie hat sat down at the upright piano near the door, wearily rolled up his sleeves, and struck the first few notes, Joe felt as though he already knew what he was going to play.

> *Beautiful dreamer,*
> *Wake unto me,*
> *Starlight and dewdrops*
> *Are awaiting thee . . .*

Jack grimaced and fiddled with his silver every time someone took a drink of their whiskey. Then the rotund twins brought up Joe's first professional fight and Jack straightened up, his eyes large.

Y'all want to hear about *my* professional debut?

We don't want to hear about that shit, Rogers said.

My first paid fight was in Springfield, Illinois, what they call a "battle royal." You know what that is? Five black boys in a ring, all of us blindfolded. A saloon basement filled with drunk white men. Couple prostitutes. I was sixteen, living on the streets, starving. Last boy standing got the purse. See, the local boys would decide who was going to win then split the money. So them other four boys knew each other and they rushed me at the first bell. I got my back to the corner and started swinging.

Fighting blind, swinging at shadows. When I knocked the last one down I told him he better stay down or I'd kill him. I got a dollar and a half for it. Afterward they bought me a beer and I got myself a spot at the free-lunch counter. Must have eaten thirty sandwiches. One boy lost an eye permanent.

It was quiet for a few moments and the pair of round gentlemen wiped their smooth foreheads again. A pair of babes in the nursery. Joe turned his sherry, the plum slivers quivering across his hands. The front door was propped open and the light of the restaurant spilled out onto the dark sidewalk. The rain was heavy now and people ran by the doorway holding on to their hats.

Well, I say. That's just . . . awful.

Not very sporting.

It's inhuman, Cohen said. That's what it is.

That's what brought me here, Jack said. Curley heard about that fight and the next month he brought me over to Chicago to fight Klondike. I came off the train straight to the ring, hadn't eaten in two days. You could see every bone in me. I had Klondike down in the third but he came back and cracked my rib. Curley gave me three dollars to get back to Springfield. Then he cabled me to come to Chicago to be a sparring partner for Frank Childs.

He looked at Joe and jabbed a fork at him.

You ever fight Frank Childs?

Knocked him out in ninety-five, Joe said.

I'm glad to hear it. The man was a tyrant. He beat on me terribly. I didn't know anything about protecting myself in those days. And when he wasn't beating on me I was cooking for him and his whole crew. And that don't mean I got a mouthful regular. Hungry all the damn time. Frank made me sleep on the floor of his room. Then one night a friend comes into town and Frank kicks me out. This is in March. It was raining and cold. I walked down to the lake and slept under a statue of somebody. I got Klondike just a couple months later in Memphis. I beat him like a drum and he quit after the fourth and the crowd chased him with broomsticks down the street to the river.

This image struck Joe as riotously funny and he threw his head back and laughed, hammering the table with one fist. The two gentlemen flinched as the silverware on the table jumped.

Quite a tale.

A fantastic story.

I done told you, Rogers said, shut your bone box or I'll take your black ass back down to the basement.

My stories *are* fantastic, Jack said, and they are all true. Right, Joe?

Joe rearranged his fork and knife with deliberate care, an absurd toothy smile stretched across his pained face. His thumping fist caused the sherry to spill over the lip of the glass and a purple stain spread across the white napkin. His calf muscles were quivering, taut as harpsichord strings.

That's right, Joe said. All true.

I'm just getting to the point of the matter, Jack said. You see, there are only two stories in this world.

He held up two long fingers.

What people *want*, and what they *get*. And these two things are never the same.

What the hell does that mean? Rogers said.

It means you have expectations, Jack said. But that's not what I do.

Oh, yeah?

Yeah. This whole little show. This world you've made.

The two round men mopped their brows again. The sheriff had his knife and fork in hand and was craning his neck, looking for the waiter. Cohen was nervously humming a countermelody to "Beautiful Dreamer" as the piano notes tinkled in the background. Jack seemed to swell and grow, larger than all of them at the table, than anyone in the restaurant. The man is a natural character, Joe thought. He was written for the stage. Joe stretched his neck and gripped the edge of the table with his fingers. Not much longer. This *can't* go on much longer.

Y'all come for my blood, Jack said. That's what you *want*.

Jack leaned across the table, looking each of them in the eye. Rogers balled up his napkin in his fist and looked away.

But with me, that ain't what you *get*.

The two rotund gentlemen seemed to be in the midst of a seizure, their open mouths perfect circles, rivers of sweat running down into their collars. Joe rotated his sherry again. The piano player dropped the tempo as he went into the chorus, drawing out the melody. Rogers spat on the floor.

You done, boy?

I am, Jack said. Just in time.

A small platoon of waiters were setting up tray stands and removing plates. One placed a thick, sizzling porterhouse, fragrant with garlic and black pepper, in front of Joe. The twins got pink slabs of prime rib lying in pools of steaming juice. The waiter set a plate in front of Jack with a small black hunk of charred meat the size of a pocket watch.

What's this? I ordered the porterhouse.

The sheriff tucked his napkin into his collar as they set an enormous slab of sirloin in front of him. Cohen stared balefully at his seared circle of filet mignon streaked with a cream sauce. Deputy Rogers was already cutting into his fat steak and the waiter topped their whiskeys and placed a carafe of blood-dark wine in the center of the table. Rogers popped a hunk of meat in his mouth and grinned at Jack as he chewed.

How's that steak, dinge?

Jack held his knife and fork, his face serene. He watched the other men eat and then reached over and tapped Joe's arm. They looked each other in the eye.

Pardon me, Joe.

Jack reached over and lifted Joe's glass of sherry and downed it in one gulp. The piano player started a popular waltz, singing in a low, warbling tenor. Joe closed his eyes and sighed as if something was released.

Matt Casey formed a social club
That beat the town for style . . .

Joe leaned over the table and put his fingers into the twin gentlemen's whiskey glasses. He picked them up in one hand and put a glass in front of Jack and then held up the other, staring at the horror-struck gentlemen who held their napkins to their faces as they struggled to swallow their half masticated meat. Then Joe poured the booze into his mouth. He held it there. It tasted like nothing but clean, clear light.

Jack grinned and tossed back the other whiskey. Cohen put down his knife and fork.

Joe? he said quietly. Joe?

Joe closed his eyes and swallowed and the liquid still tasted like nothing—an absence, a void. He raised the glass high in the air, turned it over, then brought it down on the table with a bang. He lifted his face to the ceiling, the cords in his neck straining as his voice boomed throughout the restaurant.

The valiant never taste of death but once!

Then Joe bowed his head and began to laugh again, silently this time, his head bowed and wheezing through his nose.

Joe, is everything okay?

What the hell does that mean?

Excuse me, Mr. Sheriff, Deputy Rogers?

Jack cleared his throat, head turned toward the open door. It was a regular deluge out there, the street a flowing river. He jabbed his fork in the direction of the door.

There's something you ought to be aware of. Coming this way.

The sheriff and deputy paused, chewing, before turning around in their seats. Jack was up in a flash, extending over the table and spearing the deputy's steak on his fork, hoisting it and slapping it on his plate.

Oh, bollocks! Cohen said. Jack!

One of the twin gentlemen started choking on a hunk of steak and the other immediately began hammering him on the back with his fist. The sheriff and deputy looked at the empty doorway to the street, black with rain. The piano player paused, his hands hovering over the keys. For a moment the only sound was the metronomic thud on the portly gentleman's back, his face going deep crimson. The sheriff and the deputy turned back around and saw Jack sawing through the deputy's steak. Rogers leaped up, knocking his chair to the floor with a clatter.

Son of a bitch!

Jack raised a fat dripping piece of meat up to his nose, taking a deep whiff.

This here a nicely cooked piece of beef.

Don't you do it! the sheriff hissed.

I told you, Jack said. The truth!

He opened his mouth extra wide, letting his pink tongue roll out, and inserted the meat, closing his lips and chewing thoughtfully, head cocked to one side. With a wet *hack*, the round gentleman finally expelled the hunk of meat lodged in his esophagus. His companion put an arm around him while he wheezed, both men staring bug-eyed at Jack. Joe wiped his face with his napkin and lazily reached across the table and picked up the two remaining glasses of whiskey.

Deputy Rogers fumbled at his holster and pulled his pistol. He pointed it across the table with a shaking hand.

You black son of a bitch!

Jack chewed with his eyes closed. Several ladies in the room gasped, clutching at their necks as if his dark hands had reached across the room and encircled their throats. Joe felt as if he were about to erupt into a column of fire. This is my world, he thought. This is who I am.

A bearded man at the next table stood up and in one motion Joe drank off a whiskey and shattered the glass on the floor at his feet.

Sit *down*.

Joe knotted his fists and placed them on the table. The man at the next table sat. Cohen spread his hands, a horrified look on his face.

Gentlemen, *please*!

The piano player slowly closed the lid on the keys. The

sheriff tossed his napkin on the floor and stood up, unclipping a pair of handcuffs from his belt. He held his pistol against his leg with the other hand and somewhere a woman screamed. Joe watched Jack chewing, his cheek bulging, making little side to side motions with his head as if he were slipping punches. Circle the center line, he thought. Impossible to hit cleanly. Keep going. Keep moving.

Gentlemen, let's be calm, Cohen said. We can work this out.

Rogers swung his pistol around at Cohen.

Shut up, you filthy Yid!

Jack swallowed and dabbed at his lips with his napkin. Then he squinted and pinched his finger and thumb.

Could use a *bit* more salt.

Rogers cocked the pistol and held it with both hands, pointing it at Jack's face.

I'm gonna *kill* this black bastard!

At that moment a teenage boy burst into the dining room from the street, soaking wet and waving his hat. He paused, looking around, baffled by the all the patrons who seemed mired in some kind of frozen state. He finally located the sheriff at their table by the back wall.

Sheriff! Something's happening at the jail! There's a fire! You need to come quick!

DIANA

After the storm Rabbi Cohen set up a new office in a cotton shed on the Twenty-First Street docks in the second ward. The first floor was empty, a smooth rime of contoured muck covering the walls, but the stairwells were granite and the second floor was basically intact. Cohen had a huge rectangular room with windows that looked over the docks. A desk sat next to a file cabinet pocked with rust, and correspondence and shipping manifests littered the floor. The docks were repaired and the bay channel dredged enough to receive large ships from Europe and Cohen was once again shipping a steady flow of Jewish immigrants looking for land or business opportunities in Texas.

His assistant, Mrs. Sterling, had a desk on the stair landing where she controlled the traffic of petitioners who lined up to see the rabbi. When Diana, Cordelia, and Hester arrived Mrs. Sterling waved them past the extended family of Bohemians on the stairs nursing red-faced infants and eating bread and turnips out of a sack. They found Cohen capering across the dusty floor of his office, dancing a Viennese waltz with a wooden coat stand in his arms, a Victrola on the floor next to his desk playing a scratchy recording of "Die Schönbrunner." They watched as Cohen made his turn by the window and came galloping back, catching their eye and nodding before taking off again on another spinning run across the room, neatly depositing the coat stand in the corner with a tender gesture. Hester clapped her hands.

You are a man of many talents, Diana said.

You have caught me in a celebratory mood!

Cohen went to his desk, which was piled with bristling columns of paper, and plucked a set of documents from the top of a stack.

All ready for your signature, Miss Longstreet.

With her left hand, Diana signed the legal adoption form. Cohen tossed a pinch of cornstarch over the document then waved it in the air to dry. He called out for Mrs. Sterling, who opened the door and snatched it from his outstretched hand.

For the courthouse files! Cheers, thank you, Mrs. Sterling!

He squatted down before Hester.

You are a lucky little girl, Hester Longstreet. And our friend Joe will be released today!

As expected, the Court of Criminal Appeals failed to find a true bill against Joe and Jack. Diana watched Hester as Cohen read the release notice out loud. She seemed content to leave Galveston forever. That morning Diana discovered that Hester had all her belongings, the small scraps of pilfered items and the seashells from the beach, tied up neatly in a small blanket.

Come to the ceremony with me, Cohen said. There'll be speeches and pictures and all the newspapers will be there. I'm sure Joe would be happy to see you.

Diana didn't ask if Joe was leaving. She would assume that he was and it would be for the best. Then Joe could go on with his life and this story could come to an end. All they had to do was pretend that nothing was really happening. Just like everyone else.

And yet she knew that Hester had latched on to the three of them together as some kind of destiny. But how would any of it work? What they would *be*? That night on the boat, her hand on his face, the cold wind snapping the sails, then holding the sleeping Hester on the beach while Joe sailed away into the dark with the world crashing down around her—on that night a small but vital space had opened up inside her and she knew that it would never be the same. And why couldn't she have a chance at another life?

She also had to acknowledge something else. That dark light in his eyes when they touched, the desperate ardor of his hands, a flicker of something else burning inside Joe that wasn't about her. There was another entity that drove him relentlessly on, racing against some inevitable tide. It was as if he was running for some unknowable point in the distance and unable, unwilling, or too afraid to look back.

***

They met in Clara's old office on the first floor, the desk still stacked with manifests, logs, and received correspondence from all over the world. Liverwright lounged in a chair with an unlit cigarette dangling from his mouth until Diana started talking about the money and goods flowing out of the city and then he got out his pad and started scribbling. She told him where to look and who to talk to; she handed him a stack of accounting logs. And then she told him that members of the CRC were riding with the masked vigilantes—the same masked men who murdered the Ponder children.

Why don't you tell the sheriff?

They already know.

She told him about the night in front of the jail, the masked horsemen chasing Hester in the rain, the whip. She rolled up her sleeve and showed him the bandage across her forearm, a line of dried blood that curled from her elbow to her wrist.

You'll find Mr. Craine in the hospital, she said. He was badly burned but is expected to survive.

I heard, Liverwright said. They said it was a cooking accident.

Go see him. Tell me if it looks like a cooking accident to you.

This is a grand accusation, ma'am, Liverwright said. What are you expecting me to do, exactly?

Are you a journalist?

Yes, ma'am.

Then I'm expecting you to do your job.

***

When they arrived the street in front of the jailhouse was full to the next block—a restless throng of several hundred people. A group of men in suits, including Sheriff Thomas and the deputies, members of the committee, and the mayor, were milling around the front porch of the jail. Cohen brought Diana, Cordelia, and Hester to the front of the crowd, between a set of ornamental urns planted with spiky oleander shrubs. Hester picked the narrow leaves, collecting them in a fan-shape until Cohen snatched them out of her hand.

Pretty things they are, he said. *Nerium oleander.* But you mustn't touch them or put them near your mouth. Oleanders are *poisonous*, sometimes fatally.

Poisonous, Diana said. The flower of Galveston.

We don't get to choose our symbols, Ms. Longstreet. It's an unfortunate truth.

Newspapermen and their attendant cameramen began to crowd the front of the steps around them, and when Joe and Jack were ushered out a dozen flash pans were raised.

Take it easy, fellas, Sheriff Thomas said. Everyone will get a picture.

Jack wore a navy three-button jacket, striped gray slacks, and a black bow tie, borrowed from Joe's wardrobe. The jacket was snug, just a touch too small, but his head was clean-shaven and his face was proud and defiant. Joe wore a dark suit, buttoned up tight, his hair loose and curled around his ears, a felt fedora clutched in his fist. He looked uncomfortable as the officials tried to arrange everyone for a picture. They finally decided on a pose with Joe shaking hands with the sheriff as Jack stood between them, looking directly at the cameras. The mayor and other members of the committee assembled around them, each man taking his own pose. Off to one side, Captain Brooks stood with a couple of Texas Rangers. Salazar stood in the back by the door to the jail, trombone strapped to his back with a length of twine.

The public houses on either side of the street had steady business and the crowd buzzed with a drunken intensity. About half the crowd was treating the release of the two men as a reason to celebrate while the other half, mostly blacks and immigrants from the east side, stood together with scowling faces. They were there to support Jack Johnson and to register their anger about unequal dispersal of relief and the marauding bands of masked vigilantes. Every newspaper in the state was there, and the wire would carry the story throughout the country and they were determined to be heard.

***

When Diana woke that night to find Hester gone she quickly guessed that the girl might go to the jail to find Joe. Diana told Cohen about how she found Hester surrounded by horsemen in front of the jail, how the leader of the masked men, armed with a bullwhip, spoke with a distinctive, crackling voice. How he would not reveal himself. But he would be marked now, forever.

Thousands of donated dollars are coming every day, Diana said. From all over the world. The new committee controls all of it.

Cohen sipped his tea and looked at the ceiling for a long time before saying that he didn't trust the sheriff or any local law enforcement. But the Texas Rangers were outsiders, not beholden to anyone in Galveston. He would speak to Captain Brooks.

They see Hester as the fly in the ointment, Diana said. But I will not involve her in this any further. Her part in this tragedy is over.

***

Hester started to climb the stairs to go to Joe, but Diana held her back. Hester grimaced and pulled, trying to yank her arm free.

Please, Hester, Diana said. After the pictures. Please wait.

Oh, what can you do about something like that? Diana thought. What would be the good of explaining to the child the inestimable problems and adult obligations? A child understands only the emotional aspect of things. A gift and a curse.

Then the sheriff decided that Hester, the famous orphan hero, should be in the picture as well, so they sat her on the front step, just in front of Joe and Jack, with Cohen just to her left. The dog limped his way up the stairs, settling next to her on his uneven haunches. Joe found Diana in the crowd just as the cameramen held up their flash pans preparing to shoot. They looked at each other, Joe's head slightly lowered, a lopsided smirk on his face, his heavy brows shading his blue eyes. She didn't know what this look was trying to tell her.

Joe? What is it? What have you done?

Hester sat on the step, a petulant frown on her face, annoyed that she couldn't be in Joe's arms.

Smile, Diana said. Smile for the photograph.

But she didn't. Hester glowered like a toad as Joe and Sheriff Thomas shook hands, and everyone held still as the flash pans exploded and the newspapermen counted off their exposure timing. After the photo there were shouts from the east-end crowd, some calling out to Jack, others calling for justice for the murdered Ponder children. They were hissed at by the white men around the front, and a portly man in a straw boater turned around and threatened to *shut those goddamn darkies up!* A bottle was passed hand to hand through the crowd. Then they brought Joe up to the front and the newspapermen started yelling out questions.

How's this one rate, Joe? How's this fight stack up?

Mr. Johnson is a top boxer, Joe said. He will have a long and successful career.

Say, Joe, you gonna fight again?

Joe smiled and ran a hand through his hair. The crowd grew quiet to hear his answer. A gang of children ran down the sidewalk on the other side of the street, their boots clattering on the boards. Joe seemed to watch the craven gulls banking away overhead, crying out to each other.

I will never enter the ring again, Joe said. Even for a friendly exhibition. My mother begged me to quit the game for many years. It is time I honored that request.

The crowd laughed and clapped and Joe stepped back, looking terribly uncomfortable. Then Jack Johnson came forward to answer questions and a full-figured woman in a green dress bounded up the steps and into his arms. She had milky skin and dark hair tied up with a strip of white lace. She kissed Jack's cheek and looked out over the crowd with a blazing eye.

Who's this, Jack? the reporters yelled out.

This is my girl, Mary, Jack said.

What about you, Jack? they yelled. How does this fight stack up for you?

I want to thank Mr. Choynski, Jack said, for the opportunity to box with him. Unlike Joe, I plan to keep fighting. But I'll never fight *that* man again.

He turned and gestured to Joe and the crowd laughed.

Joe's all slicked up, Jack said, talks like a Philadelphia lawyer, but he's a bully trap, folks. All his Shakespeare quotes and intellectual conversation. Believe me, Joe's as savage as a meat axe.

Say, Jack, another reporter asked, what is it with the white women? Why do you think white women seem to like you so much?

Same as any black man, Jack said. They like us because we eat cold eels and think distant thoughts.

There was a pause and then some nervous laughter. What did that mean? Jack kept turning this way and that, grinning and making eye contact with every person who looked at him. Joe stood behind him, blinking at the sky, his eyes glassy. What was the point of it all? Diana wondered. Because Jack Johnson was an unruly black man who talked too loud and laughed too much? Or was it just a chance to reestablish the preferred social order? Regardless, she knew that the story would end as it always did, with someone leaving and someone left behind. Diana just didn't know which one she was.

Joe was watching her again, his face solemn. Diana smiled and shrugged.

Whatever it is, it's going to be all right.

Joe lifted his chin, the wind pushing his hair across his face, his hat still crushed in his hand. His look gave Diana an icy shiver that climbed from her heels to her scalp—the recognition of something receding out of view.

I'm sorry. But it will never be all right.

Diana felt a choking heat rising in her chest and the crowd seemed to press closer and she clutched Hester's hand, her good arm tight across the girl's front. Her senses seemed to expand in that extraordinary magnification of sudden grief until it was almost unbearable: the sour, yeasty stench of people, the rich heady ooze of ocean soil, the salty wind lined with smoke, the pull of the mud under her feet, boards, horses, children, machinery clattering away, raw eyes always burning, burning.

Then Hester slipped away and was climbing the stairs. Diana moved to stop her, but Joe stepped forward and held out his arms and the photographers shouted and elbowed each other, their flash pans held high as Joe knelt on the top step to receive her. Hester put her arms around his neck and her mouth up to Joe's ear, her eyes closed, her lips moving.

The mayor stepped forward and gestured to the two of them.

Ladies and gentlemen, the famous orphan hero of Galveston!

Liverwright's cameraman popped his flash and others began to follow, lighting up Hester and Joe as they held each other. The crowd clapped and cheered and Joe picked her up, hugging her tightly, her feet in her buckled black shoes dangling. Hester held her doll by one leg, draped over Joe's shoulder. The burlap mask with the crooked smile covering the doll's head was painted like a blood-red skull.

People at the front of the crowd whispered and pointed at the doll, shifting and stretching to get a look. The newspapermen took advantage of the lull and began shouting questions.

Mr. Mayor, Liverwright shouted, can you tell us what happened to Mr. Floyd Craine?

Was it really a cooking accident, Mr. Mayor?

What can you tell us about the incident that happened here in front of the jail?

Is it true that Mr. Craine's been horribly disfigured?

What can you tell us about donated goods and money being shipped out of town?

Then someone in the back of the crowd threw a muddy shoe

and the mayor flinched as it tumbled past his ear and as if by some planned signal the crowd surged forward, knocking the front rows of people up against the stairs. Diana caught Hester and Cordelia and they struggled to keep their feet in the press of bodies as the arguing voices and shouted threats grew louder and there was the slapping sound of someone falling into the street and women started screaming. The committee members and others started to abandon the steps and Diana saw Balestri slip off to the side, mopping his brow with a handkerchief, trying to make his way through the crowd. He was quickly grabbed by a half dozen people, and a black man in a suit got an arm around Balestri's neck and lifted him off his feet and he was carried off in the throng. Someone snapped a harness, and a cart took off clattering down the street. Another man leaped onto a horse and spurred it through the crowd, knocking people to the ground. Diana pulled Cordelia to her and they encircled Hester as a bottle smashed on the wall of the jail and all around them men struggled, grunting and wheezing and crying out as they bludgeoned each other in a frenzy of anger and fear.

Cohen found them and led them out of the crowd and when they reached the opposite sidewalk Diana searched the confused melee on the steps. Joe was already gone.

***

They walked back to the warehouse and said their goodbyes. Cohen gave Hester a long, straining hug, holding on until she started to struggle because his mustache was wet with tears and tickling her face. In the alley beside the warehouse a couple of ladies in white dresses washed the large soup pots with steaming water, scouring them with long-handled brushes while a small boy and a girl held hands and marched through the puddles, chanting a nonsense rhyme. Cohen watched them for a moment, his arms loose at his sides.

I can't believe this is it, he said. I can't believe this is the end.

Then Diana, Cordelia, and Hester gathered him in their arms, and the three of them held the rabbi as he wept.

HESTER

They stood on the crest of the dunes and watched the waves surge toward the digging site, now just a row of shallow depressions in the sand. A few hundred yards behind the dunes the broken foundations of the St. Mary's Orphan Asylum gazed up at the clouds. Hester took Diana's hand, leaning into her, rubbing her cheek on her dress.

They walked down the dunes to the dig site. Hester thought about the sisters and the power of their belief. How they seemed impervious, beyond mortal suffering. She tried to imagine them struggling for air, buried in a tomb of sand, still praying to their God. Little Cora lying somewhere deep under her feet. Diana sat in the sand and watched her, using a hand to shade her eyes, her coil of hair over one shoulder, the ocean breeze pushing her dress around her legs.

She was leaving with Diana on a train and she would never

come back. Hester walked down to the water's edge and let the water run over her feet, the very tears of Little Cora washing around her ankles. Hester could hear her tiny lisping voice chanting in the wind.

Angel of God,
my guardian dear,
To whom God's love
commits me here,
Ever this day,
be at my side,
To light and guard,
Rule and guide.

How could the God of the sisters stand idly by for all this? Was he powerless to stop it? He didn't save the girls. He isn't going to save any of us.

Goodbye, goodbye, goodbye. I'm sorry but I'm not coming with you.

Diana stood up, looking back to the dunes where a man was sitting in a patch of saw grass. There was something long and shiny and golden that he held up to his face, working it with slow motions of his hands, playing long low notes that she felt under her skin.

Then Joe was there, walking out of the dunes carrying his jacket on his arm, hat crushed in his hand, hair lashing in the wind. He walked up to Diana and the two of them looked at each other as the water sloshed about Hester's ankles and minnows darted through the shallow water like slivers of pure light.

Henry told me you'd be here, Joe said. I'm sorry to intrude.

It's fine, Diana said. She wanted to see this place one more time.

Your arm . . .

Diana lifted her arm in the sling.

Something to remember all this by.

I'm sorry, he said.

You have nothing to be sorry about, Joe.

He ducked his head and cleared his throat, rending his hat in his hands.

Are you leaving today?

His words came out haltingly, as if he was choking on something.

We have tickets for the six-thirty to New Orleans, Diana said. We'll be in Washington in four days.

I'm glad she's going with you, Joe said. You'll make a good home for her.

Thank you, Diana said.

Joe nodded. He looked around for a moment and then tossed his coat and misshapen hat onto the sand and jammed his hands in his pockets.

I really hate hats, he said.

Diana took a few steps toward him. Hester followed her, stepping out of the watery traces of the waves. Joe's face was a strange shining color.

If there's a chance, he said. Any chance at all that . . . she's still there, that she's waiting for me, then I have to go back.

I know.

I *have* to.

I know. It's okay. I understand.

She took another step toward him.

What did Hester say to you at the jail? Diana said. Did she speak?

Yes, Joe said.

What did she say?

Joe looked away, squinting into the pale sun.

She said: Goodbye, Joe.

He smiled and shrugged, holding out his hands, his eyes glassy with tears.

Diana slipped her arm out of the sling and Joe came toward her and they embraced in stages, grasping arms, then shoulders, then Joe's hands moving across her back then spreading his fingers and pressing her to him. Diana's head was on his shoulder, his mouth and nose in her hair. The skin of her cheek brushed his face. The wind whipped Diana's white dress around both of their legs and Joe's hat tumbled down the beach.

Hester stood in their slanted shadow from the sun crossing the meridian of the sky. She knew that they were someplace else. They stood alone in a world that was not theirs, a possible world that would never be realized. They would also leave this behind.

The man with the golden horn wandered back over the dunes.

We have to be more kind, Hester thought. We have to save ourselves.

***

Diana took Hester's hand and they walked away. When they reached the dunes Hester turned back because she knew that Joe would still be standing there by the water, watching them go. She knew they would travel over the green hills to the house with the orchard and the story would go on without him. She knew that he would always have one hand up in the hair, waving, his blond hair like a halo of sunlight.

Goodbye, goodbye, goodbye, Joe.

March 21, 1901, Galveston, Texas. On the day of their release from jail Sheriff Henry Thomas shakes the hand of Joe Choynski with Jack Johnson standing between them. The two boxers shared a jail cell for twenty-three days, charged with participating in an illegal prizefight. They are surrounded by other city officials, deputies, and friends.

The young girl and dog in the foreground are unknown.

Photo courtesy of the Rosenberg Library, Galveston, Texas.

POSTSCRIPT

Clara Barton officially resigned as president of the American Red Cross in 1904, under pressure from a cohort of male scientific experts who felt her autocratic and micromanaging leadership style was out of touch with the dawning Progressive Era. She died in 1912 at the age of ninety in her home in Glen Echo, Maryland.

Jack Johnson went on to dominate the heavyweight boxing world, winning the world title in 1908 after he beat Tommy Burns in Sydney, Australia. Jack held the title for seven years, defending it eight times, finally losing to Jess Willard in 1915 in Havana, Cuba. He would go on to win many more fights, compiling a final record of seventy-three wins, thirteen losses, and ten draws. During his reign as champion he was the most famous African American in the world, and to this day Jack Johnson is widely considered the greatest heavyweight boxer of all time. He was a notoriously sly defensive boxer, nearly impossible to hit cleanly. He was also a controversial figure known for his refusal to accept or adhere to racial barriers or politics. Throughout his life he maintained that his time in jail with Joe Choynski was responsible for the change in his fighting style and his meteoric success afterward.

Rabbi Henry Cohen continued his service to the city of Galveston and helped bring at least ten thousand Jewish immigrants to America. He went on to serve his community in a variety of important ways, including educational and prison reform. Cohen served as rabbi to the Congregation B'nai Israel until 1949 and rabbi emeritus until his death in 1952. He is remembered as one of the great Texans of the twentieth century.

Joe Choynski did not retire from the fight game after his experience in Galveston. He fought twelve more times, finally retiring in 1904. His wife, Louise, recovered from her illness and they made several short-lived forays into the theater world, including a show called "A Tangle of Ropes and Diamonds" in which Joe played a college athlete with a huge chrysanthemum blossom in his lapel. Joe went on to work as an insurance salesman and a chiropractor among other vocations and later became a boxing trainer and referee. Notably, he helped train Jim Jeffries for his historic fight against Jack Johnson in 1910. (Johnson beat Jeffries soundly.) He was inducted into the International Boxing Hall of Fame and is considered the greatest Jewish boxer of all time, and possibly the greatest heavyweight who never won a championship.

Diana Longstreet is not based on any single historical figure. Nothing is known about the unidentified girl and dog in the famous photo of Joe Choynski and Jack Johnson being released from the Galveston jail.

To this day, everywhere across the world, the members of the Congregation of the Sisters of the Incarnate Word sing "Queen of the Waves" on September 8, in memory of the lives lost that day in Galveston.

ACKNOWLEDGMENTS

My wife happened upon this amazing story while researching for her history PhD dissertation about immigration through Galveston around the turn of the century. This was more than ten years ago, and the story has occupied a part of my brain ever since. Over the years I've read and consulted hundreds of different resources trying to learn more about the famous match between Joe Choynski and Jack Johnson, and all the attendant circumstances surrounding this event, including the Galveston hurricane of 1900 and the American Red Cross. The real history of this story is incredible on its own, and so at all times I made every attempt to stay as close to the historical record as possible. Some of my valuable resources include *Unforgivable Blackness: The Rise and Fall of Jack Johnson*, by Geoffrey C. Ward; *The Choynski Chronicles: A Biography of Hall of Fame Boxer Jewish Joe Choynski,* by Christopher J. Laforce; *Isaac's Storm*, by Erik

Larson; *Galveston and the 1900 Storm*, by Patricia Bixel and Elizabeth Turner; *The Complete Story of the Galveston Horror, Written by the Survivors*, edited by John Coulter; *Galveston: A History*, by David G. McComb; *James J. Corbett: A Biography of the Heavyweight Boxing Champion and Popular Theater Headliner*, by Armond Fields; *The Big Smoke*, by Adrian Matejka; *Fight of the Century*, by Thomas Hietala; *The Manly Art: Bare Knuckle Prizefighting in America*, by Elliott Gorn; *Bare Fists: the History of Bare Knuckle Prize Fighting*, by Bob Mee; *Dan Stuart's Fistic Carnival*, by Leo N. Miletich; *The Great White Hopes: The Quest to Defeat Jack Johnson*, by Graeme Kent; and many others, as well as too many newspaper, magazine, and website articles to list here. An obvious source of inspiration is Leonard Gardner's novel *Fat City*, perhaps the best American boxing novel ever written. I am also grateful to the Rosenberg Library and Museum and the Tremont Hotel in Galveston for their assistance. I was fortunate to spend a lot of time in Galveston over the last fifteen years as it is a favorite vacation destination for my wife's family, and so many of the observations and details contained here are drawn from my own experience on the island.

For me every historical novel is born not just from the historical record, but from some point of mystery, a catalyst, something for the writer to discover or explore. One of the touchstones for me is the picture that I found at the Rosenberg Library that is included in the Postscript, of Joe and Jack on their release from the Galveston jail. My eye was immediately drawn to the little girl and the dog in the bottom right corner—that was the opening to the story for me, and I felt strongly that through that little girl I could give a fuller, richer, and more true account of what happened to these historical figures in Galveston. In order to get at that truth, I created characters based on some real people, some who are combinations of the original figures, some quite close to the historical record as we know it, and others who are almost wholly fabricated. I have imagined a number of things for which there is no record, and have presumed upon the actual historical figures with the liberty that is granted a novelist. My intention was to try and reach that truth that lies beyond the poorly recorded and understood world of actualities. I hope I have honored the memory of Galveston and all the people who lived, suffered, loved, and died there during this tragedy and its aftermath.

I would like to thank my generous readers, Susan White Norman, Seth Tucker, Sally Franco Aldridge, Sara Hov, and Mike Mannon, as well as my editors Michael Carr, Kathryn Zentgraf, and all the fine folks at Blackstone. As always I am indebted to my agent, Alex Glass of Glass Literary Management, for his continued support and friendship. I need to thank my colleagues at the University of Mississippi, the MFA program, the English Department, the UM Library, and all the others who helped me along the way. Principal among all, my wife, Stacy, who discovered this tale.